RISING UP

Book One of the Tranquility Series

TANYA ROSS

*To Jack —
Be fearless
Be you
Be happy
Be*

Tanya Ross

To my husband, Kerry, who is my happiness every day.

"Happiness is like those palaces in fairy tales whose gates are guarded by dragons: We must fight in order to conquer it."

— Alexandre Dumas

Soundtrack

Rising Up has a soundtrack! Each chapter has its own music from the character's point of view. Enjoy!
To get the link and the list of music, visit
https://www.tanyarossauthor.com

Contents

Ember Vinata

On a perfect day in a perfect place with practically perfect people, even dreams should be perfect. At least that's how it was in Tranquility for everyone— for everyone but Ember Vinata.

Ember's dreams were more real than any fantasy. The moment she fell into a deep sleep, she felt herself rise to the ceiling, sensed a force pulling her out of her body into what was another time and place, independent of hour and matter. Its vivid animation and physical awareness pulled at her mind in a tug of war.

The dreams robbed her of rest, and even though her required levels of happiness peaked each day, an inner, nagging voice reminded her, "You'll never be pretty or truly happy if you don't get your beauty sleep." Those negative thoughts seemed to always intrude.

Ember had always known she was *different*. She felt everyone's emotions, not just her own, and that was enough of a burden. But the dreams. The dreams were horrible.

Her constant midnight companion was the same drama, night after night. The nightmare always began with her running. Running as fast as she could.

A sinister Someone chased her, her heartbeat the beacon leading him to her. She knew he pursued her because she possessed a special ability, rare and secret, and it was this that her assailant craved. Her frantic footsteps echoed like cracked ice through a gilded building with cold, marble floors, her pursuer's breath on her neck. She dodged mammoth books with leathery rainbow covers flying by. She reached out over and over to grab the slippery books, knowing instinctively a book could save her, but found her hands grasping only air. Finally, she melted straight into one, through its cover, landing deeply into its pages, which fanned out to cover her with safety.

Yet her black-clad, caped hunter still leaned over her, reached through, and impossibly pulled her, with one jeweled hand, out of her warm cocoon. He shoved her into a golden cage suspended in space. I know you, she thought. Yet, she searched his face, unable to determine his identity.

Without warning, her cage broke free, its pieces exploding and scattering into a stark wilderness, enveloping her in a new scene. She stood alone. A solitary sapling broke through the parched earth beneath her feet like an explosion. As it grew it gathered limbs and fire, where again, Ember saw the face of her enemy.

She wobbled, unsteady on her feet, searing heat driving her to the ground. She cowered, beads of sweat forming on her forehead. Suddenly, a whirlwind of sparkling yellow mist cascaded around her, and a strong arm pulled her to her feet. A handsome "prince"—at least that's how she imagined him—led her by the hand. Happiness gushed through her veins until they pulsed.

Just when she thought she would explode with joy, her prince fell dead in a pool of blood.

She wakes. And each time she does, she knows. Somehow, her dreams are a terrible omen.

~

IT WAS NEAR NOON, and Ember woke up, aroused by cries for help. She realized immediately, with some embarrassment, that she had been napping, and the shouts had come from her own lips. The dreams had come again, even as she dozed, after many exhausting hours spent waiting in hope for good news.

Ember sat in a neon-bright yellow-cushioned chair, the color a contrast to her black state of mind. Her mother, Talesa, lay on a stiff hospital bed, medicated on Heniprom, a treatment used at the end of life to ease suffering and pain. Right now, her mother's ghastly illness, not her own mysterious dreams, was her biggest worry.

Her mom's last two months had been a series of ups and downs. The "skin disorder" with its large swollen red patches appeared innocent at first. Starting with just one tiny spot on her mother's right arm, the illness came on suddenly, without warning. Mystifying. Unfathomable. This disease of "undetermined cause" was ultimately toxic. It made its way through her mother's system like a possessed spirit, aggressively setting up residence in every part of her body.

When Ember and her mom first arrived, they saw beauty. The hospital's intensive treatment unit was a spa-like sanctuary. Pale pink walls whispered love and calm, while fresh sunflowers in every corner buoyed their spirits with their saffron smiles. Even the medical equipment doing the monitoring, draped in crystalline veils, was a decorator statement.

It was the first time Ember had ever seen the inside of a hospital. For anyone in Tranquility to be in a building such as this was rare. Diseases had been eradicated with the introduction of genetic engineering, called GFX, which allowed doctors to correct faulty DNA. All citizens lived to be a hundred, guaranteed.

But since Talesa was admitted three weeks ago, the room had lost its charm. Today the walls appeared faded, like a Victorian valentine left in a box too long. A food tray with sweet pudding and a filet mignon drenched in buttery sauce sat stranded on the table, each nutritional offering a solemn tease, never to be consumed. Unending revolutions of the clock had now created another night, and the darkness crept in bit by bit through the cracks in the shades.

Ember tried to rouse her mom. Gently shaking Talesa's arm, Ember said with insistence, "Mom . . . can you wake up, *please!*" But the only sound she heard was the beating of her own heart.

Ember put her head in her hands, giving in momentarily to complete despair. *I feel so helpless—more alone than I've felt in my whole life. A black hole is sucking me down...* Her mother was the one who gave her life but also saw mystic strength flowering beneath Ember's timid behavior. Where Ember was shy, her mother saw sensitivity. Where Talesa saw a young adult poised for legendary Status, Ember saw a child who only felt secure when following the rules. Her mother thought she was beautiful; she saw herself as flawed. Who would believe in her if she didn't have her mom?

What even Ember's mother didn't know was that Ember was an Empath. Her gift, first of all, made her feel like a freak. From the time she was ten, she would unconsciously pick up other people's emotions. She didn't just have her own feelings, she actually attracted both the negative and positive moods from other people. If someone in her social environment was happy, Ember felt those same feelings. I affected her like a force. If she was around angry people, she grew angry; if she met an anxious person, it fed her own anxieties; and if she came across sadness in others, she became sad herself. The closer her relationship was to someone, the more she was flooded with their emotions. Even strangers bonded with her, sharing more information and emotions than she ever wanted to know. It was disturbing; often she couldn't separate what she was feeling from what people around her were feeling, and this made achieving Tranquility's Happiness Standard very difficult. She had to work extra hard at being positive.

But that was not the most bizarre thing about Ember. She could see auras around people. The colors were beautiful

—red, green, yellow, purple. There were many, as the people here were *good* and *kind*. Happy, of course. However, any dark emotions and auras radiating from people around her infected her like a virus, and it hit hard.

Because of her "talent," Ember usually chose to be alone. She'd even chosen to leave school, preferring to do independent study at home, because she didn't want to be in a classroom full of other people. It was difficult enough to handle her own emotions.

And, there was the problem. In Tranquility, all people wore an electronic device known as the Alt on their wrists. It looked a little like the Smart Watches first introduced in the mid-2000s. But technology had come a long way. Back then, the watch kept time, measured steps, set reminders, rang for phone calls, and measured breaths per minute. Now, in the year 2120, a more advanced design measured human emotions and sent all the data to a central computer at City Hall.

This cutting-edge device was what set Tranquility apart and made its citizens special. The people's ability to control and eliminate negative emotions was the key for people to rise up in society. The happier someone was, the more points would appear on the Alt. Negative emotions, like anger, jealousy, and sadness took points away. More Alt points equated to more Status. More points and Status bought better food, housing, and clothing.

Ember's life depended on the Alt. That's why her emotions—her optimism and joy—were so important. She couldn't afford to carry around everyone else's struggles. Her Alt points, like a compass at the North Pole, could spin out of control.

But her mother's life? It hung, suspended. It was a matter of life and death.

2

Will Verus

W ill Verus, another citizen of Tranquility, was celebrating.

Just yesterday, he was a Level Six. Today, a Level Twelve. Rising up so many levels was an unprecedented accomplishment. The story hit the Tranquility newsfeed immediately.

Four blocks south of Grand Avenue, Will stood on a deserted street corner headed to work. He ran his fingers through his bleach-blond hair and watched in disbelief as his very own face flashed up on a ten-foot mega screen elevated high above the boulevard. His picture then became reduced to a smaller window in the upper corner. An official-looking commentator loomed large on the main screen and began to recount yesterday's events:

"Fate entered Will Verus's life with his rescue of a young teen, age twelve, who climbed the Bird's Eye Pass Bridge immediately before the 2:15 p.m. Maglev Monorail's passing. As the Maglev sped toward the boy, Will Verus risked his own life by climbing the bridge pylons and was able to pull the boy to safety. The boy, Jesse Educari, lives in Orange Glen, and Will's heroics allowed Jesse to return home with no injury. For this amazing rescue, Will Verus is now a recognized Tranquility VIP. He will be taking his place as a Plauditor this very day."

Wow, he thought. *High profile.* A five-second wave of anxiety struck him—in, then out.

The broadcaster continued. "Remember, fine citizens. Every point on your Alt is important. You alone can rise up! You need only to concentrate on being happy. Improvements in your neighborhood, your food, your clothing, your job ... it is all within you. Make it your goal to score more points today than yesterday."

The reporter finished his broadcast for the morning by praising Tranquility's low crime rate and encouraging listeners to have a "happy, positive day." He adjusted his shiny silver tie and smoothed the lapels on his high-class sterling plaid jacket. He gave the common salute and signed off. The giant screen faded out and returned with images of fireworks and positive quotes and affirmations.

Other city dwellers were now, one by one, emerging out of early morning wispy fog, finally beginning to join him on the corner. He smiled at the rainbow of color they made. Their clothes heralded every Status hue. The founders of Tranquility were so creative!

He smiled at the easy way that the people of lower Status walked respectfully behind those of the higher classes. It was so orderly. No one forced their way ahead on the street. *Kind of like built-in manners*, he thought. A system was in place to insure proper behavior. He watched as a girl in brown fell back behind a man in orange. Level Five defers to Level Thirteen.

A few people did a double take after recognizing him from the broadcast, giving him the Tranquility salute in greeting, smiling broadly at him, or warmly praising him. He modestly waved them off. He didn't like being an instant celebrity.

It wasn't that Will didn't appreciate the points, but what

made him feel on top of the world was the opportunity to help another person in distress. He felt amazing in spite of the harrowing experience he had climbing the bridge and grabbing the boy.

Will noticed the streetlight signal change. The word "proceed" blinked in green to the rhythm of a conga beat. Time to be moving on.

Heads swiveled in Will's direction as he strode around the corner to Bliss Avenue. Not only was he freshly famous, his Plauditor's uniform made him worthy of respect and admiration.

Yet, even without the uniform, he was already used to attention. Like a reflection of his inner self, Will dazzled. His sun-kissed hair, light tan, ultra-white smile, and physically fit body would have been enough to set him apart; however, his eyes were the scene-stealer. They were like emeralds; the brilliant green color leapt from his face and sparkled.

Running footsteps broke Will's concentration. "Will!" The unmistakable voice brought a smile to his face.

Will turned to see his best friend, Weeford, closing the gap behind him. Weeford's brilliant white grin sharply contrasted with his deep brown skin.

"Hey, buddy—what's goin' on?" Will called out. "You're never out this way."

Will had his share of friends. He had always been popular. But he preferred to spend his time with Weeford, whom he'd known since they both were Level Ones, two five-year-old kids just starting out.

In those early childhood days, they both wore white, but today Weeford wore a pink long-sleeved t-shirt, tight jean-styled denim pants, and the required matching shoes, a basic slip-on with a rubber sole. Will didn't like the color. Unless it was his favorite ice cream, Pink Lemonade.

Wee closed the gap between them, throwing his arm over Will's shoulders, practically knocking him over. "Just hopin' to

catch you. Gotta congratulate you in person. You the MAN!"
He patted Will on the shoulder heavily.

"No big deal, c'mon."

Wee laughed, the noise booming out, turning heads
around them. Wee never had any volume control and had a
voice to match his vast size. "Yeah, it is! And look at that
uniform. Wooo Hoooo! Man, oh man! It's gonna take me a
while to get used to seein' you in that thing. You look good,
even for you," he joked, "but I just never imagined you as a
Plauditor."

Will's uniform was an enviable piece of fashion. A smooth
black suede, the jacket fit him perfectly. Across the back it
boasted real silver rivets, setting off a striking yellow stripe,
marking his newly acquired Status. Stripe-matching suede also
dressed up the narrow collar. The front simply zipped up, but
its heavy, inch-wide sterling zipper had a "no nonsense" visual
effect. On each wrist were cuffs, accented by single silver rivets
on each arm. His pants were a solid black knit—the better to
allow comfort and movement—but were trimmed with stripes
of yellow suede over each front pocket. Inside the jacket, a
smooth yellow knit shirt fit like a second skin. This suit stood
out among Tranquility's showy multi-colored clothing as a
bold statement of authority.

Will smiled and nudged his friend on the shoulder.
"Black's ugly, but I'm gonna try to make it look good."

"Yeah, right. The yellow stripe on that hat looks like a
halo. And you're no angel. I know the *real* truth about you."

Will laughed and gave Wee a shove. "Just don't tell
anyone," he said in his most dramatic voice. Taking off his
hat, he twirled it with his fingers and then tossed it up to catch
it a few times before dropping it at his feet.

"Well, I won't be competing with you in scoring
points. Your Alt's gotta be on fire! How many points did you
rack up, anyway?" Wee said.

Will picked up his hat and put it back on his head, its brim to the back. "Because of yesterday? I figure 16,000 points maybe. To rise up, it's a 4,000-point increase, right? I'm still in shock." Will opened his eyes wide and put his hands on both sides of his face, clowning around.

Then he got serious. He glanced down at the Alt on his wrist. Its leather band was embossed with every one of Tranquility's Status colors in a mosaic design. The Alt's face—a two-inch digital screen—was square and flat. The numbers on the black background changed constantly depending on the function being displayed. It not only told time; it was his communication device. But its most important function was its purpose—to track the way he felt every minute of his life. It measured every single emotion. This minute he was happy, but he always felt the pressure to keep his mood light.

Weeford whistled. "Won't be long you'll be moving out of Turquoise Towers and into Yellow Sunrise. Ya won't want to walk to my place."

Will said in disbelief, "Can you believe it? All my dreams are coming true. I just wish…"

Weeford shook his head up and down. "I get it. I know your family's story. Your family *still* lives in *White Sands*. And why would anyone want to live his or her life on Level One? I don't understand why your parents can't seem to rise up."

Will looked around, suddenly conscious of the people around them easily hearing the conversation about his parents. It was okay that Weeford knew everything about his family. But he didn't want it broadcast all over the street corner.

Will felt his face flush. Whether from embarrassment about his parents or guilt about feeling that way, it was an emotion to avoid. Time to put a positive spin on it. "Me? I don't want to wear white every day. Be a Level One. No living in a two-bunk, one-bath, solo-bedroom apartment."

Weeford said, "You turned eighteen anyway. You're on

your own. You do what you need to do. Your parents have a whole different idea of life."

"My parents say they want to live 'simple lives,'" Will said, "but I don't believe it. It's like they're stuck or afraid to move up—I don't know. Their lives are limited. They can't afford to buy anything they want or eat great food. It upsets me."

Weeford's face showed concern, his eyebrows looking like caterpillars going uphill. "You can't let it upset you. Their situation isn't about you. Don't let your points drop over it. Remember, they—"

"Don't worry about me. I can take care of myself—you know that. But, yeah. I know I've told you what my parents believe. And you've kept it a secret. Thanks. But now I'm a Level Twelve, I'm gonna get them out of White Sands."

"Will, how're you gonna do that? It's not like you're Elite."

"Someday, Wee."

Will gazed out across the intersection, now a hive of colors and activity, but he didn't really see any of it. His mind was in a faraway place. He badly wanted to be important, and that meant rising up. But he never wanted to do it at someone else's expense. In his heart, he knew he had a purpose, and it was far bigger than himself.

"Only four more levels to go, and you'll be a candidate for the Elite. Then I can say 'I knew you when,'" Wee said.

Will's face brightened. "As Elite, I could help make decisions to help people like my parents. I would honor my grandfather. He taught me so much about supporting our government and making Tranquility a better place."

Wee nodded. "It wouldn't surprise me if you also got an Augur Prize for what you've done. I can see that happening, too."

"You give me too much credit, Wee. If it weren't for Jesse's rescue, I'd just be an ordinary guy."

"But your Alt points don't drop—ever. Don't know how

you do it. Nothing bothers you or upsets you. For the rest of us, growing our Alt points is a challenge," Wee said.

Will knew it was true. He had an incredible mindset. Although he still had to check and recheck his Alt like everyone else, he made his point increases an unparalleled personal quest. Like a young athlete diligently preparing for the Olympics, he practiced the art of self-control until he thought his soul would bleed.

Will looked at his friend. "I try really hard. To be honest, though, I have fears—fears I'll never be able to help my parents. Letting my grandfather down. Keeping myself apart from emotional risks, like girls. Failing at my new job … it all scares me, Wee. I'm not stone, even though I want to be."

The surrounding fog was lifting, evaporating in the mystical way Tranquility controlled its precipitation. The monthly vapor acted as a cleaning process for the city, purifying their enclosed city from within. Rays of sun shone through translucent holes in the mist, making the space look other worldly. Will gazed up, his focus on the sparkle that hung in the air.

Weeford punched Will's arm. "Yeah. And now that you're a Level Twelve, you can't even date anyone with a lower Status. That's gonna be a real challenge. Who you gonna find your age who's a Level Twelve?"

"Nobody." Will hung his head. "I'm not ready to think about that, though. I just want to do what's best for Tranquility and be happy."

As if his fears literally came to life, he watched as two men dressed in bright red robes with hoods come out from Seventh Heaven, a popular restauran across the street. Sciolists! They carried a young, protesting female with purple hair toward a crimson CommuteCar parked at the curb. The teenage girl—a lowly Level One—flailed against her unwelcome detainers with her arms and legs. "Let go of me! Let go!" she screamed. The fight she put up clearly marked her as a resistor. No one acted like that, even in a Removal. It just wasn't proper.

He and Wee both turned to watch, their mouths agape, along with others standing along the sidewalk. One by one, people looked away or cast their eyes downward, embarrassed, and moved on. The girl, still screaming, and the silent Sciolists carrying her disappeared into the car. The CommuteCar took off, moving down the street as if it were a common occurrence.

"Poor girl," Will finally said. "Did you see her face? So red. She was crying." His face crumpled in sympathy, and his Alt vibrated with a surge in points. For compassion and kindness, the Alt was generous. "I'd like to help people like that."

"I've never seen a Removal in progress before, have you?" Wee said.

"No. Must be a pretty severe violation of emotion, though. She was hysterical. Not good."

"Just so long as it's never one of us," Wee said.

"I hope she gets the help she needs."

"Maybe she's going directly to The Outside," Wee said, in an uncharacteristic whisper, his eyes wide.

"Hope not. The climate out there's enough to drive people insane. I've heard things. It's either blistering hot or ungodly cold. Always gray. That—and other things. Can't believe anyone could actually survive out there."

Wee said, "I'll take my blue skies and 75 degrees in Tranquility, please. Climate control rocks."

Will's Alt buzzed a warning. The GPS tracker connected to his Alt showed he wasn't close enough to his destination to be there at eight A.M.

"I'd better get going. I don't wanna be late." Will began walking backward as he talked. "Wish me luck for my first day … I'm headed to the Plauditorium now."

"You don't need luck, Will—you might as well have 'Too Talented' written in the sky over your head." Weeford wrote with his finger in the air. "You've got it all now, buddy! Catch ya later."

Will, intent on making up time, strode forward, but stopped, turning back to his friend.

"Wee! Hang out later?" he yelled.

"Can't today. Gotta work late," he called back.

Weeford waved again and then darted across the adjacent crosswalk into Prosperity Park and blended in with the Pink Level Fours like himself, waiting in line to go over the bridge.

Will watched him until he disappeared. From his vantage point, it looked like a rainbow of colors fanned out, starting with the Level Eighteens dressed in gold at the front of the line. A peaceful process for a perfect city.

The last block to the Plauditorium was down a charming street with little shops, all with friendly facades and inviting scents. The Candy Tree was first on his left. Its picture window featured precisely carved chocolate creations, hung with red licorice and flowers made from frosting. It cost very few of his Alt points to acquire candy from the store, and it was always busy, filled with people, even this morning as he sauntered by. He grinned as he watched the children buying candy for breakfast, their faces full of smiles and their bodies jumping up and down in anticipation. *Lucky kids.* He looked past the sign that barred anyone below a Level Three from entering the store. The memory of his own disappointment as a child when he was excluded from the shop surfaced momentarily, but he quickly dismissed it. He no longer had those restrictions. His new Status would allow him to purchase so many excellent things—from tailored clothes to gourmet food.

Next door, The Wild Hair, one of Tranquility's salons, boasted its popularity with luminescent pink, green, and yellow curly cues on its facade. He sidestepped a thin, smiling woman who emerged from the door. Her bright pink hair stood straight out around her head like a lion's mane. Of course, it matched her outfit, a Level Four, through and through.

A seventy-inch monitor on his left invited prospective patrons to witness inspiring makeovers. Anyone in Tranquility, man or woman, could get a luxurious spa treatment—featuring an effervescent green solution called Lustrum—and emerge looking years younger and refreshed. No one had to worry much about appearing old unless they didn't have enough Status or Alt points to get an appointment. *Some day. Someday I might need that.*

The Detoxification Station, the third store on the street, was a bold, kelly green, the color used to represent nurturing and new beginnings. He gave a nod and a smile to the lovely models outside the door who were giving out samples of freshly minted water and cleansing minerals. Each sample not only tasted refreshing but gave each person who samples it a burst of energy to face their day. A virtual reality advertisement in the window announced the shop's special for the day. They were offering a half-off special only for Level Twelves to honor Energy, that Status Level's unique trait. Will politely passed on the offer as he thought, *I have more energy than I need.*

Staring into The Salt Mine's window next, Will pressed the app on his Alt to remind him to stop there later. He remembered he was out of Jarnish—the best tiny cracker in town. Sprinkled with sea salt, cinnamon, and coated in peanut oil, it was a sticky, addictive treat. He continued on down the crowded street with new anticipation, knowing he would be able to snack on Jarnish on his way home.

3

Will's Promise

W ill was pumped full of hope. He stopped a block away from the Plauditorium and thought again about his humble parents and wise grandfather.

A sweet memory floated to the surface of his mind—a special, unforgettable discussion he'd had with his grandfather, Blake Verus. Will had spent many golden hours with his grandpa, time he fervently wished he could bring back. He had enormous trust and love for the old man, his balding head shiny as the moon, his eyes a paler version of green than Will's own. The edges of Grandpa's eyes crinkled when he smiled, and the grooves of his smiles were imprinted on his gentle face. He knew now they were only wrinkles. Back then, he thought his gramps had simply been marked with permanent happiness pleats.

His grandpa always seemed so wise; Will knew he had to be The Most Enlightened Being in the universe. He was the one who knew all the true answers to life's puzzling questions, and yet he had the goodness and joy of the most ideal citizen of Tranquility. Will had always wondered why the old man always dressed in orange until he understood that he was a Level Thirteen, a Status worthy of deep pride.

Will had been only eight when his innocent, eager curiosity spawned the most important conversation of Will's life. It had happened only a couple of years before his beloved grandpa passed away.

"What was the world like *before*?" Will had asked, climbing up on his grandpa's lap.

"Ah. A bad place. We were starving. No money."

"Did someone steal their money, Grandpa?"

Will turned his head and moved it close to his grandpa's face so their foreheads were only an inch apart.

"Not any certain person, no. They had money in a savings account, but the banks failed. They never got their money back. They couldn't make ends meet."

Will pulled his face back, still keeping his eyes on his grandfather's, but then leaned away.

"But your dad had a job, didn't he?"

"Yep. Sent drones around the country. High demand for it, too. But after a while, no one could buy anything. Or send mail. People lived awhile on what they had. When supplies ran out, people did anything for food. They committed crimes. Even killed people. They were only out for themselves. It was hopeless."

"That's awful. You had to live through that?" Will climbed off his grandpa's lap, pushing his arms up and down on his grandpa's knees.

"Yes, buddy. That's why you *must* promise to always follow the laws we have here in Tranquility."

Will stopped moving. His grandpa's tone was stern. It scared him a little. He plucked at the pajamas he wore, discovering that the white fabric actually had white dinosaurs on it. But Will couldn't—shouldn't—think about dinosaurs. His grandpa was talking about laws. That was a lot more important.

"What are the laws? How can I remember them?" Will

rubbed his face, as if to erase the lines of worry on his forehead.

"Tranquility's laws are always in the Cloud." His grandpa pointed up.

"In the clouds?" Will asked, looking at the ceiling.

"Not an actual cloud, like the ones in the sky. It's an invisible thing. Every person has access to 'em. I have a printed copy, too. I like my printed copy. It's solid—real." Will's grandpa shuffled across the room and opened a drawer in an orange bureau. He carried the printed copy back, treating it with great honor. "Let's read it together, Will, and then I'll teach you how to memorize them." His voice cracked with awe as he began to read:

LAWS AND SOCIAL ORDER OF TRANQUILITY

Accord Number One

Every citizen will be issued an Alt from the time they are five years old. Each day's Alt measurements for HAPPINESS will be collected, analyzed, and submitted to the Elite at City Hall. All citizens must commit to be a part of the Continuum Spectrum.

Every increase in points by 4000 on the Spectrum will result in approval for advancement in Status by the Elite Council. Achievement on the Status hierarchy will result in the following upgrades and privileges, including and limited to:

- Neighborhood – citizens will be assigned to a housing area in keeping with their Status
  - Food – various levels of chef expertise and availability of foods by Status Level
    - Clothing – color assigned to the Status with potential designer availability
  - Jobs/Careers – increased levels of responsibility for leadership in the community
    - Privileges – access to store products and services
    - Transportation – available by monorail, sedans, and limousines
      - Activities – community events, recreation and theater

"So, I'll explain this, so you'll understand. Your Alt. The points on it? It's what you use to get *everything.* Food. Clothes. Toys. Your parents use 'em, too. That's what makes Alt points so important. Long ago, there was money. Now, you use your points. Understand?"

Will shook his head up and down in an exaggerated "yes."

"Let's look at your Alt, Will." The old man turned Will's wrist up to face him. "Your points. They're good. Keep it up." He gave Will a broad smile.

Will's enthusiasm boiled over. He patted his grandpa's face. "So, that's why you live in Orange Glen, and I live in White Sands?'

"Yes, Will. If you work hard at being happy, no matter what happens in your life, you could live in Orange Glen someday, too." Grandpa cleared his throat and began to read again:

Accord Number Two

All citizens who have achieved a new Status goal will attend and be recognized at Status ceremonies. This will be conducted at City Hall by the Elite, with the Magistrate presiding, on the 18th day of each month, at 7:00 p.m.

"Each year there's a ceremony. A big party. At City Hall. But just for people who rise up to a new Status level."

"How many times, Grandpa?"

"For what, Will?"

"How many ceremonies did you have?"

"Well. Let's see. That would've been twelve."

Will jumped up and down, his legs like springs. "That's a lot!"

Grandpa chuckled. "You're right, my boy. Keep listening." His voice took on a more serious tone.

Accord Number Three

The Elite and the Magistrate will determine Banishment from the Tranquility community. Banishment will occur for producing and maintaining Alt numbers below Level One over a period of six months. However, no less than eight interventions will be implemented before a citizen is labeled a REM (Resisting Emotional Management). REMs will be released to The

Outside and their histories erased. REMs are not allowed to return to the city. No deviants will be tolerated.

"This means that you always try to be happy. You follow the rules. If you don't, counselors will work with you. But there's a limit to the help. You have to want to change."

"What's 'Banishment,' Gramps?" Will climbed up into his lap. Suddenly he wanted to feel secure—to be protected.

"'Banishment,' Will, is when you're no longer allowed to live in Tranquility."

Will snuggled up closer. "Where…where would I go?" His voice quavered.

"There's a place called The Outside. If you don't keep your points up, that's where our City Hall would send you. But, don't worry. I know you'll never be banished, Will."

"How do you know?" Will's face went a little pale.

"Because I know *you*, Will. You have the proper heart, and you'll follow the laws."

"Tell me, Grandpa! What should I do?"

"Stay happy—that's all, Will. That's all. Then you can rise up in Status. I'm dressed in orange—'cause that's my Status color. But there are more. Both Accord Four and Five tell you what you need to know." He read again.

Accord Number Four

Every Tranquilite will pledge himself/herself to uphold all laws in Tranquility. He or she will devote special attention toward the Values listed below, associated with the Status maintained by the individual:

White — Level 1: Purity

Ivory — Level 2: Unity

Beige — Level 3: Respect

Pink — Level 4: Loyalty

Brown — Level 5: Order

Turquoise — Level 6: Trust

Kelly Green — Level 7: Responsibility

Royal Blue — Level 8: Peace

Mint Green — Level 9: Conformity

Magenta — Level 10: Tenacity

Lavender — Level 11: Obedience

Yellow — Level 12: Energy

Orange — Level 13: Optimism

Purple — Level 14:Nobility

Indigo — Level 15: Integrity

Copper — Level 16: Resilience

Silver — Level 17: Enlightenment

Gold — Level 18: Wisdom

Accord Number Five

Citizens will dress according to their Status. Dress code violations will result in counseling and ultimately, Removal.

"Blue's my favorite color! I'm gonna wear that!" Will's face beamed like a Chinese lantern, already forgetting his worry about Banishment.

"I have no doubt, Will. You'll do well." Gramps dropped his blue-veined dry hand onto Will's slight left shoulder and patted him.

"What else, Grandpa?" He rubbed his eyes. He was getting sleepy.

"The next part is about sickness and death, Will. But, again, Tranquility has everything figured out." He patted Will's shoulder again, this time ending his pat in an affectionate squeeze.

Accord Number Six

If, by some unknown reason, a member of the community becomes ill, Tranquility's specialists may diagnose and treat the individual. Treatments include visualization, music therapy, acupressure and massage. It is the responsibility of the citizen to heal themselves through positive thinking. Injuries will be treated with the Medela machine. Tranquilites should reach the age of 100. However, at that time, the Elite will terminate life by merciful euthanasia.

"This says you'll live a long time. You won't ever get sick."

"Sick? What's that?"

"It's when you don't feel good in your body. A few people here are Medics, but you won't need them. If you get hurt, Medics and a special machine can help you."

Will frowned. "My body feels good." He turned to gaze into his gramps' eyes. He swallowed and then stared at the floor before asking, "What's you-then-asia? Is that somebody's name? Asia?"

"No, no, Will. It's not you-then-asia. It's 'euthanasia.' The government gives you a shot, and you go to sleep. You don't come back, though."

"But *you'll* come back. You're my grandpa. You have to come back after you sleep."

"No, Will. I can't come back."

Will thought his grandpa looked sad. He was sad, too. He climbed back up into the chair next to him.

"Are you a hundred, Gramps?"

"Soon, Will. But I've had a good life. Don't you worry. When the time comes, I'll always be with you. I may be a memory, but a solid one. That you can never lose."

Will's brows furrowed, and his eyes welled up.

"Now, now." Gramps hugged him with his bear-like embrace. "Let's talk about something wonderful."

Accord Number Seven

Since Tranquility holds its members in high esteem, awards will be presented to individuals who go above and beyond their responsibilities to the City. Alt points must be higher than the majority of people of that Status. This citizen demonstrates a dedication to the Status Level's assigned value through service or written works. Recognition includes plaques, morning news announcements, and/or jewelry. The Augur Prize is one such honor, represented by a Status-determined, priceless ring.

"This means if you earn more points on your Alt than anyone else, you get a ring. Or, if you prove you have fully developed the character trait of that Status level."

"Do you have a ring?" Will asked.

"No. But I hope that you might one day."

A smile lit Will's face, and his voice grew bubbly. "Who do I ask for one?"

"Ah, Will. You don't. The prize will come if you earn it."

Accord Number Eight

Individuals who achieve Level 18, Gold, are invited to join the Elite to serve in City Hall with the Magistrate. This council determines the best welfare for its citizens, drafts laws, and recognizes citizens in the community.

Will said, "Gold! It's all about gold, huh?"

"Sort of. If you earn enough points, you become a high level. Level Eighteen. Part of the government. Make the laws. The rules. You're called Elite."

"If I'm a Leet, I can make the rules? I got lots of ideas!"

"Save 'em up, Will. For some day. Now, listen carefully. These are the last of the Accords."

Accord Number Nine

The Magistrate holds his term for life. In the event the Magistrate should die, members of the Elite will choose a new leader among themselves best suited for the position.

"Our leader's called a Magistrate. He's in charge. He and City Hall always have your best interests at heart."

"Can I be a Magistrate?"

"You never know."

Accord Number Ten

Notifications in writing made to individual citizens from City Hall will be obeyed without question for the good of all citizens and the peace of Tranquility.

"This means you need to obey the laws. Take orders. They'll keep all of us from suffering ever again like the people of the past."

Will shook his head up and down, to show his understanding, his eyes solemn as a prayer. "Okay."

"Not just 'okay.' Promise me, Will. Promise me! No matter what, you'll never betray your family or your government."

"Yes, I promise." Will raised two fingers in the air to show his pledge. "You can count on me. I'll always remember."

His mind snapped back to the present like the stretched release of a tight blind. He would make them all *proud*. His mom, especially, who told him to work hard and leave a legacy for future family members to follow like his grandpa. Perhaps at some point he could meet the Magistrate, Tranquility's leader, and thank him personally for providing everyone, especially himself, such a wonderful life.

4

Ember's Loss

E mber jumped, startled. A phone call was coming through her Alt. An upbeat tune from the city's Top 40 shattered the stillness. Its lyrics taunted her; they were a purposeful reminder that life was blissful, ideal. Yet, the music grated like a shrill saw. She was discouraged and deeply troubled.

"Hello?" She breathed into her Alt, immediately realizing that whispering was unnecessary. Her mom slept on, undisturbed.

"Ember—this is Chief Medic Abutor. Beautiful day in our fine city. Your mom—resting comfortably?"

"Oh, Medic Abutor! Thanks for calling. I've left messages for you for days now . . . I'm really concerned about my mom . . . she hasn't eaten or spoken for a week. She doesn't wake up. She needs something–something to help her! Isn't there anything more you can do?"

Ember looked around the room, searching, almost as if she could magically conjure something up to help her mom. Instead, the room's walls seem to close in. The antiseptic smell of the hospital room, partly disguised by a lavender fragrance, clung to her clothes. It added to a nausea created by anxiety.

"We've tried everything, Ember. Remember working with your mom and the doctors? Traditional healing methodologies, all utilized. Laughter sessions, check. Music therapy, throughout. Imagery used as well. There was no genetic abnormality to correct with GFX. In your mother's case, sadly —those haven't worked. Bewildered the medical team. Never even identified the disease at all. Pretty challenging finding a specialized cure. Way beyond our skills."

"But my mom's a fighter, Doctor! She went running every morning and worked her shifts at the museum just days before she was admitted here. No one in the community even realized she was sick. She was always the one engaging others in positive conversation. My mom never complained or cried. There must be *something* you can do! I'm not even able to communicate with her! What if these are my last moments with her? I can't even say goodbye!"

"So very sorry, Ember. That time has passed. We're still monitoring her Alt carefully along with her other vital signs, but there's absolutely no emotional activity on her Alt." *No wonder I can't feel her emotions,* Ember thought. *And her aura is gray and dim.* "Try some breathing patterns—they help prepare people for the worst. And, talk to your mom. Who knows? Possibly, she's still able to hear you. Again, I am sorry."

Ember eyes filled with tears as she saw the upside-down face on the Alt's screen, an icon verifying the end of the conversation.

Her eyes now on the Alt's surface, Ember realized it was time for monitoring her emotional state. She loved her Alt. Her most precious possession was sensitive and absolute, a good friend. The emotional monitoring, unlike unexpected phone calls, was a welcome activity, comforting in its ongoing presence, its feedback necessary for life to stay peaceful and happy. But this was not a typical day.

She sucked in a deep, jagged breath. Her mother's life was ebbing away, triggering a tightrope walk with Alt readings.

Depression was a severe sin in the community, the Alt noting it with ease. What would it read now?

Ember tapped on her Alt. Place her index finger . . . wait ten seconds . . .

Her reading came up, blinking neon pink. Respiration rate — twenty-five breaths per minute, heart at 100 beats per minute. "This is accelerated . . ." She caught herself talking aloud. The "C" measurement—the Cortisol hormone secretion protecting the body from stress—was elevated. She had to concentrate.

Ember's Alt vibrated and started to ping. To her dismay, a downward arrow popped up in the display. It appeared as a solid form but soon began to transform into a repeating downward arrow. A bar of red appeared at the bottom of the Alt's face, indicating that she had bottomed out in the red zone! *Don't panic,* she thought.

Her tears threatened to break free, but Ember couldn't allow herself the freedom to cry. A tear had its price. A tear was a *risk*. Even a simple, reactive thought was fatefully significant. Ember gazed out the hospital window tonight and sighed. As with all nights, every window was wet with rain. The raindrops were like tears, tracing with their tracks her difficult journey.

In spite of what was happening, it was vital to battle emotions. Even death was not an excuse to be weak or sad! She had to breathe deeply and be calm! Think positive thoughts!

As if she was on the outside step of a moving merry-go-round gripping the iron bars, Ember hung on. A thought settled into her unbalanced psyche—a reflection back on her early schooling when she had her Empowerment Teachings. Those teachings throughout her life had successfully enabled her to overcome negative energy. Ember concentrated on slowing her heartbeat by repeating a common mantra: "Happiness is a choice that requires effort."

Ember struggled not to cry and kept reaching over to squeeze one of her mother's hands from where it listlessly dangled over the side of the hospital bed. Her childhood history came to mind, memories streaking through like meteorites in the night sky. She saw her mom pushing her on a swing when she was four. She saw the homemade birthday cake, iced in pink, that her mother placed in front of her; saw, too, how her mom brought sparklers out for an extra surprise, her own eyes as bright as the fiery shreds. She remembered notes in her lunchbox with positive affirmations and heard her mother singing as she dressed for the day, not hitting the proper notes. She saw her mom pouring essential oils into Ember's bathtub, remarking they were "magical." She saw her mom at forty, graduating to Status Level Fourteen, her face radiant as a pearl newly formed, as she received a set of silky purple clothes. Each change in status meant a new color to wear. Purple was the color everyone wore at Level Fourteen, but Ember thought that the color looked more magnificent on her mom than anyone else in Tranquility. All these scenes projected in her mind as if in an old-fashioned film, now crushing toward "The End" in the final frame.

When Ember was eight, she achieved the first level on the Continuum's Spectrum. Her mouth curled in a smile as she remembered the beautiful white dress her mother had sewn for her. In a special Status ceremony called Renew, Ember graduated from wearing pale pink, the color of all Tranquility's children, to wearing white. White symbolized purity of thought and new beginnings.

Ember squeezed her eyes shut, willing these memories to take hold and register on her Alt. Love was the ultimate emotion. Pure. Stronger than all. She believed that love could prevail. As if in confirmation, she felt a vibration on her wrist . . . an encouraging sign.

Mom's ruptured breathing from the hospital bed grew

louder. Could her mother feel the love, too? She breathed in deeply, willing her own breath to repair her mother's.

"Mmm . . ."

What was that? Had she heard something other than her mom's irregular breathing? One of the machines made a soft whirring sound . . . okay . . . the machines were making adjustments.

"Mmm . . ."

Ember sat up in her chair. *Wait! It* was *Mom making that noise! Maybe Mom was rallying?*

Ember leaned in toward her mother. "Mom? I'm here . . . it's Ember, Mom." She put her hands on her mother's face. "Mom . . . I love you. Please . . . can you talk?"

Only silence answered.

She had been so hopeful that what she had heard was more than just breath. She placed her hands around her mother's face and silently begged her to respond.

Ember closed her eyes, again remembering the carefree days with her mom before the illness slithered stealthily into her near-perfect body. The most dominant memory . . . her mother's shining blue-green eyes noticeably twinkling when she smiled, her hugs all comfort and selflessness, her values exemplary.

Ember took her hands gently from her mother's face. She turned her eyes to the clock on the wall. The clock's muted ticking was both a comfort (all clocks in the city at large were programmed to soothe), but yet, the tick-tock was a reminder that time slowed down for no one, not even in Tranquility.

5

Ember's Hope

"Em . . . ber." The word was weak, barely audible.

Ember's head whipped back around. "Mom! I'm here, Mom! You're talking!" Ember cried.

"Don't wear . . ." Talesa's voice faded out to a whisper.

"Mom! What? What shouldn't I wear?"

"No . . . time . . ." her mom's eyes were still closed, but her mouth quivered.

"Mom! Please! What are you saying?" She implored her mother to help her understand. "I need you to fully wake up, Mom . . . Mom!" A whoosh from behind distracted Ember from her mom's labored whisper.

The unanticipated rush came from the automated door, blowing in a stubby medic with red hair cut in a smooth bowl shape. *Go away.* Ember's heart was tumbling once again— an intrusion. Right when Mom was trying to tell her something important!

The medic, wearing a bright yellow uniform, stomped in. "How's she doing, darling? We want to make sure her medication is high enough that she has pleasant dreams, you know." Medic Redhead, or whatever her name was, walked briskly to the bed, turned up the medication sliding into the tube, checked her mom's vitals being measured on the Alt on her wrist, fluffed the pillow, and smiled.

Ember was ready to burst. She jumped out of her chair and ran to this new person. She'd interrupted, but maybe she could help. "Medic! My mom talked! I haven't been able to talk to her for two weeks, and she actually spoke!" Tears blurred her vision, and her whole body vibrated with nervous tremors.

"Ah. Sometimes that happens . . . and it's a blessing," Medic Redhead murmured. Her eyes, twin puppy-dog orbs, bore sympathy, but her face was tight.

"Yeah. But it's not just a fluke. She's coming back. I know it!"

Ember pushed down a rising instant hatred for this woman. The medic could help, but it was clear she wouldn't. What kind of medic was she, anyway? Ember clenched her fists, her frustration getting the best of her.

"Can't you just . . . can't you at least look at her Alt? If she spoke, there's emotion. She's still alive—feeling stuff!" Ember rushed over and picked up her mom's wrist but saw nothing on the Alt's screen. How could there be darkness when her mom was full of light?

"You need to understand. There's nothing to change your mom's situation. It won't be long now, dear. She needs to rest, so let your mother enjoy her peace. You just be happy! She's not feeling a thing." She moved toward the door, her shoes squeaking against the floor's shiny tiles. She turned as if she had a last-minute thought. "Those who can," she paused for a beat, "die . . . without feeling sad . . . are the luckiest people." Medic Redhead then slipped out the door, but not before offering Ember a "thumbs up" and a radiant smile.

Ember forced a weak smile in return, but was totally confused. *Didn't this woman fathom what miracle had just occurred?* In spite of the medic's warning and her lack of help and hope,

Ember was ebullient. Maybe her mom would speak again! Everything suddenly seemed to be looking so much better!

Ember turned back and keenly watched her mother. But, to her dismay, Talesa had now slipped back under heavier medication. She was deeply sleeping.

Yet Ember was convinced her mother could still hear her. "I know you wanted me to hear something important, Mom. What did you try to tell me?"

The minutes ticked by to the familiar swaying of the clock's pendulum on the wall. Ember sat, watching and hoping. A tear escaped, and she quickly wiped it off, as if the Alt couldn't see it. She checked her Alt to gauge the random teardrop. Her pulse quickened as she again saw a dip in the readings.

Ember knew she was going to need all the strength she could muster to get through whatever was going on here. She simply could not lose any more Alt points today! The best course of action was to meditate on the imagery she had been taught. She dreamed up a fifty-yard race in her mind, where she crossed the finish line and won the ribbon. It was one of her "go-to" simple emergency responses. The deeper she could go into the dream, the more the Alt readings would level out.

But as hard as she tried, she couldn't get deep enough into the meditative state to refresh her mind and spirit. Her mom's face—and words—continued to enter her thoughts. She again squeezed her mother's hand hanging motionless over the side of the hospital bed. With her finger, Ember traced the pale line where her mother's ring had once graced her finger.

Suddenly, a bell chimed merrily through a speaker above Ember's head. It played a modernistic carnival-like tune. It was obviously some type of alarm. It had an urgent sound because of its tempo, although the bells were soft and insistent. Ember gazed around the room. She couldn't read the medical monitors under their willowy shrouds. They picked up every little change; they were the most precise pieces of equipment designed by science. Perhaps—probably?—in spite of Medic Redhead's comments, the medical staff had realized her mother had spoken?

In the hallway, the flurry of beating wings turned out to be footsteps marching to the beat of the alarm. In a matter of seconds, an assembly of young men and women reverently entered the room. *More medics?* she thought. The noise of the alarm faded to nothing, and Ember felt a chill creep like a bug up her spinal cord.

Ember glanced around, turning her head, hoping to find answers somewhere—anywhere. Her eyes filled up, the tears silvery drops of misery. The team approached her without words, pulling her by the arms into a circle with them, placing her carefully in the center. Each of the six put their arms on one another's shoulders.

"What's this? What's happening?"

Ember gazed desperately around the circle, her eyes scrutinizing the faces of these newcomers for answers to her confusion. Their faces seemed happy, yet oddly disturbing. All were smiling, but the emotion didn't seem sincere. She yearned to yell, scream, demand answers, but she stood frozen in place, unable to utter a word.

Then, each of them released their hands, and in the same way they entered, began to file out the door. For a moment, Ember stared after them, too nonplussed to even move.

"Wait!" she was finally able to cry. But the door was already closing. "You're needed here!" *Where were they all going?* It was clear that the alert chime was to notify the medical staff of a great change. "Come back!" Frantically, Ember turned back again to her mom.

The bed was empty.

6

Xander Noble

W hile Ember grappled with staying true to her Alt in spite of personal tragedy, another resident of Tranquility, Xander Noble, was just as busy resisting.

Thinking back, Xander knew that he was a true rebel, even in his very young years.

In elementary school, he was indifferent to what was being taught. Emotional Training had been a waste of his time. Why couldn't he speak his mind? Wasn't how he thought important?

But for the most part, it aggravated him to see other people being upbeat all the time, trying so hard to please. To Xander, it was phony. By the time he was in middle school, he began to realize that life—and people he knew—would always be this way. He found himself upset 'round the clock, especially going through adolescence, and he had never been able to control it. To Xander, life was a series of ups and downs, and his negative feelings were part of who he was at his core. He had never wished to accumulate either material items or achievement, so the system here in Tranquility was, without a doubt, not designed for someone like him.

He found himself regularly depressed but unwilling to take the steps that his teachers recommended to "get better." He sometimes tried to tie his hopes to what Tranquility leaders had promised would help him. But those measures didn't last long, although he did enjoy Tranquility's Fun Zone on the south side of town.

The Fun Zone was one of the "helps" Tranquility offered to people who wanted or needed to boost their Alt points. Shiny rainbow roller coasters spanned up six stories or cruised simple tracks in a loop. Of course, even here, one's Status determined which rides were available and which were off-limits.

If none of the roller coasters were to a person's liking, or available per one's Status, no one lacked entertainment in the Fun Zone. Rides were experiential: "Airplane Acrobatics," a vintage airplane from the 1960s doing unpredictable daredevil stunts. "L Extreme," a sky-high elevator drop at a hundred miles an hour. A cruise through space . . . a rolling rapids water ride. The Fun Zone was full of laughing, smiling people. For Xander, a few thrill rides lifted his mood, but after an hour or two, the effects had left him; after a time, he simply quit going.

People who knew him marveled at how his physical features mimicked his mischievous and dark nature. Yet, in spite of being the opposite of a Tranquilite ("Trank" for short), the shadowy side of his personality was profoundly charismatic; he quickly drew people to him, and as he aged, his sex appeal seared many a heart. Every inch of his now six-foot, lanky frame screamed confidence and allure. His jet-black hair and pale skin were a model of the "bad boy, good boy" war that waged within him. Adding to his his look with heavy midnight eyeliner, Xander styled his hair unlike others in the city. They wore their hair longer on the sides and combed down in the front. Combed straight up on the top and short on the sides, Xander's rock star hair set him apart, and made him kind of famous. He loved that—all the attention. It made his life in Tranquility almost bearable.

Xander preferred to wear fashions on the edge; it pleased his artistic nature. So although he had never earned the privilege of wearing the bright colors of higher Status, he wore what he pleased. He designed and sewed many of his own most extravagant outfits. The Elite colors of indigo, magenta, and gold were his favorite, the colors of their society's uppermost rungs. When he wore the colors of Levels Fourteen and above, people listened to what he had to say. He was *somebody*. He loved the high regard people leveled his way.

People in authority were often the target of his disrespect. One evening, Xander was on his way out. Dressed in an indigo-hued light-weight silk jacket and tight pants appropriate to a Level Fifteen, he was ready to impress. He was on his way to a club in town, a place where girls and fancy drinks could make anybody's day more fun. He was being a good citizen, of course; going after things like that would definitely make him happier. Too bad his Alt points would prevent his getting the best spot in the club. And his drink would be barely alcoholic, but it would do.

A Plauditor stopped Xander on the street corner. The guy was a Level Seventeen—high up. Even if he weren't, a Plauditor was a government agent, and all citizens gave them the ultimate courtesy and respect, even going beyond the common manners required of all Tranks.

"Hey, citizen," the Plauditor said after giving the Tranquility salute. The man's face was wreathed in a smile, his hazel eyes twinkling with a joy that Xander envied. "Your Alt points—are they high tonight?"

"Don't give two squeaks about my Alt. Never have." He continued to walk by, his careless attitude showing up in the shrug of his shoulders.

The Plauditor put his hand over his heart, as if the reply

stopped its beat. "Is there anything I can do to help improve that for you?"

Xander stopped, even though he had no desire for conversation. He looked the Plauditor up and down. "Let me think . . ." He paused, as if he were truly giving it some serious thought. "No. You're just in my way. Don't you have anything better to do than to bother people already out for a good time?" Then, impulsively, he unstrapped his Alt, and tossed it to the Plauditor. "Catch!" He laughed.

The Plauditor's eyes opened wide in alarm. "Oh, heavens!" The man looked as if he'd seen a massive spider crawl up his pant leg. He picked up the Alt from the ground and dusted it off. But he didn't hand it back. Instead, he looked at it, shock registering on his face at the point levels. "Your Alt shows less than baseline levels. And you're throwing it on the ground! Inappropriate! Emotional issues! I must report this." He pulled his wrist up to his mouth, ready to speak after his finger poked on a sad-faced emoticon on the screen. "Your name?"

"I'm Batman."

The beefy, perspiring Level Seventeen looked at him as if he were a lost puppy, his eyes full of compassion. But he didn't laugh. At all. "I'm taking your Alt to City Hall. A Sciolist will take it from there."

Xander was left to stand there alone, his plans for the night ruined. Without his Alt, he'd have no access to the club. And, to be truthful, the bouncers probably wouldn't have let him in anyway. Not if his points were at baseline.

In his young life of seventeen, Xander had been punished for similar violations over forty times. From his wardrobe offenses to his snarky words to people in authority, he arrogantly rode the limits.

At age five he received his Alt, same as everyone else; Xander wore it, but was unmindful of its presence. It vibrated to remind him to check its face, but Xander figured he was what he was, so other than "checking in," he dismissed the readings and went about his life.

Xander was of the Noble family; the city had always valued them. His parents and several aunts and uncles had served in city government and in the Good Works agencies that were focused on keeping the citizens happy and safe from negative influences. Xander's mother, similar to many of the women in Tranquility, helped sew and design the clothes that each Status group was entitled to wear. His dad was a manager in the Transportation Department. He had been proud of his heritage, but often he wondered how he had ever been born into such a family. It was a puzzle.

As he grew older and the Alt readings remained often in the Red Zone, Intervention Teams came and picked him up. He'd had both Sciolists and Plauditors in his life. No one in Tranquility could expect less than being counseled, the city leaders hoping they'd be reformed. Xander had experienced many sessions. These sessions, known as Purging, lasted hours, depending on his attitude and the patience of the counselor assigned to his case.

He would be whisked off into a large fifteen-by-fifteen-foot room painted and decorated with all the eighteen Status colors in Tranquility. Gems the size of dinner plates sparkled on the wall, each one a glittering, colorful equivalent to its relevant Status. He smirked as he read each Level's label stenciled in gold leaf.

The first time Xander went for Purging, he didn't know what to expect. Once in the office, he decided to make things difficult for his Counselor.

"Xander. I'm Winslow Liberalis." Winslow extended the city salute of acknowledgment and acceptance, pulled out a chair from the table in the center of the room, and sat down, as if he was the paragon of all things proper. "I'm here to help you with your anger and negative feelings today. You will keep your Alt on your wrist at all times, but we'll be looking at your Status Points on the big screen on the wall there." Winslow pointed toward the white wall in front of them.

Xander studied the man across the table. He took in his platinum-framed glasses and white-coiffed hair. "Hey. I certainly hope you can help me, Win," Xander replied with enthusiasm, sarcasm dripping from every word. "I just don't know what I'll *do* if I can't get my act together." Xander ran his right hand through his spiky hair, as if feeling absolute desperation.

"Now, Xander. Of course I can help you. If you'll just choose to open your mind and your heart, young man, you'll learn to take your citizenship here with the earnestness it deserves. Then, we'll not need to see each other again. This day is yours, and I'll be here as long as it takes to get you purged out." Winslow straightened his gold tie and buttoned his gilded coat, as if to prove how serious this business was.

"Whatever you say, Win. You fix me."

"Xander, there are certain principles you need to understand. We can't expect to be happy when we are busy criticizing our fellow citizens or delight in anger. And I see you're dressed in the color of a Level Ten—magenta—today. You know that's taboo. Level One citizens can't wear that. You should be wearing white, Xander. White."

Xander smoothed his hands down the lapels of the magenta-colored velveteen jacket he wore and then adjusted his coordinated shirt cuffs peeking from underneath. "Well, that's one thing you guys just don't *get*. I need freedom to express myself. I designed and made these clothes myself. Sorry you can't appreciate my talent."

Winslow sighed, as if to say he wasn't going to fight that particular battle. "The best choice you can make is to purge. Purge negative emotions from your heart and mind. Do that now, before it's too late. A positive attitude toward life will give you a positive self- image. And that will lead to rewarding relationships with friends and family. Civility, Liability, Stability, Possibility. Understand? That's what we all want here.

"Not easy or satisfying." Xander, uncomfortable with the lecture, shifted in his chair, feeling like a trapped squirrel.

"Dealing with negative emotions is simple if you look at negative emotions for what they are. They're quite finite. They have a limit."

"Do they, Win? And what's that checkpoint? Or is that what you're here to find out?" Xander popped up from his chair and paced, wishing the interview was over. All he wanted was to be left alone. Why did he have to be compared to other people? And didn't they realize that the more they pushed him to be happy, the darker he wanted to be? He would never allow them to get under his skin.

"Xander . . . Xander. Please sit down." Winslow gestured to the now-empty chair, and waited, with unlimited patience, for Xander to return, not bothered one whit by Xander's slouch once he got there. "Do you know how to swim, Xander?"

"Of course, '*Lieutenant.*' We're taught that in grade school, but you already knew that . . ."

"When the school first taught you to swim, did they drop you into choppy waters, Xander?"

"No. They wouldn't do anything like that to a student. Everyone's Alts would rage into the Red Zone."

"Right, Xander. Correct. First you learn to swim in calm water. Then later, once you know how, you could swim just fine, even if the water had a strong current and was thrashing you about. That's the best analogy I can show you, young man."

"That's bull. Not even close." The image of swimming in a pool full of sharks came to mind. Now, that would be the proper comparison.

"If you're calm and emotionally balanced, it will help you to make good choices. Allow you to be a productive citizen.

We all win here, Xander. Tranquility provides us security and peace, but everyone has to do their part." Winslow sat up and smiled, looking pleased with himself.

Xander stared back at Winslow and blinked. "And just how're you gonna teach me to become who you want me to be?"

7

Xander's Memory

"Now that you're with me, teaching you what you need to be will not be all that difficult. The machine in the center of the table is a Neuroscope. It picks up your current Alt readings. It'll help us magnify your feelings and see exactly where these negative feelings come from. And here is a headset."

Xander reluctantly took the tiny button-sized transponders for his ears. "Why do I need these?"

"You've got to listen and see." Win pointed to a device on the table. "That's a neurotransmitter. It's a special process, and one I may have to repeat in other sessions. Now, are you ready to begin?"

"Do I have a choice?"

Xander looked at the thing on the table. About four inches tall and a foot long, it was actually beautiful. Down its center was a purple stripe with a faint checkered pattern lit from within. Each side of the stripe had panels that glowed pink, while a turquoise base illuminated the base. What faced him was a lens. Its circle of mint green was like a shiny eye, with two black cylindrical knobs on either side. Two other buttons above the lens on both the right and the left side reminded him of what a primitive robot's eyes might look like.

"Your choice is to remain in Tranquility . . . or not." Win sighed, as if this was a delicate decision. He stared Xander in the eyes, finally dropping his gaze as if burned by the fire there.

"Okay—let's see what ya got, *Sir*." Xander wondered if the Neuroscope was already measuring his defiance. But, okay. He had nothing to hide because he didn't care. Xander closed one eye, examining showy colored gems hung on the wall. They were as big as his head. He squinted, trying to estimate the difference in measurement between them. *Five inches apart,* he thought. *Perfect, of course.*

Win's voice filtered back to him. He wondered how many minutes the guy had droned on before he tuned back into what he was saying.

". . . a lot of sessions. Now we need to take you back through your whole life, Xander. We need to explore how your anger is rooted in your childhood. I'm going to ask you now to search your memory. A time when you first felt a challenge to following the behavioral expectations in Tranquility."

Xander watched a gnat briefly land on Winslow's face. No matter how perfect Tranquility was, it couldn't get rid of pesky little insects like that one. He marveled that Winslow didn't seem to even feel it. He smiled to himself, wondering how long the bug would crawl around there without Winslow breaking the conversation to deal with it. The gnat was a lot like himself. *Just like they can't get rid of how I want to feel,* he thought.

Winslow said, "The Neuroscope will measure your thoughts and feelings and your vital signs, like the Alt. It's in your best interest to be as open as possible." Winslow gestured with his hands, as if trying to impart more wisdom through them.

Yep. The gnat was still there, and Winslow droned on.

"When the Neuroscope's numbers accelerate, that will show me what the actual triggers are for your . . . um . . . disorder. So, Xander, let's think of that moment when you first noticed that your emotions became a problem."

Xander remained silent, still trying to buck the system, the moments ticking by one by one. But as hard as he tried, there was no stopping the process. An invisible force pulled on strands of his brain; he was being hijacked. The system locked in on his subconscious.

A scene immediately came to his mind, and he began to talk. He didn't want to. The words just flowed out. "I was 13 . . . All the students at Felicitous Middle School earned extra time at lunch for 'kind and considerate behavior' and for showing their 'smiling faces' all week long. I was stoked about having the long lunch hour . . ."

Winslow tapped his fingers on the table. "Now that we have that memory at the surface of your mind, the Neuroscope will project your Alt readings on the screen. The *entire experience* you are envisioning will follow." A wide electronic screen hidden behind a panel in the Purge room revealed itself, dropping down and rolling out to cover the wall in front of them. "Both of us will see exactly how this event happened, Xander."

Xander squirmed, feeling overexposed, like being hit with a spotlight while totally nude. He watched in wonder as the once private memory rolled along just like a historical biopic.

Twenty kids sat in a classroom at white desks. Each student was synching their Alts to the screens on their desks and to one on the wall.

Shazz! That's my middle school classroom, he reflected. *That takes me back . . .* Positive words and instructions for proper breathing techniques for stress relief were on the board. *Ah... it's Empowerment Strategy day,* he realized. The teacher—*oh, yeah, Mr. Dictus droning on . . .* "With each increase in Status comes more responsibility" . . . "Thirteen-year-olds are no longer considered children," and "Each young person has to be analyzing emotions" . . ."Eye those Alt results carefully throughout the day . . ."

Xander closed his eyes, but it didn't dissolve the image in his mind.

A large display board in his now virtual middle school classroom emerged from the ceiling with bright and bold colored lights. Students' points flashed up on it in both numbers and pictures. Xander saw his own scores on the Leaderboard; his were at the bottom, of course. *Whatever.*

The name and scores of the best performing student were at the top of the board: Ember. Xander snickered in real time, noting the excitement on Ember's face. *What a kiss-ass,* he thought.

"Congratulations, Class," Mr. Dictus said. "A moment ago, I viewed the live tracking of your Alts. You've reached a class total of 1000 points today. You can see how working hard pays off, especially when you are all so happy about that hard work! I'm awarding you extra time at lunch." He put two thumbs up in the air and slapped the table next to him with gushing exuberance. "You are dismissed! We'll see you all back here for an exciting and uplifting afternoon studying history."

The Ember girl, her face glowing like moonlight, turned to another female student seated next to her. "I'm so glad we get more time at lunch. I can practice my visualization skills to impress Mr. Dictus!"

The other girl smiled and nodded enthusiastically. "You wanna practice together? We could eat lunch and then—"

"No thanks, Lorna. But you have a great lunch!" Ember grabbed her brand-new lunch pail from its resting place on the floor and rushed out the door to the crowded eating area. Xander followed her out. On her way, she called out to others. "Hi, Jexa—I love that new outfit! Hey, Toff! How's it going? I heard you aced our math test." Her voice vibrated with fondness. Some students lobbed back a few positive compliments of their own before going on their way. Other students responded with smiles and waves, followed by the upward arm gesture, their single index fingers creating a zoo of Number Ones, a gesture of trust and acceptance.

Xander hooted as he watched the scene from his virtual reality chair. Ember was throwing out those stupid comments just to score more points for herself. As if she actually heard him from the future, she slowed her steps and checked her Alt for her current reading. This was getting more and more entertaining. He realized he was not only getting to relive his own memory, but he was seeing what went on behind the scenes that day.

Ember stopped to admire some artwork in a display box window, making sure she left encouraging comments on the guest log. Her Alt must have pinged then; she looked down at it and smiled. Walking further along the sidewalk under the shade of the corridor cover, she made her way to the end, where it stopped at a broad wall. She stepped onto iridescent tile in front of a four-foot by eight-foot mirror, illuminated even by day, with clear, crystal light bulbs.

"Welcome, Ember, Level Three. Your clothes are neatly pressed today, and your smile is bright. Have a most perfect day." The mirror's voice had a bell-like sound, crisp and soothing to the ear.

There she adjusted her skirt and removed a brush from her bag, dreamily running it through her strawberry blond hair. Returning her brush to her bag, she pulled out a pair of round framed sunglasses with beige rims and slipped them on, pausing to admire how they looked in the mirror. She glanced around and moved away, now dedicated to impressing the world. But instead of walking out into the main quad, Ember walked out of the open corridor and around the building, away from the students. Their bulging masses congregated around the soda fountains and ice cream dispensers.

Winslow's voice intruded. "Keep watching carefully, Xander. I don't want you to miss what's important here."

At Winslow's prompting, Xander continued to study her moves. *She kind of looks like a spy,* he thought. *She's looking around and ducking behind a building! Oh—it's the Yoga Studio. It's pretty isolated back there . . .* He had to admit, though, he could relate. He had also sought daily retreat from the crowds.

She thoughtfully removed her sunglasses, placing them next to her, settled herself on the ground and opened her lunch pail, pushing buttons within the lid. Within two minutes, layers of different substances created real fare on their own within the lunch pail's interior. It was the perfect result of 3D printing and nutritional analysis provided by her Alt.

She's happy by herself. No real friends, though, he guessed. Shade from a lonely tree embraced the space, and it was quiet as a bug's whisper.

Within a moment, he watched himself step out from behind a shade-shrouded wall in front of Ember, as if he were making an entrance as an actor in a dramatic play. He smiled at the way his clothes defied the rules; his eyeliner was painted on thickly; and his black hair, accented with purple, rocked.

"What's up?" he blurted out.

Ember jumped and put her hand to her chest. Her face went pale. "Shazz! You scared me to death!"

"Didn't mean to, of course." His voice was blustery and loud.

Ember's brow furrowed and she stood up. "What . . . what are you doing back here?"

"Eating lunch." Xander unshelled a peanut, threw the shell on the ground, and popped a nut into his mouth. "Why? You got a problem with that?"

"Well . . . I come here every day. It's kind of . . . you know . . . my own place. I like to be by myself at lunch." Ember took a deep breath and looked at him through lowered eyes, as if meeting his eyes would burn. "You know . . . you need to be kind and considerate." She glanced around at the tree, the warm, speckled cement sidewalk, and the white brick wall.

Xander realized, even without knowing her well, that those were solid, protective, and dependable pieces of her world. He said, "I guess you're gonna have to find another place. I'm feeling *very positive* here. It makes me smile, and I think it will make me so happy for the rest of the day. So, sorry. I was here before you." He stepped forward, stamping the ground with a heavy right foot. "This spot is now taken." He smiled, but it was the vicious smile of someone who was enjoying the situation to its fullest extent.

8

Xander's Lesson

T he electronic screen in the Purging room became brighter, and Xander blinked.

"Xander, pay close attention to the indicators on the side of the screen," Winslow said, tapping the table. For a while Xander had been so lost in watching his own performance that he had forgotten where he actually was. *Stupid Winslow.*

Xander refocused. There were numbers on the screen. He saw that these were now Ember's numbers—not his. He could see how Ember's points were deflating as he bullied her. The digits revealed her respiration levels. She was in a panic.

He, by contrast, was clearly not ruffled, standing there just as if he owned the place, relaxed, contented, and happy.

The screen-star Xander continued to gaze down at Ember as he tossed another peanut into his mouth, adjusting position to catch it just before it bounced to the ground.

Ember stood up and shuffled from one foot to the other; Xander shifted in his chair before the screen.

"Focus, Xander," Winslow commanded.

Noticing his chair was askew, Xander straightened it out and pivoted to a forward position. He noticed that the gnat d finally left Winslow's face and had landed directly on the table in front of him. He put his thumb out and squashed it flat.

"Xander—what are you thinking now?" Watson probed.

"That girl is sure weak. Here she's supposed to be the best student in the school, and she's going all to pieces."

"Keep watching, Xander. You're on the verge of discovery."

The scene continuing on the screen again captured Xander's attention.

Without warning, words gushed out of the girl's mouth and hung, electrified, in the air. "You have no right to be here! Look, I don't know who you think you are, but this is my place!" She wrung her hands, as if to recapture and take back the words.

Her bravado is such an act, he thought. *How pathetic. Let's see how far this can go.*

"I know who *I* am, Ember. I'm Xander from your pre-lunch class. And . . . really? There's no sign or anything saying that it's yours. Look at the wall." He gestured around. "Is there a 'No Trespassing' sign on there? I'm claiming this part of the sidewalk." Xander pointed straight down. "And I'll get points for 'finding moments of solitude.' That's a quote from the rules book. And remember—don't start something we'll both regret."

"You're not Xander from class. You're a . . . a . . . monster!"

Getting under her skin! She's gonna lose it! Xander leaned forward in his counseling chair, fascinated. This was getting more and more interesting. He remembered it all, the thrill of it. *What a rush!*

"Maybe if your food was somewhere ELSE, you could LEAVE!" Ember swooped down and grabbed the lunch pail resting next to Xander. She hurled it as far as she could across the pavement. The metal clattered, a tin cacophony. Peanuts showered the cement like BBs, and a slightly overripe banana splatted its guts on the adjacent wall. An unopened water bottle cannoned down the sidewalk, out of sight, and a sandwich of peanut butter and pickles bounced its way to a thud—right in front of a Quad Supervisor's feet.

Perfect. He couldn't have planned it better if he'd tried.

Ember's Alt reading had alerted the attentive, devoted supervisors on campus. With the school's GPS tracking system, Ember was easy to find. She was out of control. Anger was poison for Alt readings. He watched her close her eyes and sway on her feet, as if the angry outburst made her dizzy.

The outtake stopped for a second, and Xander looked at Winslow to see if it was Winslow or his own brain that had temporarily stopped the mind film. But it then went on to right itself after the pause, simply then replaying the moment before the interruption.

Xander rendered an endearing smile for the Quad Supervisor, as if he was innocence personified. "Listen," he explained, "I honestly don't know why she's so upset. We were just talking. I tried to cheer her up," he said.

The no-nonsense supervisor directed Ember to climb aboard a utilitarian mini-cart, and they buzzed down through the buildings to arrive at the center of campus. Some students stared at the truck as it whizzed by; many, however, remembered to avert their eyes. A pariah was best ignored.

Xander chuckled. This session hadn't been bad at all. It was sooo entertaining.

Winslow grabbed the armrests on Xander's chair, spinning him away from the room's screen to look him full in the face.

"So, Xander," the counselor said, "It's power, isn't it? It's not enough for you to have self-control. You need to be in control of other people to be happy. This session has shown me that you have a deeply serious disorder."

Journal Entry #5427

We thrive on happiness here. It is our very blood. There isn't one thing that the people of our city lack in order to be peaceful and merry. I often lie awake at night wondering how I can make our Tranquility even more perfect—more visionary. I've read and studied Sir Thomas More's Utopia, which is an amazing blueprint for our society. Our municipality is based on More's original ideas. One of my favorite excerpts is this, paraphrased slightly in more modern language:

"If a man wants a position and goes after it with selfishness, he loses it for certain. The office and the people live in harmony and love among themselves. The Magistrates never conduct themselves pompously or cruelly to the people. Instead they wish to be considered **fathers**, and by being like fathers, will qualify for the love and respect of their citizens. The people award them all kinds of honor, more voluntarily because they are not required to do it. They have few laws which are their constitution. Because they adhere to the constitution happily, they don't require many laws at all."

Of course, I AM such a Magistrate. All I desire is to be esteemed for the goodness I can bestow.

—Serpio Magnus, Magistrate

9

Ember's Exit

After the inexplicable circle in the hospital room, and no one to question, Ember gathered the few personal items left in her mother's room. A tablet, now dark and needing a charge, marked the end of Talesa's long days of reading. Her mother's purple satchel with clothes, makeup, brush, and toothbrush couldn't stay behind, either, even though there would be no use for it anymore. The items were heavy in Ember's arms as she collected them and pushed her way through the crystal glass door.

The hospital's elevator was modern and slick, welcoming Ember with bells and audible greeting: "Have a beautiful and tranquil day."

Ember stepped out, feeling like she herself had died. She forced herself to stop at the front desk to see if she could determine what steps she should take next. Where did her mother disappear to, and why? Was the hospital now in charge?

A long-haired brunette woman in a mint-green skirt and jacket proudly sat behind a sheer plexiglass table in the lobby. *"Level Nine,"* Ember thought. *"She's only a Level Nine."* As Ember approached, she absorbed the strong sympathy flowing from the matronly figure. In spite of the pity, the woman assumed an authoritarian air as she looked above her half-glasses and focused her attention on Ember as she approached the desk. Ember took a deep, cleansing breath.

"Hello . . . I'm Ember Vinata. My mom . . . just . . . died. I need to know what happened to her . . . I mean, I know she *died*, but she—she actually disappeared out of the bed. Can you tell me where they took her? I need to make sure she's being taken care of . . ."

"Ember. I'm so sorry for your loss. But you don't need to worry. She didn't 'disappear.' Your mom is in good hands. Kelasts take charge of deceased persons. They're compassionate and dedicated men and women, treating her with loving care. So much depends on it, you know?" the woman said. "By the way, I'm Gladys."

"Good to meet you, Gladys, but I still have questions!"

She didn't think it was good to meet her. That was a lie. Couldn't this Gladys see that she was bleeding on the inside and needed help? She observed the room, noting its emptiness. She was the only person there besides the receptionist. The level-coordinated colored chairs lined up against the wall had to be all for show. Because why would there be people waiting? Nobody got sick. People didn't just *die*.

"As people in Tranquility pass away, they become even more precious to the well-being of our citizens," Gladys continued. "We don't want anyone to worry about their loved ones. Tranquility has arranged special transport for them. That is the way it's done, and so you can go home and be at peace. Is this your first death experience, dear?"

"Yeah. And this is my *mom*. I really loved her!"

Take a deep breath. You're gonna be okay. She concentrated on the positive self-talk. Maybe if she was stronger, this lady would answer her questions.

"Are you able to manage your emotions? What is your Alt registering?" Gladys prodded.

Ember looked down in shame. "I'm not doing well with my readings. This has been so, so horrible."

"I know you realize what's at stake, Ember, so you need to continue trying hard and just trusting all of us in Management. We have everyone's best interests at heart." Gladys smiled a thousand-watt smile at Ember. "So, go on home. And remember, if your Alt readings don't come back up by tomorrow at this time, your Status *will* be affected." Gladys then picked up a stylus, handed it to Ember, and asked her to sign the tablet to show she was leaving the hospital.

Sad and confused, Ember spun out through the revolving door, almost catching her royal blue jacket on her way through the turnstile.

She was not half a minute out the door when Ember felt her Alt vibrate. She pushed back the sleeve of her jacket to check its message. Her Alt continued to show a downward trend and was registering strongly in the red zone. *"Shazz! Second Alt alert of the day. I need to get home. Security. And meditation! That's what I need . . ."* Ember felt new peace at the thought.

At the curb, she looked at the array of CommuteCars waiting for passengers. There were ten cars lined up in the circular queue on the street. Luckily, she found a royal blue car with "Level 8, Peace" painted on its side, five cars down the street. This was the car she needed, the only one that could transport her home. Setting down her mother's belongings, Ember pulled her Status Card from her jacket pocket. The royal blue plastic blinked in the sunlight as she inserted it into the car's door slot to activate her account. After a short bell, the polished door slid open, and a friendly robotic voice and blinking lights reminded her to remove her card. Ember grabbed her gear and slid inside.

"Welcome to Tranquility CommuteCars," the dashboard announced. "Make yourself comfortable and relax. This will be a lovely drive. Please respond with your desired drop-off location."

"Home," Ember replied.

"Home," the car responded as it pulled out onto the street.

Ember forced her sagging eyelids open. Her stomach growled, and her throat, she realized, felt cottony. She snuggled down into the bucket seat, but not before pulling a lemonade and churro from the food dispenser in front of her. She needed to restore and stabilize her mood. Her primary purpose today would be to pull her Alt's points up.

EMBER'S THIRTY-MINUTE ride was a blur. She must have fallen asleep after devouring her first food in over a day. Then she woke abruptly, shaking off sickening images from her recurring dream of running, giant books, and a pool of blood...

One of her favorite songs, "Power Up," piped through the car speakers, accompanied by the car's honey-voiced computer. "You have arrived at your destination. Thank you for using CommuteCars, Ember. Have a perfect and very happy day."

Like a zombie, Ember moved from the car to the steps leading up to her door at the Purple Vale complex. Her fingerprint opened the orchid colored door, and she hesitated before stepping inside. This was a first. Not only was the heart of her home gone with her mother, but Ember would not be permitted to remain in a Level Fourteen complex. Now she would be on her own. She was old enough as an orphan, even though she wasn't eighteen. She would be expected to move into a complex for her own Status, now that her mom was dead. She was not sure how much time she had before City Hall would enforce the location change for Status. That is, if she didn't fall out of her own Level Eight. Her personal grief was an emotional enemy that needed conquering. Especially now that she was on her own, she would need the things her Level Eight Status would provide.

But Ember was not prepared for what she saw upon

entering their home. She gasped and then felt the breath leave her body. The interior was in shambles. Their personal belongings were thrown about the room; even the walls were bare, the artwork stripped off, lying in bizarre places around the Great Room. Overturned furniture was slashed on top and underneath as well. Lamps were dismembered. Books from the bookcase, their spines askew, were sodden butterflies, their pages scattered like leaves. The one thing that still looked untouched was the fish tank where Jonas, their two-inch gold-fish, swam about peacefully, oblivious to the destruction.

She felt the blood in her head seem to evaporate, and she swayed on her feet. Grabbing the wall to steady herself, she then sunk down, defeated, onto the floor. She didn't know if she could take even one more step into this chaos. Who had been in their home? Why? Putting her head in her hands, she broke down, tears dissolving whatever makeup she had left at the end of the day. All alone. What was she going to do?

Again, she felt a pulse on her arm. Her Alt was crashing, the third time today. Its frantic buzz mirrored her panic. *Get in control. Think.* "Happiness is a choice," Ember whispered.

Looking to her Alt as comfort, Ember pressed the "H" icon in the right-hand corner of its face. The "Help" icon was for emergencies only, but this had to be an emergency. She didn't know what else to do.

A female voice emanated from the Alt's bejeweled wrist-band. "We understand you are in distress. How can we help?"

"Someone . . . has broken into . . . my home and made a mess," Ember said. "And my mother . . . has died. I have . . . no one to help me. Could you send someone out . . . please?" Her Alt showed a two-point increase with the 'please' on the end of her request, but Ember couldn't appreciate the gain. Not with the accompanying warning on her Alt. She was suddenly sweating. She pulled at her clothes, now too hot. Her hands trembled, and the quakes traveled down her arms and legs. Her heart pounded too fast, too hard. She tried taking a deep breath to calm herself, but her breaths were sharp and shallow. Her vision narrowed and darkened. Closing her eyes, she saw bright pins of light. It felt like she was dying.

The electronic voice continued. "According to your Alt, you are having a severe emotional crisis, Ember. Aid will arrive shortly. Please breathe deeply and meditate while you watch your Alt's screen. It will provide you with a stress-relieving exercise."

Ember took a jagged breath that failed again to fill her lungs. Thank goodness for the excellent response team at Tranquility's City Hall. They were going to take care of her. Someone was coming. All she had to do was wait.

10

Will's Introduction

T he door, shiny black as a crow's wings, still operated on hinges, unlike most others in the city. Its weight was a surprise. A heavy metal, the door displayed an engraved sign with letters in gold: Plauditorium. Filled with anticipation and without hesitation, Will turned the knob and, with more effort than he thought he'd need, pushed the door open.

At first, he was puzzled. A warm earthy fragrance, just short of what you'd call sweet, greeted his senses. He stood, pondering it for a moment, his eyes sweeping the expansive room for clues. But he suddenly realized he carried the same odor himself—his suede jacket multiplied a hundred times. Every Plauditor wore one.

Even though he'd slid in just before eight, Plauditors were already there, working zealously. Warmth spread through his heart as he beheld uniformed Plauditors, many at stations around the room watching hundreds of flat screen telemonitors on the walls. Since Tranquility was an entirely enclosed bubble city, it was a full-time job to observe people's daily activities so they could remain safe.

Will ventured further into the room, where fifty staff

members were dressed in identical versions of Will's own uniform. The accent colors on their uniforms were different. There was no doubt as to each person's Status. He noticed none of them wore their Plauditor hats. He took his off, nervously putting it under his arm.

As Will entered, the Plauditors raised their right hands high above their heads, palms out, one finger up, acknowledging his presence. He gestured back, making sure he showed his respect and acceptance to all.

In close to what would be the middle of the gymnasium-sized room, Will's name appeared up on a screen in bold letters, along with his current Alt reading, which he noted was in the high 900s today. There would be no hiding his emotional state here. *As it should be*, he thought.

He crossed the room to his laminated bright yellow desk over which the silver and acrylic screen hung suspended in the air. He tossed his hat on the desk. Sitting down, he tested out the comfort of his chair. *His* chair. Shiny. Plush. And even though his chair wasn't the best in the room—he was just a Level Twelve, after all—he felt like a king in it. Being a Plauditor was the start of something big.

He noticed a series of buttons on the right arm of the chair and tested them out. Whoa! Vibration. He grinned. That first button was there to offer massage, a relief from any stress the job could have. As if there was stress. He couldn't imagine anything that could upset him here.

He felt like a little kid, pushing the buttons, finding the second one to be a gentle heat that warmed his seat. *Cool.* Button Three—immediate chilled air swirled around him. He found another dial he could adjust to personalize the force and temperature. He tried to guess Button Four before he pushed it. Fragrance maybe? Or music. Probably music.

Someone cleared his throat behind him, making him jump. A man hovered directly behind his chair, so closely Will could feel his breath. Will swiveled and stood up, somewhat embarrassed at being blind to what was going on around him. He'd need to improve if he was going to be a decent Plauditor.

"So. Welcome, Will! Great to see you! Honored to have you here." The man's right hand jutted out to shake Will's. The silver metallic stripe on his uniform shone like a wet dime. A Level Seventeen!

Will reached out to shake his hand, to discover the fellow offered the Tranquility salute instead. Will returned the gesture, amused by the gentleman's height. Will's five-eleven-foot frame towered over him. The guy was shorter than any adult male he had seen before, probably just over five foot.

"I'm Tedman Adoravi, Chief Plauditor. I'll be showing you around and introducing you to a few key people. Then we can put you to work!" Tedman laughed heartily as if his statement was the biggest joke of the day.

"Great! I'm game," Will said. He wondered when he was going to get training for this job. All he knew was he had to watch the monitors, report problems, and be an influencer for happiness in the city. As structured as Tranquility was, there had to be a vast amount of information to learn. A kernel of doubt snaked its way into his mind. Was he up to this? All the learning? His lack of experience at doing anything bothered him. *That's a negative thought, Will,* his conscience prodded. *Let it go.* He forced a smile, took a deep breath, and remembered this was the opportunity of a lifetime. *I was meant for this,* he told himself, as he brushed a small piece of fuzz off his jacket sleeve. *Not tolerating that lint either,* he mused.

"So. How's your family?" Tedman asked, as he gestured for Will to follow him.

"Good. They're happy I'm here." Will trailed behind Tedman, who walked surprisingly quickly on his stubby legs.

"So. What do you do in your spare time?"

"Umm . . . just hang out. You know, with friends." His mouth was strangely dry.

"So. Yes. But you're a city celebrity. What's that like?"

The man has a strange affection for the word "so," he thought. *Weird, but whatever.* Will didn't have any trouble being conversational. He'd always been outgoing and polite to a fault, so he couldn't shut this guy down, but the small talk grated on him a little. Questions about his family, his friends, and especially his newfound fame he certainly didn't want to share with his new boss. More than anything, he just wanted to get started on his job.

"I'm adjusting," Will said. "I hope the spotlight disappears soon." No sooner had he said that, than he passed under a broad halogen can light hung from the ceiling. He smiled wryly, the irony of the double meaning not lost on him.

Tedman led Will over to an adjacent room. They stood just outside the door and peered in. "Broadcasts are made here. Everything—absolutely everything—that is broadcast comes from here."

"What if the equipment fails?"

"Never happens." Tedman shrugged his shoulders. "If it did, the city couldn't get information. But this keeps the news central. The Magistrate's daily speech, Tranquility News, and 'feel good' stories. We do it all."

"Who can broadcast?"

"The five people you see here in this room are the key writers, communicators, and anchors. Eventually you might create public service announcements. Plauditors cheer up the population. That'll involve separate training."

Will's eyes scanned the production room. On the wall was a large canvas. A colorful portrait of the city's mascot, a Halcyon with molten eyes, looked back at him. The wings seemed to vibrate with deep magenta. Magenta symbolized the universal harmony that was the promise of their community. Flecks of blue for serenity accented the tips of those wings and its reflective eyes. Throughout Tranquility, citizens celebrated their good luck and happiness with paintings of this symbol in corridors and on buildings. According to legend, the Halcyon was a bird that had the power to calm.

Shiny knobs and slick cameras flanked the five people inhabiting the powerful broadcast room, filled with both small and large screens. They seemed heavily engaged in the daily programming. The broadcasters, two in purple suits, and the others in yellow, lavender, and orange formal apparel, were discussing ideas, their voices a tangle of highs and lows. One fellow—the orange-clad Level Thirteen—looked to be fine-tuning the equipment, making sure the broadcast system was operating effectively. Will thought, *I hope it won't be long until I can advance to broadcasting. I'd love to be on camera.*

The arm Tedman placed on Will's shoulder broke his concentration. Tedman led him back out into the primary room, his short legs somehow able to generate some unusual speed. Will hurried to keep up. "I'll show you the main unit here. You'll 'cut your teeth' in this room. If you work hard at being a Plauditor and your Alt points stay high, you'll be in line for a broadcasting position."

Most of the Plauditors' eyes in the room were riveted on their monitors. Every person appeared focused on the job at hand, and while the projected Alt scores showed a room full of cheerful people, he could tell the employees took their jobs very seriously. *Their jobs make them happy*, he mused.

"So. I see your desk neighbor has just clocked in. Let's head back over to your station so I can introduce you," Tedman said.

It's not the most social place I've ever been. I see a few people I recognize, but most of them are older and in higher Status groups than I am. I hope I'll have a chance to meet more people.

As if Tedman heard his thoughts, he stretched out his arm and put his hand on Will's shoulder. "We're going to make sure you're happy here, Will."

As they approached, Will looked to either side of his own workspace. To the left of him, instead of another workstation, was a table-sized cart holding doughnuts with colored frosting, a carafe, and an assortment of multi-hued cups. No one would sit on that side of him, then. He loved that he could grab a snack whenever he wanted. How much better could this job get?

On the other side of Will's area, a young man who looked to be about five years older than him swiveled around to meet Will's gaze. A square face accented by a turned-up nose broke into a toothy grin. His smooth auburn hair reminded Will of a hairstyle model, its thickness combed back from his forehead and cropped straight across his neck. He held a cup in his hand and spilled it slightly as he put it down in a hurry on his desktop.

"So. Austel, meet Will," Tedman boomed. "He'll be your right-hand man, so to speak."

"Hey, Austel. Guess we'll have to tolerate each other." Will grinned. "Looks like I'm takin' up residence."

"Great. Just don't upstage me, okay?" The light words had an oddly serious tone.

"No worries about that. I'm fresh in, remember?"

"Yeah. One that's famous. A hot shot. And I'm just a Level Eleven," Austel said with mock humility. His wide brown eyes reminded Will of a dog's, soulful and innocent.

The guy's a nerd, but not a weak one. He noticed the fellow's muscles, a sharp contrast to his bookish appearance. Instead of a handshake, Austel gave Will Tranquility's acknowledgment gesture. Will responded, arm up, index finger raised.

"We'll be a great duo, bro," Will proclaimed.

Austel put his hand over his heart in an overly dramatic gesture. "Indeed. You honor me, new comrade."

11

Will's Investigation

wo days on the job at the Plauditorium, and Will was starting to feel useless. Although being a Plauditor was a huge honor, he was also finding it to be entirely boring. He'd received his training, and afterward he knew for sure: he was made for this. He rubbed his eyes. Staying awake and interested was the problem with the job. It was a long day when the whole job was watching the monitor.

Everything was always so peaceful in Tranquility. Crime was nil, and everyone was always considerate and kind. The situations that made a Plauditor blink twice were when someone was in trouble or needed encouragement.

It was clear from the start, though, that Will was the One —the One chosen exclusively for those types of emergencies. His experience saving young Jesse from the train had shown his mettle and his self-sacrificing nature. So, he was a logical choice when there was an at-risk situation. Although it would be infrequent, Will relished the opportunity to get out into the community.

A huge part of a Plauditor's job was to encourage the citizens if they were experiencing an emotional crisis. They were the city's intervention teams, helping people before they were referred to counseling or purging. Will was perfect for that. He could stay calm and focused; his Alt numbers would stay stable and would pulse upward when he could affect someone's day in a positive manner. It was then that he truly loved his job. During these first days, multiple people had already commended Will for his sensitivity to others. His response was a modest smile and deep blush.

"Umm . . . Will? Austel spoke up from behind his screen.

"Yeah?"

"You know any people who are Elites? I mean, personally, like a friend, not professionally." Austel turned toward Will, his head tilted to the side, thoughtfully. His fiercely gathered brows jutted over his questioning eyes.

"Hard to miss them in those gold clothes, but no. I don't know any personally. Everyone's always polite, though. Why?"

"Just wondering. I've met a few Elites. They're friendly, yes . . . but I don't feel connected to them. Like they're above us —I mean *way* above us. A goal of mine is to have friends in the Elite. Possibly be one myself one day. They have it all." Austel brushed a flake of tiny debris off his lapel; in spite of resembling a dog, Austel was as fastidious as a cat.

"I'm sure you'll get there, Austel. If you're upbeat, there's no ceiling. Hey . . . let's have a competition with our Alt points. You in?"

"Only if you want to lose, Golden Boy."

Will grinned. "How long you been a Plauditor?"

"Two years to the day. Best job ever." Austel picked up the cup on his desk and held it up, as if to say "cheers."

"Not much experience then." Will teased. He'd been trying hard to break down Austel's barriers. He was such a serious guy and maybe a little jealous. Will didn't want bad blood between them. That would breed negativity. He couldn't have that.

"I've got enough, bro. I'll help *you* whenever I can," Austel laughed.

"Whatcha do when you're not workin'?"

"Go out with girls, what else?" Austel gave Will a wink, as if he was suddenly a best friend.

"Anyone special?"

"Nope. I like to date around. Plenty of girls want a Plauditor."

"Yeah? Good to know. I'd better keep this job, then," he replied, happy that he had finally broken the ice with Austel.

Will switched the view on his screen to see what was happening at the transportation hub of the city. He watched the monorail stop to let "Tranks" board, but his heart lurched when a high alert broadcast blasted through the Plauditorium's speakers. "This is Tedman. Attention, all Plauditors: A Level Eight Trank's security and Emotional Management are in crisis! Will Verus: respond to Abode Twenty-five in Purple Vale. Help Center reports break in and multiple Alt crashes."

Will stood and yelled out into the workplace. "Who's got the Purple Vale sector?" Will's eyes panned the room. "Certainly, someone in here saw a problem . . ."

A Level Thirteen Plauditor seated by the window jumped up. "The camera showed nothing! I would've reported it. Look for yourself!" she called out.

Will thought that was ridiculous. Why wouldn't the camera show a break-in? But the girl sounded sincere.

He turned to Austel, seated to his right. "Go with me?"

"No time to waste," Austel replied. Austel shoved his badge into his pocket and grabbed his hat, taking a moment to set it on his head perfectly.

Will grabbed his shiny new badge and his Tranquility ID card and dashed through the door to a curb-bound black vehicle with tinted windows. He inserted his card into the door and whipped inside.

"Go, go, go!" Austel shouted as he jumped right in next to him.

Within minutes, they arrived at the Purple Vale

sector. And seconds after that, they were knocking on Number Twenty-five.

The door immediately opened, and Will stifled a gasp. Although her eyes shone with tears, the girl in the doorway was a beauty. It caught him off guard for a moment, and he worked to recover himself.

The Vision spoke. "You got here faster than I imagined. Thank you so much." Peering beyond, he glimpsed a disheveled interior and knew they had their work cut out for them.

From his pants' pocket Will drew out his Factive, a pocket-sized appliance used for note-taking, "Our pleasure, Miss . . ." He glanced at the little screen. ". . .Vinata."

The poor girl looks more like a body for the Kelasts to collect. In spite of her beauty, she was pale as a cadaver. Will could tell without a doubt that the victim was in a severe crisis.

"Call me Ember, please. Come in— if you can find a place to walk."

Will entered through the door to find he was forced to tiptoe through debris scattered everywhere. An entire purple-gilded bookcase had its collection strewn on the carpet. The lack of books seemed to broadcast its loneliness, its bareness sleek, but startling. Portraits and still-lifes pried from the eggplant-colored walls lay upside down or were stripped from their frames, their positions now marking a north, south, east, west design. Whatever lay shattered on the ground in pieces was unrecognizable, just a mosaic of color and brilliance. Lamps appeared dissected, save for one which proudly stood at the edge of the fireplace, its light still stubbornly shining amidst the chaos.

Austel whistled. "Whoever did this was pretty upset here. And I can see where you would be, too. Look at this place."

The three of them made their way further into the Great Room. "Anything been stolen, Ember?" Will continued to glance about the room, recording a few notes on his Factive.

"I haven't . . . seen anything missing, but I haven't even been upstairs to the bedrooms. I thought I'd better wait for you to get here," Ember admitted.

Austel said, "I'll check up there." He dashed off, taking the stairs two at a time.

"So, Ember, can you think of who might've done this? Anyone you know getting treatment for Emotional Management issues?"

He was suddenly nervous, worrying about the impression he was making on the girl. *Do your job*, he thought. But his heart was racing, and his palms began to sweat. A wave of panic set in, followed by confusion. Hope, fear, and insecurity were all converging in the pit of his stomach at the same time. *Pull yourself together.*

"No, I can't imagine . . . I mean, I don't know anyone like that."

Will took a deep breath, hoping it sounded like frustration over her lack of information, instead of the emotions he was feeling. "Think hard. When someone has to submit to Purging sessions, they could go a little haywire. They're already struggling with controlling emotions. Those people are monitored closely, but you never know."

"Honestly, I don't know anybody who's even been counseled. I live kind of a quiet life."

A yell from upstairs interrupted the conversation. "Clear. Just a mess all around. Taking notes now."

Will called back, "I'll handle the Great Room and kitchen then." He turned to Ember. "First, though, we'll get you stabilized." Looking at his factive, he stated, "Three complete Alt crashes today." *You might not know anyone who's been counseled, but you're about ready to be in that situation,* he thought. "Let's find you a place to sit . . ." Will found a plushly upholstered chair and with a hefty lift and push put it back in an upright position. "The break-in's upsetting. But I see your first two Alt crashes happened earlier in the day."

Will motioned to the cushioned chair. "Sit. Please." Ember gratefully sat down.

She looks exhausted. "My name's Will—Will Verus. And my partner," he pointed to the ceiling, "is Austel."

"You look familiar. Have I met you before?"

"No." Will shifted his weight and dropped his eyes. "I'm a little embarrassed . . . I was on the morning news. Maybe that's why?"

"Yeah. I remember seeing something like that."

"No matter. Not important, not at all. Now, can you tell me about your day?"

Ember sighed. "It's hard . . . hard to talk about." She looked down at her hands twisting in her lap and then put them flat on her lap, smoothing them across her dress.

Will hoped his demeanor was soothing. He didn't want to hurt her in her fragile state, so he softened his voice. "Take your time, Ember."

"My mother died this morning." It came out in a rush.

Wow. Now Will understood. The information stunned him. *How much could a person take in a day?* "I'm so sorry. No wonder you're sad."

She shook her head up and down, speechless for an extended moment. "Yeah. I don't know how to get my Alt readings back up. I don't want to be counseled. I feel so . . . alone." She placed her hands on her face as if to hide from the world around her. He watched as she realized her hands were shaking, and she dropped them to her lap, clasping them in an iron grip.

"Can I help you? Some deep breathing and visualization, Ember? It'll help you feel better. Then we'll see what else needs to be done. You've gotta get a handle on your emotions."

"Yes . . . thank you."

"May I sit here next to you? Or will that make you uncomfortable?"

Ember gave a weak laugh, although Will was sure she was not finding this funny at all. "Of course. I trust you."

"That alone will help your Alt points. Close physical presence to another person'll help." Will sat down next to Ember. The chair seemed to forgive the extra body, but it was a tight squeeze.

"Take my hand, Ember." At her touch, his chest tightened, and a tingle traveled down his spine.

12

Will's Salvation

E mber grasped Will's hand and squeezed. He put his other arm around her, and an overwhelming urge to protect her swept over him.

"First thing to do is practice deep breathing. Your training. You remember it, right?"

"Yeah, of course."

"Okay, breathe with me now. Seven rounds of deep breaths in through the nose. Hold it, then let your breath out through your mouth."

She looked at him with doe-like eyes, and he saw a vulnerability that surprised him. Yet it was the trust in her eyes that freaked him out. Here she had just met him, and she was hanging on his every word, following each command perfectly. He wondered if the trauma of the moment made her act this way, or if she was always so trusting of people she didn't know.

Ember took jagged breaths. Her eyes closed in concentration. He could see she was trying hard just to get the breath pulled in smoothly. He was vaguely aware of Austel's footsteps upstairs and the ticking of the clock in the room, and yet they seemed far, far away. She wasn't the only one concentrating. He was wrapped up in the moment.

"As you exhale, let go of all expectations. Exhale all tension, fear, and exhaustion. Allow your physical, mental and emotional body to melt away."

He thought about that melting part. Her emotions should melt away since they were so sad. But the idea of her melting physically away . . . he was glad that wouldn't happen.

"Empty yourself and enter stillness. Enter silence . . . Now, once you are in that same space of quiet calm, repeat your mantra seven times." *She seems to find it possible to repeat her personal mantra and breathe. That's a relief.*

"Happiness is a choice. Happiness is a choice. Happiness is a choice . . . " Her voice was soft, breathy.

"Feel yourself becoming one with the state of tranquility. Open your heart and connect to the positive emotions and the love you have inside."

This girl. He wondered if she had a lot of love. He hoped so. She certainly seemed to need people—almost as if she was starving for them. How was she all alone here? Certainly she had people to love her.

"As you continue, you'll release fear, doubt, hesitation, and resistance. You'll become a channel for happiness and peace. See yourself as an overcomer. Your Alt will register these desires."

Will watched Ember begin to relax. Her shoulders came down from their tight position. He noticed the muscles in her arms and hands slacken. Her hands no longer tightened into fists.

"How're you feeling, Ember?"

"Better . . ." Her voice was weak, breathy.

"We're doing one last thing for calm. Then we'll look for clues on this break in." Will reached into his pocket and pulled out some magnetic music transponders and handed them to Ember. "Just place the dot on your earlobe—it'll stay attached.

Then I'll play music. It'll help your brain produce more Alpha waves. About twelve minutes long, okay? During this just relax and close your eyes. I'll be looking at your Alt to see if you can get some point increases."

Ember adjusted the dots as she placed them on her ears. "Thank you."

Will soon realized the music was making some headway. Ember's Alt was responding. He watched, elated, as her points increased and her breath became steady. The Alt registered a change from a low of fifty to a more stable one hundred. He continued to hold her hand, hoping that even the blood rushing through his fingertips would help to comfort her.

This girl took his breath away. He noticed her long lashes rested softly on her face as she shut her eyes to concentrate; the smallest frown formed a crease between her eyebrows. Tendrils of her hair, shiny and copper, had escaped from the rest, adding a slightly disheveled look to her appearance; however, it took nothing away from her beauty. In fact, it added a vulnerability that was endearing. She was exquisite. He felt a hot wave ignite his entire being, an uninvited stir the force of which he had never imagined. His palms now damp, he diverted his thoughts to one of the more mundane paintings staring up at him from the floor.

The music ceased, and none too soon. It had been a long twelve minutes. Ember opened her eyes. Will smiled and exhaled. Ember's Alt showed its points were back in the normal zone. One hundred fifty and going up.

"Ember . . . how are you feeling?"

"Like I've been drowning! But I feel like I'm back on dry land. Thank you."

Will was reluctant to get out of the chair where he was snuggled with Ember but pushed his body to rise. "I think we can continue the investigation now."

Will made his way around the messy room, Ember shadowing his moves. After a few moments, she lost her "deer in the headlights" look, and Will noticed her adjusting her dress and running her fingers through her hair. She seemed to be fully back in the moment.

Will began by snapping pictures, using his Alt's camera app. Take a shot, replace a vase on a pedestal. Photograph the sofa and restore it to an upright position. He and Ember cleaned up the earth dumped from potted plants with their hands, and rehung pictures. *Why would any citizen of Tranquility be so destructive?*

"Ember, the person was looking for something in your place. Think again. Is there anything that might be missing? Or so valuable that someone would take this risk?"

"I can't think of anything. I haven't taken inventory. I'll have to let you know," Ember said, her voice still unsteady.

Just then Austel came bounding down the stairs, entering the room like a fireball. "Took pictures. Most everything's back in order, as best I could."

Ember smiled at them both, but Will imagined the warmth was all for him. "Of course. Thanks again so much. You're so helpful."

"Will, let's wrap up. Back at the Plauditorium we'll put it all together. See what we can make of it."

"Right. We'll see you again, Ember, once we can issue a formal report. In the meantime, stay safe. Make sure you're monitoring your points frequently. Hopefully, you won't have to call us again." Inside, Will thought, *I hope you do.*

The duo marched over to the door and extended their arms, fingers up. Ember, smiling, raised her arm in response.

As the door swung open and Austel stepped out, Will stopped. An epiphany struck him. How had he missed it? "Your home's monitor camera, Ember. Is it working?"

"I think so. Let me check." Ember moved across to where the hidden camera was mounted next to the fireplace. "It's blinking and following our moves . . . so yeah, it's working." For proof, she waved her hand in front of the lens.

"Great," Will responded, although his bewilderment deepened. Somehow the camera had not captured any of the break-in but was working well. "Again, take care, Ember."

He closed the door. His feelings were on an out-of-control elevator ride to the top floor. Time to check his Alt. The numbers blinked into place, and as he suspected, they hit an all-time high.

13

Xander's Win

Xander cringed. After witnessing his abuse of Ember in the middle school memory Purge, the counselor insisted he come back yet again to talk about other experiences nearly identical to that one. Winslow assured him each confession and visual experience would completely rehabilitate him.

Xander shook his head, trying to rid himself of the many memories he'd viewed with the counselor. Winslow insisted that wanting to be in control was a weakness—but isn't that what Tranquility was all about—control? In every episode where he sought command over another, Xander was pushed, prodded, and exhorted to remember, confess, and analyze. It all pointed to the same conclusion. Xander was dysfunctional; he couldn't be happy unless he had the upper hand—the influence, the authority.

The customary appointment that day took a different turn than Xander expected. After all their sessions together, Winslow had reached a frustrated decision. "The medical professionals will have to provide the next steps, Xander." He pushed a button on the wall, pulled a form appearing from a slotted window, scribbled something illegible on it, and handed it to him. "Please. Give this to the team outside the door, Xander. They'll be taking care of you. Good luck."

"Really?"

"Really. I've done all I can."

Xander couldn't wait to get out the door. *Yes! No more sessions with Win!* He did a fist pump in the air.

Immediately, a middle-aged man dressed completely in red, his eyes spaced apart enough to give him an alien look, met Xander before the door even finished its final click.

"Xander, I am Esryn. Do you have your paperwork?"

Xander looked the man up and down with disdain. "Yeah…here ya go." Xander dropped it in the man's outstretched hands, to see it miss its mark and float to the floor. And he wasn't going to stoop to picking it up. That would be beneath him. He eyed its presence on the floor and, for some proper fun, slid his foot over it. Esryn jerked Xander's paperwork out from under Xander's foot and pushed him down the corridor.

"So, what's your *Status*, Esryn? Red's no Status color."

"Sciolists don't have Status. Red is only for us." The Sciolist answered him in an emotionless voice. He never turned but continued walking down the brick-lined hallway.

"Another crappy rule. Red looks great on me. I should be wearing it *all* the time." Xander hoped to get under Esryn's skin, but he meant what he said. Red had always been his favorite color. Impossible to find fabric, though. He'd never been able to get an outfit made.

"Red's only for the Sciolist Team," Esryn repeated, this time in an irritated tone.

"Right. Well, you stay *special* . . . Hey, Sciolist—you takin' me to the crazy house?"

"You need help."

"And you don't? What're you but a worthless pawn?"

The corridor ended abruptly at a cardinal-colored door which opened to a short sidewalk to the street. An undersized red car waited at the curb. The car's door opened at their approach. Esryn shoved Xander inside. "Solace Institute," the Sciolist said, and the car shot out of its spot.

Xander kicked back, checking out his red ride. He sat behind Esryn in a small, uncomfortable seat built for one person. The vehicle was boxy, but compact. As red as the scarlet painted exterior, the control buttons inside gave no clue to their purpose. He shuddered a little, wondering if they might be there in case of resistance. The interior roof was thick with a fuzzy upholstery. He couldn't resist running his hands over to feel its fluffiness. The plush headliner was almost comical, considering the car's purpose was anything but soft.

"Esryn. You like your job?" Xander asked, grinning.

No answer.

"Maybe that's where I went wrong. I shoulda been a Sciolist! Controlling other people. I hear I'm made for that."

The Sciolist hardly moved, his posture stiff. His voice was emotionless. "Don't talk. Outside the building, we don't talk to emotional resistors."

"You'd get infected or something?"

Silence.

"You got a personal life?" In spite of the lack of answers, Xander was enjoying himself.

Still nothing.

The Sciolist hardly moved, his posture stiff as a cadaver's.

Up ahead loomed the treatment building, a massive glass-paneled atrocity where Esryn gestured to him to exit the auto. A sign read "Solace Institute." Esryn accompanied Xander to a narrow waiting area with chairs in every Status color flanking the walls.

The Sciolist shut the door and left him alone.

Xander's mind raced. He hardly dared think about what the Solace Institute meant for him. Winslow tried to repro-gram him without success. But Winslow wasn't a mental doctor. If this place could actually help him, would that be good? Could he ever be okay with being told how to think? How to smile? If only people understood that he didn't want to intentionally hurt people. It just seemed to happen. Maybe this was the lifeline he needed . . .

An hour later, Xander was listening to his assigned medic. "You'll take these according to the directions on the label. Please, don't miss a dose." She held the bottle up. "You're going to feel a lot better!" Extending a glass of lavender-colored purified water, she placed two orange pills in his hand. She then clasped her hands in a prayer-like gesture, optimism oozing out of her beautiful pores.

This medic should be a model instead, Xander mused. Her symmetrical face and long legs made him far happier than the pills she was gently placing in his possession.

"You're completely gorgeous, Medic . . .?"

"Spero. My family members are all in altruistic professions. Our surname means "hope.""

"Well, Miss Spero. You do give me hope! But not from those pills . . . Have you ever thought your beauty is being wasted on losers like me? You could be a model for Tranquility's clothing design studio. The Spectrum Colorhouse needs some new figures. And you fit the bill."

"Thank you. You seem to be an upbeat guy. I'm sorry we had to meet this way." She fidgeted and stepped back.

"Yeah, that's a shame—but what do you say we get together later? I could show you a good time."

It wounded him to see her eyes glaze over in pity before she rushed out without a reply, glancing at the Alt on her wrist.

Xander knew the medication, Abacinate, was the last-ditch effort to help him become a "Trank" in spirit and deed. But there was *no way* he was going to be medicated into bowing down. Perhaps it worked for others, but not for him. Sneaking out the door and down the hallway, he didn't look back as he exited, feeding the pills to the trash receptacle on his way out.

Once he got home, in a final act of rebellion, Xander removed his Alt, hoping that he would somehow just simply fall off the radar. It took two hours before his luck ran out.

~

A DIFFERENT SCIOLIST came back to collect him. He wondered briefly why it wasn't Esryn again. The new creep took him to a small, waiting room off City Hall's main corridor. Xander surveyed the room, scoffing at the bright red walls. Recessed lighting did nothing to quiet the bold color. *Irritating room*, he thought, *meant to intimidate. Good try.* However, he only had a few minutes to reflect on the obscene color choice before the Sciolist came back for him. "The Magistrate is ready for you," the Sciolist droned.

Xander shrugged his shoulders. "As you wish. You're in charge . . ." He gave him a mock bow.

In spite of his bravado, deep inside he suddenly wished it could have been different. That he could have somehow fit in. That he could have actually been saved. What if he could have pulled himself together? But now, here he was. He had to stand up for himself.

They walked down an adjacent hallway, the Sciolist mute during the short fifteen-foot walk. Again, a red door. But when it opened, no red washed the walls; instead, walls the color of sand were ironically serene. A chamber, perfectly round, made it both serious and elegant. Soft lighting showed off columns —eighteen of them, to be exact—and the space was vast. The pillars looked to be made of steel. In the center of the room was a colossal crystal globe sitting on a platform of ornate iron filigree. Light reflecting from the glass was mesmerizing.

The Sciolist ushered Xander forward toward the crystal. *The hot spot?* he wondered. "Stand here," the Sciolist said.

"Right by the crystal." The Sciolist shoved him into place. He felt an immediate surge of anger so strong it left him weak. He noticed the Sciolist take up a position beside the door. Within seconds, the floor transformed. Where it was flat before, it was now becoming a dark opening, like a monster's maw. He cringed, wondering if it would swallow him up. A desk emerged from beneath, as well as a giant throne. The desk, constructed of heavy concrete, displayed two words etched into the front: "Tranquility Justice."

14

Xander's Exile

Xander faced the Magistrate. His black robes defined a broad man with a beady stare and straight ebony hair that reached his shoulders. This man, then, was the cherished and revered leader of Tranquility, the one every citizen worshipped.

"Xander Noble."

"Yes, Your Majesty." Xander gazed back defiantly.

"Your Alt has shown over 1000 negativity registers on The Continuum." The Magistrate creased his hawkish face with a frown and shuffled some papers in front of him.

"I guess that would be correct."

"I understand that all efforts to rehabilitate you have failed."

"Yeah. Who the frik cares? Not like *you* do, our Great Kindhearted Leader."

"Since that is the case, and since you have violated your contractual agreement, we now decline your citizenship in Tranquility."

"Well, that's a big sacrifice," Xander said with dramatic sarcasm. "You can bring me down, and throw me out, but I'll never give up my freakin' identity." He looked around, pretty sure he could make it to the door again, if he tried, before someone could catch him.

"Have you anything to say that would excuse your behavior as a citizen of Tranquility?"

"No . . . only this. I'm strong enough to survive. You won't see me begging to be one of your brainwashed citizens."

The Magistrate narrowed his eyes, which were dark as pitch. "Very well. In keeping with the law, you're being given your wish." He smirked. "You are hereby stripped of your citizenship and your family name and classified as REM. The acronym defines you as 'Resisting Emotional Management.' Most unfortunate. You no longer have access to the city or to any of its benefits. Your family will not acknowledge your existence, including your past. You are hereby erased from society, exiled to The Outside." He waved a veined hand in dismissal. "The Sciolist will take care of you from here."

The red-clad Sciolist did not speak, but with a burst of energy, took deliberate, exaggeratedly hurried steps to the front of the judge's bench. He handed Xander a pile of what looked to be thin fabric, charcoal gray. The Sciolist asserted, "Your REM clothes."

Xander snatched the rough, bland apparel. "You expect me to wear . . . *this*?" Xander replied, holding it up to the light. "Not my style," he joked.

The Sciolist boomed, "Put on your clothes!"

Xander stood, his stance mulish. When he didn't immediately show even a flicker of movement, the Sciolist took control, stripping off Xander's flamboyant clothes and shoes. *This is the definition of humiliation.* His arms reflexively covered his naked body, a sense of vertigo threatening to throw him off balance. He swallowed rapidly, wishing he could just disappear. At last, Xander jerked his arms and head through the short-sleeved shirt and his legs through the shorts like an angry robot. He was dressed.

Then, hustling toward him, the Sciolist captured him by

the arms and shoved. There was no happiness campaign here. His time was up.

Across the room a screen went up. Xander saw heavy, red curtains monogrammed with a monumental "T" on each side. As he had no choice but to slide along with his prosecutor, he stumbled, off balance, toward the curtains. Xander watched the weighty curtain draw up, as if the next stage of his life was being unveiled. There was no getting out of this.

Xander shifted his weight into a more threatening position. He growled in frustration, a deep guttural sound. The Sciolist, unflappable and eerily calm, unlocked the ponderous scarlet door before them with a large, old-fashioned golden skeleton key from his pocket and pulled it open. He threw a thumb out, gesturing to Xander to move on into what looked to be a simple hallway. Xander crossed his arms and shook his head from side to side as if he had an actual choice, in a firm "no." Finally, the Sciolist gave Xander a brutal shove where he stumbled like a disorderly drunk into the coldness of the corridor. "You'll find no happiness or peace now, REM."

The door shut with finality behind him, and he heard the lock screech. He winced as it thudded into place.

Xander found himself in a hallway. Cement floor and brick walls in gray surrounded him, unwelcoming as a morgue. He immediately felt like a lost soul. His eyes darted up and down, checking out any options he might have. He could see that the hallway stretched ahead, until, at some point, it took a sharp turn, obscuring it from sight. His bravery suddenly evaporating, Xander hesitated, but there was nowhere to go but forward.

He cursed under his breath. A bead of sweat ran into his eye where it burned like acid. He wiped the sour smelling sweat off his brow with his arm. Straightening his embarrassing clothes, frustrated that they were already riding up his crotch, he yelled, "Frak!" And with that, he started his pace into the unknown.

The grey, brick-lined tunnel was punctuated every twenty feet by undersized flickering light bulbs that threatened to wink out. Not great lighting—but at least he could see.

Xander relaxed a bit, as he realized the tunnel just looked industrial, not menacing. *I already know my fate is set, he thought. I am a REM—there's no going back. But maybe, even for me, I'm being overly negative?* His thoughts somehow restoring his spirits, Xander traveled a distance of 100 feet before he realized that with each step, the lighting became dimmer and the hallway became colder. It might as well be a tomb. There were no sounds. No creatures stirring. The smell, though, was another story. Nothing that he had noticed at first, Xander sensed how the tunnel reeked of age and neglect. He inhaled the moldy smell and coughed.

The kicker, though, was the cold. Xander was not used to this kind of climate; the frigid air gripped him, forcing his teeth to chatter, especially dressed as he was in his issued clothing of a thin t-shirt and shorts. Stripped of shoes, the concrete floor sucked the very life out of his feet.

Little by little, the lights on which he had depended winked out and disappeared. Finally, it was dark as pitch. He threw his arms out in front of him, and then shuffled over to the wall on his left where he at least had a physical support.

Feeling his way along the walls, Xander hoped for anything that would give him answers. Would there be an end sometime soon? And what would he find at the end, when it dumped him Outside? In the inkiness surrounding him, Xander imagined stars, but he had never been good at the Visualization Technique, and now he understood that, regardless, this present reality could not be altered with his mind. Step, step, step, step . . . each step, each breath, a sentence, an obvious punishment. Darkness swallowed him up little by little as he took curves and slopes leading him downward into mystery.

He began to lose track of time. How long he had now

been walking? Probably miles . . . at least a couple of hours . . . who knew? He trudged along, his progress slow but steady. He stopped, sensing a new odor. Among the smell of decay, Xander detected the scent of smoke. Why smoke? Was there fire?

A fleeting thought. Would his parents even miss him? He had broken ties with them long ago after they politely asked him to move out of the house. He was a disgrace, even to them. He imagined they'd just be glad to hear he got what he deserved.

Xander knew he had reached his limits. He was by now exhausted, thirsty, and confused. He still felt the cold grabbing his body with ghostly fingers. Cold . . . so cold. Suddenly, he bumped into a wall. The wall was deep-freeze cold as well, but when he ran his hands over it, he found that a primitive metal door handle protruded into the space.

Still having no glimmer of light, Xander grabbed ahold of the doorknob. In spite of himself, he prayed. To Whom or What he did not know.

Xander turned the knob and pushed himself with all his weight into the heavy door. It was stuck, as if rusted into place or warped from the dampness. Finally, after pushing with all his might, and pressing himself onto the door handle, it opened with a groan. He stepped through. The tunnel, with its twists and turns, its long path, deposited him into . . . what? His eyes revealed a whole new view.

Hot. The sky was gray, and he stepped out onto sparse, parched brown grass. After being in the deep freeze, the air, scorching and dry, was akin to a dragon's breath. Just a minute ago he had been freezing, but now, already, he began to sweat. Even the air was suffocating. It hurt to breathe.

His eyes scanned the arid landscape. All he could see was parched, flat earth. There was no sign of any life anywhere.

He had no hints of where to go. Which direction, even?

He would have to launch a discovery tour. *Damn it. What choices do I have now?*

With nothing recognizable as far as he could see, Xander quickly made up his mind. His remark to the judge about being able to survive would have to prove accurate. His life depended on it.

Xander stood against the outer side of the tunnel's walls and slid down it wearily. He sat, both to rest and to reflect on what he was going to do. He gazed across the landscape. A plume of diffuse gray smoke in the distance snaked its way into the heavens. He felt a sedative-like heaviness descend on him.

XANDER WOKE UP, startled. Something was running down his leg. He shook himself to fully wake and shake off what he thought might be a spider crawling on his calf. Arriving at a fuller consciousness, he realized what he felt was a rivulet of sweat. Then, the crushing memory came back—The Outside. He was sunburned and sticky, bleary and confused. He scratched his back and stomach. His ugly clothes were wrinkled and prickled his skin.

With a grunt, he pushed himself to his feet, realizing that his clothing was the least of his problems. So thirsty. His mouth was a shriveled fissure. He would have to start looking for a way to find food, water, and maybe other REMs? Would he find others like himself somewhere in the vast landscape? Or was The Outside a death sentence?

With an earnest sigh, he propelled himself forward into the wilderness before him. Water, food, and people in that order, he determined. It was going to be a challenge.

He had no sense of direction, but his sense of time and his blistered, aching feet told him he had been walking for a few hours. He had discovered nothing to suggest that he would even survive a day or two out of the city. The trek had been long, and Xander was sighed with discouragement. The air of the place still weighed heavily on his lungs.

Just when he was ready to break down in frustration, he saw in the distance what looked to be a small copse of trees. At least those would offer him some shade for a time, and if they were growing there, some way to find water nearby.

Ten minutes later, he arrived. To his dismay, the trees, anorexic at best, were partially cut, obviously for wood at some point in time, and more or less dead. Someone had been here, but now no one was around; he was still alone. Except for the faint smell of smoke in the air, the surroundings offered no shred of humanity or animal life. He sank down on a section of cut tree to rest, sagging against its shredded form.

Putting his head in his hands, he stared off into space. He couldn't go another step; this was the best place for him to make a camp. It would have to do for today. At least he wasn't dead yet, he rationalized. He would prevail! At that, a joke he'd heard pushed its way into his thoughts: never knock on Death's door. Ring the bell and run—he hates that. Xander chuckled. Yes, he would, indeed, have to be running.

He bent down and picked up a couple of sticks, one about three feet long, the other about a foot. He could use them to start a fire, if he found food. No need for warmth. The sun, while lower in the sky, was unrelenting.

Suddenly a tiny movement captured his attention. A lizard, about six inches long, was watching him from a nearby rock. *Dinner!* he thought. The lizard cocked its head, blinking with its bright, beady eyes, content to bask in the sun. Xander inched his way closer, never making eye contact with his intended meal. He realized that he was close enough that he could bash the lizard with one of his sticks. He stood perfectly still, measuring the distance with his eyes. Finally, he let his stick fly. Thwack! The stick hit the lizard square across the middle. It was oozing liquid, but still somehow alive, its head and legs jerking spasmodically. His fingers closed around the writhing creature. Xander squeezed it hard until its eyes bulged out, and it flopped across his knuckles, dead. He would stay alive another day.

Journal Entry #5484

There is much to do as the Magistrate of Tranquility. No one knows —except perhaps the Elite—what difficult things I must handle on a daily basis.

Most days I'm satisfied with what the readouts show, but once in a while there are people who can't maintain their contentment. They obviously don't try hard enough. When that happens, I'm the one who puts the plans in motion for intervention. It's a heavy responsibility, and I don't take the task lightly. I can think of several, just this month, who have been disappointments.

Today a REM, Xander Noble, was exiled to The Outside. When I monitored the Continuum Spectrum, I found the city's scores had already improved. Even one REM disturbs our peace. I feel responsible for helping all of our people to remain emotionally stable and happy.

And, yes, I become disappointed. I'm also often sad and angry. But I wear no Alt. As the Magistrate I am free to exercise my emotions. Sending citizens to The Outside is not a pleasant task. It would make anyone question their own humanity. So, I willingly take this on, to be a proper judge of others' emotions. Every day I realize what uncontrolled emotional highs and lows could do to our citizens. These unbridled emotions I experience and tolerate are exhausting, but necessary. I accept and bear the burden, but I often wish there would be someone trustworthy to take this on.

Because of my responsibility, I have no family. I have chosen to be alone. A family would complicate the decisions I must make. My city is my family, so I gladly sacrifice any other blood ties. The Elite body is my clan. They support me in my needs and follow my recommendations without question. It is through me that the Elite can help govern Tranquility.

—Serpio Magnus, Magistrate

15

Ember's Inventory

Two days after the break-in, Ember was still getting her living quarters organized to where she could find everything. Putting her possessions back together, though, was a calming experience. She was still raw from the last few days' traumatic events, but her Alt numbers had at least normalized, thanks to her dedication to Tranquility's best mental exercises and her return to a routine.

She still missed her mother terribly. The place didn't feel like home anymore without her mom there. When she felt especially lonely, she wrote letters to her mother about how she felt and what had happened since her death. It wasn't like she was truly talking to her mom, but she could make believe her mother would receive the letters. In them, she promised her mom she would try hard to become the person her mom would want her to be. In the end, the positive energy she put into it, and her make-believe life with her helped her. Dwelling on the loss would not bring her mother back or help her move forward.

City Hall had not wasted much time notifying her that her days in the Purple Vale sector were numbered. One short day after she had returned from the hospital, the eviction notice was posted on the front door. Ember pulled a five-by-five card from a stiff white envelope. A royal blue background imprinted with an old-fashioned white key formed a frame for "Home Sweet Home" written in script. Below was listed her new address at Number Twelve, Blueberry Way. She would have to be there within two weeks, where all the Level Eights like herself lived, provided she could stay in control of her points and maintain her Status. Although not nearly as plush as Purple Vale, the Blue Riverfront development would represent a new beginning for her.

Along with the notification about the move, Ember received a purple envelope with the seal of the city holding the flap closed. Breaking the seal, Ember read the letter inside:

"Tranquility's leaders are sorry for your loss. We understand this is a traumatic period, but one we trust that you will manage with dignity and optimism. As you know, every cloud has a silver lining!
Items previously owned by the deceased will need to be returned to the city. Talesa Vinata's Alt is especially important. In your loved one's honor, the Alt will be smashed, its parts rearranged artistically. From there it will be encased in a crystal jar bearing Talesa's name. The jar will sit in the City Hall Memorial Room with many others who have come and gone before.
The rest of the deceased's possessions are on the attached list. Please be sure that you account for every item on the next page. These items will go to the Clearing House where they will be recycled and made new again for someone else to own. We

respectfully ask that you begin this process
immediately so that you may heal quickly. We
determine that one week from the receipt of
this letter should be sufficient. Again, our
deepest sympathy in your bereavement."

As Ember examined the list, she realized what a daunting task she had before her. She looked over the extensive inventory, pacing the floor with a nervous energy. She would have to check off hundreds of items.

Finally, Ember recognized she had procrastinated as long as she could. In exactly twenty-four hours she would be deemed late for the collection. She stroked her Alt, feeling the safety and security it offered her, before grabbing a box, scissors, and some packing tape and heading down the hallway to her mother's bedroom. It was time to pack up Talesa's things.

In great haste, she made the bed, resisting the urge to put her face in her mother's pillow. Smelling her mom's personal scent and perfume would send her back into mourning—not an advisable place to go. The closet was next, and again, Ember did not hesitate as she lifted each soft, pristine garment out, folded it, and placed it in the box she had brought. So many lovely purple clothes . . .

She was proud of her own efficiency as at last she headed to her mother's dressing table under the broad, bright window. Talesa's makeup was still scattered about, something that Austel probably felt was better left to Ember to arrange. She would normally place items back into the special little drawers that were painted with delicate flowers and calligraphy, designating each drawer for a purpose. Talesa always reminded Ember that organization was a shining personal attribute; it allowed the mind to stay focused. The more organized a person's possessions, the more a person's life would imitate the process.

Ember picked up all the pieces of makeup, again placing

them in yet another box, the final one of the day. She pulled open each of the wooden drawers of the dressing table, still finding random items that Austel had tried to position after he had taken inventory. A few beaded necklaces, glimmering earrings, and even underwear were stuffed into the dressing table in a haphazard fashion, lonely artifacts of a life gone too soon.

Into the box they went, and Ember pushed to shut the last door front, symbolically making the collection more final.

"What is wrong with this drawer?" Ember wondered aloud. "Shazz!" Ember tried to shut it again, and for a second time it stuck, its front protruding for about a half inch. *Pull it out, push back in. What was so hard about that?*

"I'm going to have to take the whole thing out!" Ember yelled out to the room at large, throwing her hands up in the air. She felt a strange tickle down her spine. Anger. *Breathe. Be careful. Get those emotions in check.*

Grabbing the defiant drawer with a hand on each side, Ember eased it out until it again became stubborn, refusing to give up its position. As she pushed up on the bottom, Ember blew out a frustrated blast of air, and then with a Herculean yank, freed the drawer from whatever anchored it to the table. Ember tumbled backwards, landing in heap not unlike a half somersault. She lay there for a moment, rubbing her hip, its throbbing like a displaced heartbeat. As she tried to sit up on the floor, her feet and legs mulishly refused to move. It was behaved as if they belonged to someone else. "Graceful much?" Ember muttered. Her Alt vibrated, reminding her that her negative self-talk was registering on the scale.

Ember righted herself at last and picked up the drawer which had landed on its side. She realized instantly that the thing was empty and had probably become stuck from recent disuse. She slid it back into its casing, but still could not get it to fully close. "Shazz! What's goin' on here?" Taking a deep, discontented breath, she pulled it out again, entirely dislodging the drawer from the table. With the determination of a keen detective, she peered more closely into the hollow recess of the dressing table. Something that looked like gauze was lodged in the very back.

She reached her hand in, grabbed, and pulled the wad out, realizing it had been hooked on a tiny nail. Unfurling the gauze, she gawked at the discovery. Her heart skittered like an escaping mouse. She had found her mother's special ring.

16

Ember's Secret

T he dazzling amethyst and diamond ring had been on her mother's finger "twenty-four-seven" for the last three months, but when she became sick, Talesa put away all her jewelry and, sadly, never put it on again. *I wonder what it's doing in the back of the drawer,* thought Ember. *I could have completely missed it!*

Ember held the ring up to the light, and memories of the Day of the Ring and the Ceremony sprang to the surface. She was instantly in another place and time, and she felt infused with love . . .

"Mom . . . I'm so excited you're getting this award. So proud, too!"

"Thanks, Ember." She beamed her characteristic smile. "I have to go up on stage now. See you right after in the reception room."

Ember had smoothed her deep blue evening dress as she made her way to her seat in the front row of the theater. Talesa's joy radiated from her. So incredibly strong, it didn't even take Ember's empathic talents to sense it.

The lights dimmed as Talesa made her way onto the stage and seated herself in a highly decorated purple chair. Seventeen other chairs, making a total of eighteen, were a rainbow of color. The seats held men and women of all ages, each person's smile bigger than the room.

Then the Magistrate stepped to the podium. It was the first time Ember had ever seen Serpio Magnus in person. She was awe-struck. People thought him to be a chivalrous, compassionate individual, but to Ember, he seemed rather fearsome. The man was tall, which alone was intimidating. His black hair, sparsely iced with delicate strands of lustrous silver, reached almost to his shoulders. Regardless of his age— unknown but estimated to be around fifty—he radiated good health and perfect skin, unmarked by lines. He must visit the Youth Restoration clinic all the time. Or maybe they even came to him . . . Ember felt his presence strongly, his inner strength and emotional luster almost bowling her over. When her gaze reached his eyes, as piercing as steel points, he scruti- nized her with intense curiosity in return.

"Good evening, Tranquilites! Welcome to our twenty-fifth annual Day of the Ring Ceremony. Tonight we have eighteen distinguished citi- zens who are to receive an award. Each ring, the Augur Prize, represents and symbolizes the special qualities of these individuals. We name them for the first Magistrate of Tranquility, Bahram Augur, who began using a circular band to symbolize Tranquility's never-ending Emotional Contin- uum. All eighteen levels are being honored here tonight." The great Magistrate's hands shook with excitement, and, to Ember's dismay and revulsion, several droplets of spittle shot out from his mouth over the podium. "The Commission nominated these individuals, but also vetted them, determining who was most worthy to receive this prestigious award. It is an immense honor."

She snapped back into the present. Ember polished the ring's stone with the bottom of her shirt and held it up to the light, where its prismatic facets glimmered like stardust. It was as breathtaking as she remembered. The amethyst stone, three carats in size, sparkled in a solid gold swirly "T" criss-cross setting. Two tiny diamonds set off the amethyst on each side. Above and beyond its monetary worth, it was priceless for its symbolism. Nothing comparable could be purchased with Status points.

She grabbed the possessions inventory from the top of the dressing table, frantically looking for the ring's presence on the index, hoping against hope that it had been overlooked. Her heart sank as she saw it listed in bold directly above the Alt.

I can't part with this. One thing of my mom's to remember her by . . . I've got to keep it safe! It's like she left me something to comfort me.

She slipped it into her shirt pocket, knowing that putting it on her finger would be impractical. The ring would never fit her, as her hands were diminutive in comparison to her mom's. It wasn't something she would wear around every day anyway, and it wasn't hers, but it could be a special keepsake to keep and treasure forever.

Picking up the box she had packed, she left the room, and closed the door behind her. The furniture and heavy items would be left to the movers to clear and move. She pasted a smile on her face—she knew the value of the external to affect inner feelings—and went downstairs. All was now packed, including her own possessions. She set the box down on a nearby table, dragging her fingers across the top as if to say goodbye.

Next, she would head down to City Hall to inquire about the move and turn in the inventory list. It would have to be stamped and notarized. She picked up a pen off the table, signing her name in bold lettering, affirming its completion.

The ring seemed to burn in her pocket. She had never before done anything so rebellious. Her palms were damp with moisture, and she squeezed her hands together to keep them from shaking. Her Alt vibrated a warning. *Shazz!* Her points were dropping. She immediately forced a smile onto her face and thought about going down to the Fun Zone later to help balance her emotions.

A short while later, Ember emerged from the blue CommuteCar in front of City Hall. She had seen City Hall, of course, but she had never been inside. She was young, inexperienced, and naïve. City Hall was not for people like her, but for the Elite—the government who provided them with peace and happiness. She had never had a reason to be there.

After passing the ten-foot iridescent "T" statue in front of the double glass doors trimmed in gold, she entered the building. Looking up, Ember determined the building stretched to the skies, as it was either open at the top, many stories up, or had a glass ceiling at some point. In the lobby, a massive wooden desk, gold, easily twenty feet long and seven feet high, dominated the room. The front of the desk was laser-carved, the carving with faces of former and current leaders of Tranquility etched deeply into the smooth grain. They were meant to be encouraging, but Ember found them unnerving. They were so realistic! Each face had a softly shaped smile and vibrant looking eyes. Flags of all colors lined each side of the room, about eight feet up. Each flag, each color, a Status.

Ember strode with what she hoped to be a convincing, purposeful confidence up to the front desk where she planted her feet in a wide stance, her eyes glued to the woman behind the counter.

Behind the desk was what appeared to be a person, but Ember quickly realized she was mistaken. Ember felt no emotional energy, saw no aura. It wasn't a person at all. Its hair glistened unrealistically under the overhead chandeliers, and its eyes blinked a little too sluggishly. A rose-colored blush dusted the cheeks on snowy skin. Its slender arms moved fluidly on and off a keyboard like a pianist in recital. Shiny, pearly teeth highlighted a bow-like mouth, lips an ideal shade of peach. "She" was picture-perfect. Her name tag had A.S.P.E.R. written on it in bold gold letters. In fine print were the words "Alt Spectrum Policy Enforcing Receptionist."

Ember glanced around, hoping to find others in the room. Real people. There was surely someone else. But the foyer was empty, except for herself. Nothing to do but go forward. "Hello. I'm Ember. I have to register my mom's personal effects and ask about a few other things."

The supermodel robot behind the desk listened intently and politely. "I'll be *happy* to help you, citizen. Please insert the face of your Alt into the Alt Reader on the desk." Ember hesitated but did as she was told. "Thank you, Ember Vinata, Status Eight. Now, what did you wish to accomplish here?"

"My mother passed away last week. I . . . wanted to see about a memorial. I was told the Kelasts take care of the dead? Where would I find them?" Ember leaned forward, placing her hands firmly on the marble desktop. The support would keep her from swaying.

A.S.P.E.R. responded, smiling broadly in her mechanical way. "First, you must submit your Inventory List. Have you been able to collect everything?"

"It took a while, but yeah," Ember said. She smiled at A.S.P.E.R. as she pulled the folded itemization from her pocket and handed it across the desk.

A.S.P.E.R. retrieved it effortlessly and lifted it up to eye level to "read." With a tilt of her head, she seemed satisfied. She pushed it through a slot in the massive desk. Immediately, it shot out from another aperture. A.S.P.E.R. grabbed it and imprinted "Approved" with a laser hand tool. "The Clearing House and City Hall will match your list to the items you have packed for recycling. At that time, you will receive a notice that you have satisfied all requirements for the End of Life Possessions Collection. You may go."

"No! I need to find out where my mother's remains are. There's been no one to help me." Ember threw her hands in the air.

A.S.P.E.R. blinked several times and typed in something on the computer keyboard in front of her. "I'm sorry. The Kelast portfolio indicates that you are not privileged to have this information. You must go."

"Wait. My mother was a Level Fourteen and had access to classified documents. She had clout with the Elite in City Hall. She knew the Magistrate *personally*."

A.S.P.E.R. replied, "Seek comfort, then, from the living. Have a positive day." The lovely robot turned away.

Ember clenched her fists, daring her Alt to find her guilty. *I don't care what I have to do. I am getting to the bottom of this.*

17

Will's 1025

Will hadn't stopped thinking of Ember since he had left her. Not only was she beautiful and sweet, he knew she was alone. Absolutely alone. He was still disturbed that the break-in had not been solved. And, in spite of all Tranquility's security features, he feared for her safety. There was something jiggy about the whole thing. It was, of course, the right thing to do to check up on her to see if she needed any other help. He smiled.

He entered her number on his Alt.

"Hi, Will." The sound of her voice tightened his throat and turned his body to mush.

"Ember . . . just wanted to follow up. It's customary. We have to make sure all is back to normal. How're you doing?" Will pushed a button on the chair's arm to lean way back in his chair at his station, his eyes searching the ceiling. Trying to sound professional was taking some effort.

"I'm fine. I've put everything away and gone down to City Hall to submit my inventory list. I'm cleared for the move."

"Good, good. Wondering if I can come by? I'd like to wrap up the incident report . . . and . . . well, it would be great to see you again."

"Actually, I'd love that."

"Sure. And, maybe I can help more with your clean up?" An excuse for a chunk of time with Ember.

"Um...actually—I haven't been able to find out what happened to my mom's body."

"What? Her body?" He could hardly grasp what she was talking about. *Why would a body be missing?*

"Yeah. Weird, I know. She also tried to tell me something in the hospital. Maybe you'll give me some advice?"

The poor girl. "Say no more. I'm on my way."

WILL SMILED BROADLY when Ember opened the door. His memory hadn't deceived him. She was a beauty. Her hair shone as if buffed by strawberry sunshine, set off by the royal blue tunic she wore.

"Come in, Will. Hopefully the place looks better than it did when you were here before. Don't mind the boxes, though. I'm getting ready for my move." The boxes rose up in stacks throughout the place, blue stripes on each marking them for a new community.

"Yeah. Different. More like a cardboard maze." He intentionally bumped into a stack of boxes. "Or a fortress." He laughed.

Ember chuckled. She led him through the towers of boxes to the leathery purple sofa. "Sit down, please. Can I offer you something? Water, soda, coffee?"

"No, nothing, thanks. Just wanted to make sure your points are up and you didn't discover anything else amiss. That way I can sign off on this report." Will held up the Factive and waved it.

"I'm doing okay." Ember sounded defeated instead of okay. "But I do have some things you could help me with. What friends I do have aren't in a position to help me, but you work for the city. Can I trust you?" She gazed at him with eyes full of hope.

Warm feelings flooded him, and Will felt his Alt vibrate. "That's what I'm here for." *And for a few other reasons,* he thought.

"I found something of my mother's, and I want to make sure it stays safe with me. And I can't get any answers about where they took her body. Is that normal?"

"The Kelasts take care of the deceased. You've been to City Hall about the Kelast transfer?"

"Yeah—no help at all. In fact, the clerk told me I couldn't have access to any information." Ember's face seemed to droop. She resembled a wilted flower. He noted she quickly realized her slip, recovered, and forced a nervous smile.

Will's eyebrows went up. "Hmm. It's not a secret or anything. The Kelasts take those who have passed on to the city's mortuary. You know the building—'Irides.' There the person who's passed is placed in a sarcophagus the color of the person's status. Then there's a Celebration of Life at City Hall. Family and friends each bring a single flower to place together in a large bouquet. Afterward, the body is taken to a vault beneath the city."

"That sounds lovely. But I don't know anything about that. It's as if someone didn't *want* me to know about that."

"No—there has to be an explanation. I'll bet you the notification just slipped through the cracks." He put his hand on her shoulder. "I'll look into it. I'll put it in the system and see what's going on."

"That would be wonderful!" She reached out and gave him an impulsive, tight hug, and then let him go. She looked up at him. "I don't know what to say."

Will thrilled to the look of appreciation in her eyes. And her hug made his head spin. "That's no problem at all. As soon as I find out, I'll let you know. And," he said, "it would make me happy to take you to the Celebration when the time comes. I wouldn't want you to be alone."

Ember beamed and Will was feeling good. He could make both of them happy, and he could perhaps get to know her better. Dinner somewhere afterward, maybe.

She broke his reverie. "So . . . there's another thing."

"Hit me up."

"I'm pretty sure that whoever broke in here was looking for something, and it might have been this." Ember pulled her mother's bejeweled ring out of her pocket, extending it.

Will whistled. "That's some ring. The Augur Prize."

"My mother's. I couldn't bear to turn it in to the city with the inventory list. I'm worried that City Hall will discover soon that I didn't return it. I want to keep it, Will. It is so special to me. Something of my mom's I can keep forever."

"Could I see it?" Will took it from Ember's fingers, turning it over in his palm and examining it with sharp focus. "Hmm . . . did you notice there is a tiny number engraved inside?"

"A number? No. I actually haven't looked at it too intently. I'm more concerned with keeping it with me. I sometimes hide it in my pocket to protect it. When I hold it tightly in my hand, though, my Alt points go up. It's like the love my mother had for me is in that ring."

"Well, there's definitely a number, a '1025.' Here. Look closely." Will held the ring toward the light so Ember could see. "You might be right that someone was looking for it when they came here and trashed this place. It's certainly valuable. Your mom must've been a stellar citizen to have earned this."

"Yes. I wish you could've known her."

Will put his hands on her shoulders, hoping she wouldn't think it was too forward.

"Me too. Listen, I want you to call me at any time if you think anything at all is wrong, okay? I'm going to look into your mom's celebration, and I might find out what I can about the number in the ring, too. I know all of this is going to work out for the best. It has to. We live in an ideal place. Promise me you'll call if you need me, Ember?"

"Yes, of course. And you'll call me as soon as you find out anything, right?"

"You have my word."

18

Xander's Independence

Xander had slept well, in spite of having no
comfort. He didn't even remember going to sleep
and found himself slumped over in an L shape as he
awakened. *It's a new day . . . time to get this party started,* he
muttered to himself.

Again, he began his journey out into the unknown. It
wasn't long before the unforgiving, flat, dry landscape, the
persistent heat, and the lack of companionship unraveled his
usual bon vivant spirit. The air was heavy. His body sagged
with a drop-dead weariness he would expect of someone three
times his age. For the first time, worry hung like a web about
him, threatening to bind him forever with the sticky threads of
self-doubt and fear.

When he began to cry, he yelled in frustration. He was
unbreakable! And yet, here he was, acting like a child. Feeling
more vulnerable than he ever had in his life, he wiped the trai-
torous tears away with a brutal thrust of the heel of his hand
and pushed forward.

He put one foot in front of the other, each step a victory
over the last. His eyes burned now, the salt of his tears
becoming sandpaper in the wind. Was he getting farther and

farther away from any hope of life? He didn't know. He'd had to have trudged along another hour but imagined he saw ahead of him a dip in the landscape. What could lie ahead? The bleak flatness evolved into a corrugated terrain with course ripples. This was an unexpected, fresh panorama. He picked up his pace, a tentative optimism propelling him over sand-spun dirt and periodic sprays of scraggly weeds.

He blinked his eyes and shook his head. Had he seen a shimmer? He narrowed his eyes, squinting into the sun.

There it was, for sure. An undeniable sparkle. *Unless I'm hallucinating, it's gotta be water. If not, I'm gonna die.* He had gone too long without a drink.

At last he came close. He dropped to his knees, this time shouting for joy. The hollow did contain water. About six feet wide, its shallow surface generated a subtle glimmer. It was a miracle. The five-inch depth gave him just enough volume to fill his hands. His gratefulness turned the water into an elixir such as he had never known.

He hated leaving the spot, and yet he couldn't stay here, could he? Especially not knowing when—or if—he would find water again. Yet he saw no signs of any other people. *Either they've found a better place, or no one is alive out here.* He needed to journey on.

He had counted eleven thousand merciless steps along the rugged landscape when he noticed milky, thin smoke in the distance. No question now—that was where he was headed. He imagined other people who also wanted emotional freedom might be there. Others like him—REMs. He could maybe finally live his life without constraint.

Several hours later, acrid-scented smoke seared his nostrils. He smelled sulphur, a wicked burnt odor. *A hint of some life?* He was encouraged, and he picked up speed. He saw ahead the outline of a city on the horizon. Its black shape rose up like a giant from the brutal earth.

Those buildings look bombed out, he thought. *What happened here?*

A short distance away, he rubbed his hands together and broke into a grin. A few people—*people!*—were going in and out of the buildings, some of them dressed in clothing identical to his, but in various faded shades of black, grey and brown, certainly a sharp contrast to what one would see in Tranquility. *I'm gonna have to get some fashion sense going on around here,* he thought. *These people don't realize what they could have. Maybe I'll even make myself a fashion icon.* He stood tall, his confidence returning, as he strutted toward the closest building. He was already thinking about his future.

Xander looked for the door of the building, and found it easily, although the building itself did not look inviting. A tarnished sign overhead read "Base 4." The words had been scratched into the metal.

As he entered, he was surprised to find about a hundred people. Each of the people appeared hard at work crafting what looked like tools.

A man stood nearby. Xander approached. "Hey, is there someone in charge here?"

"Well, now. You're new," the stranger replied, his voice raspy. "Welcome, fellow REM. Did you just get in? It's not easy to find us."

"A minute ago! By the way, I'm Xander." He began the Tranquility salute, and then remembered it wasn't necessary here. He lowered his arm and sized up the guy. Tall and skinny, his curly hair was white as snow. A short, fuzzy beard made him look older than he probably was. His actions were quick, and his blue eyes sharp.

"Gabriel. No matter . . . you can check in at the 'main office.'" Gabriel laughed at his own feeble joke. "Won't offer ya much, but at least you can learn something about this place. Two buildings over—sign says Base 1. Good meetin' ya . . ." Gabriel casually waved him off, as if Xander was unimportant, and went back to his work.

Xander lost no time in finding his way back out the door. Now that he knew where he was going, he looked about the place with acute interest. After all, this was going to be home.

Sidewalks protruded from the ground in bits and pieces, often revealing bare dirt. Vegetation was sparse to nonexistent, a carbon copy of where he had come from earlier. The surrounding buildings were in various stages of demolition, their concrete walls covered in a moist film, like tears of misery. Dark black hulls rose up like concrete monuments to despondency. The sky was dark, the sun occluded by clouds. Or perhaps it was the smoke again, he didn't know.

Off the "road" he spied what he imagined was once a park, now a home for colorless trees and cadaverous plants, reaching their skeleton limbs to the sky. Broken swings creaked as if still full of joyful children, a slight wind dusting their chains. He gave a shiver, his mind recreating something alive. When life was real. When people could have lived their own dreams.

This place is bizarre, he thought. *It's going to take some adjustment. But I'm up to it.* Before he knew it, he had made his way to Base 1. A massive building, a shadowy wave, loomed above him. Several stories high, its windows, some cracked and some totally shattered, were obscured by dark shades. At the top was some type of steeple, piercing the sky. Xander felt suddenly exposed, and for a tiny moment, intimidated by the ghostly isolation.

Xander opened a heavy iron door and stepped inside. The interior was dim but still allowed him to notice the crumbling walls and the graphic graffiti landscape. A musty smell glommed onto his clothes, reminding him this place was a victim of its neglected history. A lone male sat at a small wooden desk playing some type of mandala game.

"Hey, there," Xander spoke up. "I'm Xander."

No answer.

"Hellooooo? Are you deaf?"

"Got it. You're new. Sign in right here." The sooty young man behind the desk barely glanced his way. He extended a clipboard and a pen, cracked near the top.

"Sure thing." Xander grasped the items and put them to quick use, handing them back to the clerk. "Glad I finally found some people. I was startin' to wonder if I was gonna be on my own. So, what's the deal here? You guys got some sort of 'welcome brochure' or somethin'?" Xander grinned. *Might as well make an impression.*

"Yeah, right," the greasy-haired REM replied. "It's each one to himself. You gotta figure things out, dude. We got a place to work—Base 4— so you can make tools to help ya capture food. It ain't much. There's a stream up along an old train depot. You can borrow a container for now but boil the water. As far as shelter, find a building that's got what ya want, and it's yours. Ain't nobody in charge."

"You have a name?"

"Graham. Like your grandma's crackers."

Graham seemed to be as funny as he was physically. Tall and desperately skinny, his voice was high-pitched, almost squeaky, like he'd been sucking helium balloons that affected every other word. His chin sported a thin patch of hair, like a goatee. The facial hair did even more to make him look like a cartoon character. Xander wondered how Graham kept such a small amount of facial hair. Nobody out there would have any shaving tools.

Xander grinned. "Well, Graham, I'll be seein' you around." Xander turned toward the door set on making the best of his new situation, but paused. "Wait . . . you said there's no leader here?"

"Nope. We're REMs for a reason, dude."

Xander felt a fresh energy. He suddenly saw the pieces fall into place. Destiny had found him. He would become Leader of The Outside.

Journal Entry #5515

My favorite event of the year is the Day of the Ring. What a magnificent display! So many fine people—so many beautiful colors assembled on stage. I have watched with pleasure the everyday authentic expression of true happiness and success. It is a great reminder to the people of Tranquility; each person can rise up—can distinguish themselves as model citizens. The annual Augur Prize Ceremony this year was even more glamorous than years past. I feel confident that my choices for the recipients will highlight ideal lifestyles for all Tranquility citizens. When I congratulate the people and describe their accomplishments and their Alt numbers, it's elevating for everyone, even me. Each year more and more Tranquilites attend the Ceremony, dreaming about a ring that could perhaps, someday, be theirs. Great planning between the Elite and me goes into choosing the recipients. These are very unique individuals. Special preparation goes into the prizes for those with high Status. It is an affair marked by illusion and joy.

—Serpio Magnus, Magistrate

19

Ember's Ailment

E mber sagged from the weight of the elephant on her shoulders. Of course, it wasn't real, but it might as well be. She read Will's vibes accurately. She perceived the rush as he entered the apartment. Her Alt vibrated at regular intervals. His ardor seeped into her bones, filling her every cell. Or was it her own excitement at being with him? Ember had to admit she was all tingly when she looked into his eyes.

In any case, her Alt points were climbing; she viewed the surge as new hope.

Her Alt erupted, music redirecting her focus. An unexpected call. "Hello?"

"Hello, Ember. It's Austel from the Plauditorium. How're you doing?"

"Much better. Thanks, Austel. How can I help you?"

"Just wanted to finish up this report. Making sure you haven't had any other situations we need to notate."

"No, I'm good, but thanks. Will was just here this morning, making sure the report was finalized. He's pretty much taken charge." A swell of appreciation for these great people affected her like a sugar rush.

"Will was there?" Ember observed an awkward beat of silence on the other end. "Oh, sorry then."

Ember rushed to answer. "No problem. I assumed Will was completing the investigation."

"I'm the lead in the case since I'm senior to him. I'll have to give him a ration about that." Austel laughed.

"He was super helpful."

"It's no big deal. I'll make sure we get this wrapped up. Glad you're more tranquil, Ember. You're a great citizen."

"Thanks, Austel. Goodbye." Ember hung up the phone, the verbal reassurance a virtual hug.

It was time to get back to a routine, at least until she had to move to the new digs. That would take some getting used to, but in the meantime, she could get back to her job at Peaceful Paws, the animal shelter across town. She adored the cats and dogs; they were great therapy for her. Her empathic talent allowed her to read about each critter's disposition. She knew immediately which ones were most in need of love and care. In return, she experienced their enormous love.

Her heart suddenly light, she sprang up the stairs to put on her blue uniform and put up her hair in the customary bun she wore to keep it out of the animals' way. What to do with the ring? She was loath to leave it behind. Picking it up from where she left it the night before, she transferred it into her jumpsuit's upper breast pocket. Right over her heart, it would stay with her all day.

As she left home, she waved to the room's camera, hoping perhaps Will might see her from the Plauditorium. She closed the door with finality, and skipped down the marble tiled steps, calling for a car on her Alt.

Her senses suddenly overwhelmed her. The world tipped. She gasped for breath, tottering on legs that suddenly trembled. What was happening to her? She managed to make it to the street's edge, where she plopped down on the curb. A headache equivalent to a fiery thunderbolt struck her, and there was no one there to help.

Just then, the CommuteCar pulled up next to where she sat on the concrete. She stood up as if in slow motion and inserted her card into the vehicle's identification slot. "To the Plauditorium," she rasped. "And call Will Verus."

The CommuteCar seemed to take a thousand years as it motored down the city streets. These cars were not made for harried passengers hurrying to arrive at a destination. All CommuteCars were programmed to no more than thirty miles per hour to keep the roads safe and tranquil. Ember gripped the side handholds anyway, as motion of any kind was not her friend right now. Her Alt lit up, picking up Ember's accelerated heart rate and the sweat that was drenching her hands and forehead.

EMBER WOKE when a beam of sunlight kissed her face with a gentle glow. Her eyes opened to Will's presence in a chair nearby. She immediately sat up, embarrassed at having her arms over her face and her legs splayed out in a total disregard for dignity. How must she look? Her Alt chimed, registering the change from sleep to alertness.

"Ember. How are you feeling?" Will couldn't help himself. He reached out and touched her face. In his mind, he substituted compassion for worry.

"Confused. How long have I been asleep?"

"About two hours. Do you hear the music?" Will pointed up to the ceiling, where Ember heard a low, New Age song playing. "I made sure you got some auditory healing harmonies."

"Will, thanks for helping me. I didn't know where else to go." She felt sheepish. "But I feel just fine now." Ember swung her legs around and stood up, discovering she was energized and refreshed. "Yeah. I feel great, actually. Must have been something I ate." She cracked a broad smile and perceived a broad rush of compassion emanating from Will's inner being.

"Can I get you anything?"

"No. I was planning to go to work, but now I'll just head home." Ember realized she was starving. "Unless you have Jarnish?" She raised her eyebrows and looked at him hopefully.

"Just so happens I have some, girl." Will winked at her. "You really feeling better?" She soaked up the worry he was struggling to control.

"Yeah—honestly. I feel fine. Much better than when I got here." She wanted him to put his concern aside. *Would his Alt pick up compassion or would it register anxiety?*

"Okay. But I'm gonna keep an eye on you. Have a seat at the table, while I get you some Jarnish and hot cocoa."

"Great."

Will pulled out a plush chair, grabbing her elbow and escorting her into it as if she were royalty. "Give me a sec." Will rattled around in the kitchen area. As he began pulling cups out of the cupboard that had automatically opened behind him, he glanced her way. He held the mugs under a decorative spigot attached to a silver module. Hot chocolate poured out, perfectly filling the mugs. "Got a bit of information with you, too. I researched the ring number."

Ember turned around in her chair, the hair on her arms standing up. "You found something out already?"

Will strode over with two plates, the coveted Jarnish, and mugs of cocoa swirled with whipped cream. "Comfort food." Will smiled and placed the steaming chocolate offerings in front of her. "Yeah, some success . . . but first, log into your Alt. I want to make sure your readings are positive. You need to be strong enough to hear it."

Ember's eyes widened, her eyebrows forming a question

mark. "Of course, I am! I'm tougher than I look!" She laughed.

"You sure?"

"Okay, Will. I'll give you the proof. I need my early afternoon reading, anyway." She placed her finger and awaited the results. Frowning a little, she noticed the health icon blinking. *It's detected my fainting spell.* But her points showed positive for happiness. *Probably because I'm here with Will.* "Look. I'm fine. Magnificent!" she declared, turning the Alt's face in his direction as if he could see the numbers. Taking a bite of Jarnish, she sighed with delight. "Is there anything this good anywhere else on the planet?"

"This stuff helps. Mood elevating." He grinned. "So, I first researched number 1025 and got no results—nothing. Next, I checked the city's records for the Augur Prize, trying to find the number that way. Got a list of recipients, nothing special. Doesn't help. Merely an account of the first group of citizens to ever receive rings. In that very first group, City Hall issued rings to citizens Level Fourteen and above. That's odd."

"Not that odd. It takes time for people to distinguish themselves. Especially the initial group who were probably older."

"Yeah, I agree. But the people who received the Augur Prize in the first 'class'? Each one is now listed as deceased."

Ember tried to keep her face composed, but a frown won out as she processed the information. "They're all . . . dead?" Her thoughts bounced around like out-of-control ping pong balls. "What—? Now that *is* odd."

"I thought so."

She looked straight into Will's eyes, hoping to glean more than his words. She felt Will's emotions seeping out, a steady line of droplets, as if from a wet umbrella. She sensed his seriousness. He was unsettled, his aura a red arc.

His Alt's going to register his apprehension, she reflected. She needed to make light of this discovery for Will's sake, even though she was working through it herself. "C'mon,

Will. Those citizens—well before our time. That list isn't answering any questions about my mom's ring that I can see." She took a swallow of her chocolate, grateful for its warm comfort.

Will said, "Right. But each person on the list had a number. I don't know if the number was also engraved on each band, but maybe. Was hoping to find the recipients and talk to them about theirs. Now, I can't. Have to find out another way."

"What other way? Records will be sealed." Ember fought back a wave of frustration. *Will is helping. He's gonna find a way. He's got to.*

"I'll figure it out. *Gotta* be in the system somewhere. And if it is, I'll find it. Trust me?"

"Totally." She reached out and squeezed his hand, her heart melting a little at the touch.

"You still keeping your mom's ring safe? You're gonna to be asked about it sooner or later. We've got to be sure it's safe. Keep you above questioning."

She loved the way he said, "We've got to be sure." He was in her court. "Of course. I always have it with me." Will could know she carried the ring. He was the one person she could trust. Ember looked around to make sure no one was watching before digging into her front pocket.

The blood drained from her face. Her stomach dropped, and a wave of panic threatened to overwhelm her. Her pocket was empty.

20

Will's Lost And Found

"It's gone!"

Will gaped at Ember. "What? *Gone?* How?"

She looked at him, wide-eyed, and shook her head, as if she couldn't process it.

Will reached out and touched her arm. "You must have left it at home. Let's hope you did."

"No. I had it when I came here. I'm sure of it. I deliberately put it in my pocket."

"Well, we'd better look around. It can't be lost, Ember!"

Both began searching the room, especially around the place where Ember had been lying on the cot. They searched the floor and the area from the front of the building to the lounge. Nothing. It was as if it had disappeared on its own.

"Maybe when we brought you in front outside. Let's look out by the curb." *It has to be there,* he thought. *Maybe lying on the sidewalk. I carried her. It could have fallen from her pocket.*

They dashed outside and began a frantic investigation. From cobblestone to cobblestone and to each shrub along the path, they explored the scene, but to no avail.

"Now what?" Ember said. Her Alt began making noise as pure panic registered on it.

"Well, you can't exactly report this. I'm just going to have to keep looking around the Plauditorium. Check the CommuteCar, too. You could've lost it in there when you were feeling faint."

Will felt Ember's eyes on him, but this time, he didn't like it. She seemed to be stripping him down and laying him bare.

"Will, are you sure you didn't take it out of my pocket?" Ember was looking at him with the eyes of a tiger seeking prey.

"What? Ember! I didn't even know it was *in* your pocket. Had no idea!" Will put his hand to his head, hoping this new development was some sort of dream.

"I think—I need to go. I'm feeling better now, and it's late. I have to figure out what to do next. Best that I'm at home." Ember raised her Alt to see its face and clicked the app for the CommuteCar. "Should be here in five."

Will felt defeated. *I was helping Ember, but now she just has more problems.* Her pale face and disappointment—now appearing to be directed at him—were stones in his stomach. Why would she distrust him? He looked at his Alt, trying to figure out how much his discomfort was affecting the reading. *Shazz!* A dip in his points. *No!* Will began some positive mind tricks. *All will be well...I need to find out how to help Ember find the ring.*

"Ember, let me wait with you."

"No thanks, Will. Appreciate the offer, but I've taken enough time away from your job. I've been selfish enough. Thanks for all your . . . help today."

At that, Ember strode past Will to the curb—her back to him was like a cement wall.

Will reluctantly headed back inside to his station. His shoulders sagged and he walked with his head down. He felt totally defeated. He'd have to pull his mood up by sheer resolve. He looked around the Plauditorium. Everyone was working. As if the bottom didn't just fall out of the world.

"Austel, thanks for watching my screen while I was with

Ember. Was everything quiet?"

"Hey, Will," Austel said in greeting. "Nothing to report—your sector's just fine. But is everything okay with Ember?"

"She feels better. Perhaps all the trauma she's suffered caused a temporary physical crisis. She seems back to normal. But . . . " Will hesitated, "she was having an issue with her emotional status."

"An emotional crisis? Again?" Will could practically see the wheels turning in Austel's head.

"Yeah, well . . . she's been through a lot. And, she lost something. While she was resting. You didn't happen to see anything lying around, did you?"

"Like what? Didn't see her bring anything in with her." Austel took his eyes briefly off the screen to search Will's face. He narrowed his dog-like eyes and adjusted his glasses. Then he glued his eyes back on the screen, leaning forward a little to zero in on the image.

"Never mind. My responsibility. Just—just keep an eye out, okay?" Will took a deep breath and felt better being able to involve Austel. The guy was observant. Perhaps he'd discover where the ring had gone. In the meantime, he wasn't sharing that Ember had a ring she shouldn't have.

"Sure thing. Let me know if I can help at all. Looking for ways to jump my points today."

"Yeah, okay. I'll let ya know."

Will returned to closely monitoring the screen in front of him. His watchfulness was demanding, although it was rare to see any problems at all. It was tranquil, just as it should be.

No sooner had he let that thought go, and his eyes became riveted on the screen. A tan-colored, boxy vehicle, unmarked, glided soundlessly through an intersection and then disappeared around a corner. At that point, it dropped off his screen, no longer in his sector. He had never seen a vehicle identical to that before. It was no CommuteCar, that's for sure. Appearing to be over ten feet tall, its height alone was bizarre. The thing was like a life-size moving trunk or chest on wheels. While Will had only had a few seconds to observe it, it was clear that the vehicle had heavy metal sides, reinforced by substantial steel girders. It was an intimidating conveyance, yet its wheels seem to glide on air.

It confused Will how quickly the transport entered and left his screen. Almost magic. It was so strange, he even questioned if he had seen it at all. *I'd better report this, and now.*

Will pulled up the GRID notification form from his screen's task bar. GRID stood for a specialized software form — Gathering Rare Incidents Data. He hesitated before filling out the report. How would he rate the peculiarity of the vehicle? It didn't seem to be causing a disruption, but in terms of its irregularity, he might have to place high importance on it. After only another moment of indecisiveness, he clicked the "10," signifying an alert of the highest order.

Will turned to Austel and swiveled his chair so their conversation could be confidential. Will didn't want to be overstepping anyone's authority or causing undue panic.

"Austel, I just cited an unidentified transport I saw on my screen. A weird, tan-colored vehicle with high sides."

"Hmmm. That is odd. Push your replay so I can see this thing." Austel leaned over to peer at Will's monitor.

Within seconds, Will replayed the footage of the bizarre carrier in a small window on his screen. "What do you make of it?"

"That's clearly an alien vehicle. It's excellent you reported it, but I have more experience with these types of situations. I'll take this on, Will. I'll make sure the GRID gets to the people at the top."

"Really? Just wondered how important it is," Will said.

"You'll learn, Will. Anything at *all* that's suspicious is paramount."

Will wished he could have had the total responsibility for himself, but that would be selfish and not conducive to his or

Austel's happiness. *What a day.* His mind was littered with questions. He had to talk to someone he could trust. Weeford Modestus, his good buddy—it had been a while since he'd talked to him. After work he'd grab some dinner and head over to Wee's house. No invitation was needed; they had grown up together and had always had each other's backs. Only half an hour to go and he'd be on his way.

"By the way, Will," Austel remarked, interrupting his thoughts. "I let City Hall know about Ember's brief illness here. As you know, sickness is a symptom of decay in emotional control. She may need intervention."

WEEFORD OPENED the door of his unit, tucked away in the Pink Peaks complex, greeting Will with the Tranquility salute and then a bro handshake. "Will, buddy! Great to see ya! Beginning to think you were too good for me now that you're up the ranks!"

Will chuckled and playfully slapped him on the back. "You know it, bud!" He smiled, feeling the warmth of the camaraderie and long history with his schoolmate. He still felt honored to know him. Weeford's skin was the color of a ripe fig, his hair black as Will's Plauditorium uniform. His seven-foot height dwarfed anyone in the city. That's why his nickname, "Wee," was such a joke.

Samkhat individuals like Wee were especially valued, admired for their bravery in overcoming adversity and misfortune. Most of the Samkhat came from places where their race and backgrounds caused them more hardships than anyone else, especially during the final world war, when many were victims of genocide. Now here, he was safe and secure, a chemical engineer for the city.

"Just about ready to sit down to dinner. I'm happy to share." Wee pointed to a plate of food on the table. "Got some fresh rations delivered today, but I know you'll be slummin' it a little, you being a Level Twelve and all." Wee grinned. "Level Four food will leave you wishing you grabbed dinner on the way here."

He headed to the kitchen where dishes clattered and a door slammed. He returned with another plate and silverware. Wee scooped some of the dinner from his own plate onto the new one, pushing it across a tiny white and pink laminate table. "Snag a chair."

Will relaxed into the leather chair, which was more comfortable than attractive. Its rosy color was designed to inspire warm and comforting feelings, but those emotions were far from his mind. "It's been a challenging day, Wee," he admitted. "I'm exhausted."

"You're not letting it drain your points, are you? That's not the Will I know. What's goin' on?" Wee began eating with gusto, wasting little time with proper manners.

"There's this girl . . ."

Wee stopped eating, his fork in midair. "A *girl*. Really, Will? She better be piping fine for you to be risking your Alt points. And, what's her Status? You can't just be with anyone."

Will looked at Wee, not surprised at all about his reaction. Confessions were new territory. "Yeah. She's beautiful all right. And," he blushed, "she's only a Level Eight." He saw Wee throw his arms in the air in frustration.

"What're you gettin' into, Will? A Level *Eight*? How long has this been a 'thing'?"

"Not long. I just met her, and we hit it off. I know she's too low for me, but I can't think about that. She's perfect, Wee."

"Yeah. Perfect for somebody else. How you gonna keep this big Status gap under wraps? Someone's gonna intervene, you know that. And, she's okay with you being a Level Twelve? C'mon. She's gonna be in trouble, too."

"I need to be careful—you're right. But I might not even

have to worry. Here's the thing. I thought we had an extraordinary connection, one worth going out on a limb for, but something happened today. Now there's a strain between us."

"Okay, so spill it. What'd she do—no—what'd *you* do for this to become a fiasco? And who is she anyway?" Wee delivered an oversized bite to stuff his cheeks full.

Will spent the next fifteen minutes explaining how he met Ember and how she made him feel glowing hot from the inside. He explained how he'd be willing to sacrifice everything for her, how he was investigating her mother's passing, the break-in, and the unusual fainting spell he had witnessed today, finally leading to the suspicious looks Ember had given him before saying goodbye at the Plauditorium.

"So, this ring, Will. Even knowing about it, won't you be at risk with City Hall and with your job at the Plauditorium?" Wee's dark eyes regarded him soulfully.

With anyone else, Will would never have confided the loss of the ring, but he would stake his life on Wee's loyalty to the secret.

"Yeah, but it's worth it. She needs help, and I want to be the one who figures it all out." Will picked through his food, the noodles, crisp beef, and spinach leaves a real disappointment.

"But she might think you took the ring?" Wee tapped his fork restlessly on his plastic plate several times, the noise like a nail gun to Will's heart.

"That's what I think, but I'm not dwelling on it. I can't. But I need to convince her. I had nothing to do with the ring's disappearance. How can I make her sure of me again?"

"You gotta find the ring, that's all. In the meantime, set your mind at ease. Two weeks ago, you didn't even know she existed. Just get back in that zone. Let your detective skills do the rest. I'll help you do whatever you need—as long as it won't affect my Status. A man's gotta live, right?"

21

Xander's Gang

"**G**onna find my castle where I am KING!" Xander yelled out loud to the sky at large, trying his best to stomp heavy footprints into the dust.

As he strolled down the god-forsaken "street," he marveled at the crude scenery. Burned out trees resembled giant, goblin specters, their shadows deepening the gloom that pervaded empty pathways. Dried leaves scuttled by, for some reason in a hurry to get where they were going. Another wounded building defied gravity, but it rose up proudly on the left, nevertheless. Multi-storied, its oxidized front door was no longer attached to the structure, but resting on its hinges, sideways, a ballerina on point. *Might as well check this out for a residence. At least it's central.* He ducked his head inside the open door but couldn't resist the urge to topple the door on edge, sending it crashing over with a slight touch of his toe.

Entering the edifice, Xander was struck by the deep cold of concrete and the earthy smell of moss and neglect. It appeared to be some type of old-fashioned office building, its single cubicle compartments in various stages of degradation. *There are possibilities here…a booth here, a nook there…could be a pretty good apartment...* He looked around with approval, already imagining what could be not only his home, but also a place where he could gather others. He rubbed his hands together, both in gleeful anticipation and in defiance of the crisp chill radiating from the walls.

A clink, like steel on mortar, broke the silence. The clatter dissected his thoughts and he turned, trying to make out the source of the noise. Xander hadn't seen anyone inhabiting the building, but it was vast. It was possible that it already had occupants.

"Hel-loooooo! Anybody here?" Xander called. He turned about, listening.

A shuffle. A muted voice. "Yeah. Up top."

Xander looked up to find a man, probably in his forties, with matted auburn hair, an uneven beard, and hazel eyes sitting on a cross beam about fifty feet from where he stood. He held a metal rod in front of his torso, as if to protect himself.

The top stories were visible through massive holes above Xander's head. He wondered if there was any place where the ceiling was actually intact.

"Hey . . . there. You surprised me. You live here?"

"Yep. Been here ten years. Got a spot up high where I can see out. Quite a view, too."

"Great. I'm lookin' to settle. Anyone else in the building?" Xander sauntered over to where he could gaze up through the rafters.

"There's just Bixby on the third floor in the corner, and then me. That's it. I'm Jasper."

"Xander."

"Well, help yourself—you find an open space, it's yours."

"I'm decidin' I like it down here just fine. I think I'll take it!" Xander laughed.

"Well, welcome then. Just don't do too much exploring on your own. It's a dangerous place out here."

"Nothing that I can't handle, Jasper." Xander wondered why the guy didn't want to come down. It was hard looking up and yelling back and forth.

"Yeah? Well, there are people around that aren't too friendly. It isn't Tranquility, ya know? And most buildings are unstable. You got lucky with this one."

"Doesn't sound too bad. Sounds like it's just the challenge I need."

"Then there's the Greelox."

"Greelox? What's that?" Xander asked.

"They're cats. Giant cats—about ten times the size of a panther. Cats you don't want to run into. Body and markings of a tiger, but sinewy. Spikes across their backs. Big teeth. Claws. Genetic experiments gone wrong. Aggressive and cunning. Aren't tons of 'em, but we've all seen one on the prowl at one time or another."

"Thanks for the warning, pal. Another reason why only the brave come here, right?" In truth, Xander's boldness began to evaporate. "And I smell smoke. Where's that coming from?"

"Out east. You don't want to go out there either. If you do, you're gonna be shot. Transport vans from Tranquility do their business there."

"Business? What kind of business would any Tranks have out here?"

"You don't know? Story is they burn bodies out there."

Two WEEKS after settling into his new home, Xander felt more satisfied than he'd expected. He had built basic but sturdy furniture. His bed frame, constructed from the front door, supported a hole-pocked mattress he found under a beam about a mile out from Base. He learned how to make tools, hunt for food, and cook just about anything over an outdoor fire. Animal skins he sewed together himself with sinew kept him warm at night, along with the fire he built in his brick-lined fire pit.

Soon after putting his first piece of furniture in his new "apartment," he met Bixby, the other inhabitant of his building, a reclusive fifteen-year-old who reminded Xander of a scarecrow, his golden hair stiff as straw, his body angular. With an icy-blue stare and adolescent whiskers, he was hardly Mr. Personality.

Bixby had some tumbled-down stairs that led up to his living quarters. It wasn't the day they met, but Xander's first trip up to Bixby's place made him wonder how long it would be until the stairs would completely crumble. Each climb up or down shed tiny pieces of concrete off the edges of various steps. An iron railing meant to support the structure stood a good two feet from the stairway and bent at a weird angle halfway up. Xander was thankful after the first time he'd made it up and down without anything falling apart. After that, he told Bixby to come down to his place. He had too much at stake to risk dying on a dilapidated staircase.

"The kid"—that's what came to mind when Xander thought about Bixby, even though the guy was only two years younger than he. Quiet and nervous, he made a point of keeping to himself.

Each day going forward, Xander initiated conversation with Bixby every time the guy came through the building, catching him before he trekked up to his area. Xander was curious; he wanted to find out what made this odd guy tick. One day, he blurted out, "How'd you end up here, Bixby?"

To his surprise, Bixby turned and walked over to Xander, who was lying on his lumpy mattress. "Had a mental illness. Got sent out for damaging property," he said quietly.

Xander gave a low whistle. "You do okay out here?"

"Yep. Nobody cares what I do here. And if I wanna bash somethin' up, it's no big deal."

Xander smiled. "You just bash away. I'll plan to call on you for protection, then." Interesting to discover what kind of people made up the REM population. A mentally ill basher. He could maybe use somebody like that.

The next day with not much to do, and no other people to talk to, Xander headed back to Base 1 and visited Graham. The guy who handed Xander the clipboard when he first discovered the camp could be a good connection. Graham certainly would know everyone in Camp.

"Graham Cracker!" Xander called out as he entered the primitive "lobby." "'Member me?" In the gloom, Graham was still playing a solitary Mandala, just like he was the first time Xander met him.

Graham sat on a stool, its seat shredded, two legs supported by a board slanted up underneath. He looked up from his game. "Yeah. 'Course. How's it goin'?"

"I'm gettin' settled. But wondered if you'd take me on tour? Show me the ropes around here?"

Graham pushed a group of pebbles off the board and stood up. "Hmmm. 'kay. Gotta cook dinner first."

Xander laughed. Graham's squeaky voice was hilarious. Graham turned away, walked over to an area in the corner, and picked up a rat by the tail. It was dead, its beady eyes glassy, its tiny feet curled up. "You hungry?"

Xander winced about having to eat rat, but he didn't hesitate. He hadn't had food for over a day. Food was scarce. Too scarce. "You sharing?"

"Not much here. But, yeah. I'll share. Seein' how you're new and all."

Xander helped Graham pile up some rocks and sticks that Graham had gathered sometime earlier. With some friction, the fire was lit, and the rat roasted on a short metal rod, rusted on both ends, but long enough to do the job. Graham held the rat over the fire, patiently turning it around as the fire licked it until the smell of cooked meat made Xander's mouth water.

Graham said, looking at him intently. "Do ya ever wish you weren't here?"

"Here? Like dead?" Xander threw a small rock into the fire.

"Naw. Outside."

Xander gave him a wry smile. "It's tough. Tougher than I thought. But, no. Tranquility . . . I couldn't deal. But . . . my parents. My whole life I've been a disappointment to them."

"Yeah? Mine too. Before I got sent out, Magnus sent word to 'em. Told 'em I was the definition of 'failure.' Magistrate's last words to me when I went tunnel-bound broke me. He said my mom cried so much they had to put her at Solace. Got no idea how she's doin' now."

"That's rough, Graham. I don't know about my folks. Far as I know, they weren't told ahead of time. Sciolists came and got me. But they were prob'ly glad."

"Doubt it. Parents love their kid."

"Yep," he said, his throat tight. "Guess they did. Tried to raise me right. But I didn't listen. I even stole fabric from my mom that she needed for her clients."

Graham raised his eyebrows. "Dang. What the heck for?"

"Wanted to make clothes. Got to make an impression." Xander stood up and straightened his REM clothes, grabbing the fabric to gather it in front of him. He paraded like a model back and forth by the fire. He had the strut down perfectly.

Graham laughed. "So what'd your mom do?"

Xander plopped back down. "Just talked to me. Tried to make me sorry. I wasn't. I was always rogue. In school, I got in trouble constantly, not just for my lame Alt points. When I was fourteen, the school told my folks to send me to Panglossian Academy."

"I heard about that place. Never went." He wiped his forehead in a "whew" motion.

"Be glad. It sucked so bad. Talk about a brain wash. Each day up at 6. Hot yoga. Exercise half the day. Classes on how to raise Alt points. Memorizing the Accords. I hated every minute of it. So, I left." He grinned.

"You walked out?"

"Broke out. We were keyed in. Went back home, but my parents struggled with their Alts when I was around. So, I made myself scarce—wasn't home much. Then the real counseling started. Purging. Winslow. The rest is history."

"Your parents mighta loved you if they paid for that place. It's in the upper price bracket."

"Strange way to show love. I never forgave them for it. Told 'em one time that they'd made me worse, sending me there."

As they tore off pieces of rodent, the two guys compared their pasts. By the time they'd finished the meal, what little there was, they'd shared more than food. They joked about girls being fun, but how they were the biggest mystery to understand. Graham gave Xander advice about ways to survive The Outside, including finding whatever he could to eat. They made wisecracks, laughed, and argued over who'd get the last piece of rat. Eating what little was there, even as they ate slowly, took no time at all, but the time slipped away into an hour, and then two. Xander had made a friend. Finally, someone understood him.

Xander pushed himself up from his squat by the fire. "So, Cracker, how 'bout that tour?"

"Not much to see, but I'm game." Graham stood from his sitting position in the dirt, dusting off the dirt on his already filthy clothes.

"Great." He made a grand sweeping gesture toward the door. "Ready when you are."

That day, Xander met about thirty-five people in the camp. People here were not too trusting, but he could relate to that. Most REMs were men, like himself, but four fairly young women would make his nights a little warmer, he hoped. Within moments, Xander had disarmed and charmed them with compliments and promises.

~

As THE DAYS WENT ON, he worked hard to build rapport with the REMs. He'd listen to their complaints. He'd offer to help fix something up or hunt. He visited the "apartments" of each REM and hung out. REMs found his sense of humor and sarcasm attractive; he was a lot like them.

The key was to win over one at a time, then encourage groups. His sense of humor and problem-solving began to make him popular. Then, he gathered them together, a few at a time, and he would perform skits for them. He acted out all the parts of stories he remembered from school or books.

He wanted to get his new friends thinking about being a group that depended on each other, not just random individuals roaming around, doing as little as possible. When he'd gathered most of the camp together, he told a story. *This will get these REMs thinking.* He stood up in front of his building on a concrete pad, cracked in the middle. He towered above them as they sat around, waiting to be entertained.

"This story's about the body," Xander announced before starting.

"Whose body?" a middle-aged REM yelled out. The group laughed.

"Not mine, I hope," a girl, Iris, said, a serious look on her face.

"Nobody's body. I mean, it's everybody's. Just listen!" Xander said. "One day parts of the body complained. 'We're doing all the work while the belly gets all of the food.'" Xander made his voice whiny and pointed to his stomach. The group laughed. They were warming up.

"My belly needs food," Graham said, laughing loudly. The others started chanting, "My belly needs food. My belly needs food."

Xander held up his hands and waited for them to calm down. He grinned and went on. "The body believed the belly was lazy."

Exaggerated oh's and ooo's rippled across the group.

"They decided to hold a meeting to discuss how unfair this was."

"Yeah! A meeting!" Gabriel, the white-haired REM said, raising his fist in the air.

"After a very long meeting, the members of the body voted to go on strike until the belly agreed to take its proper share of the work."

The group murmured to each other. Xander listened to them, trying to keep a straight face. They all thought the strike was a good idea.

"The body parts didn't do anything for several days. The legs stopped walking, the hands stopped moving, and the teeth stopped chewing."

"Good strike, yeah?" Jasper said.

"With the starving of the belly, the legs became more and more tired, the hands could hardly move anymore, and the mouth became parched and dry. Eventually the entire body collapsed and died."

There was dead silence in the group. Jasper broke the spell. "So, the belly was the most important?"

"No, Jaz. The whole body had to work together. Just like us. We're a team. Every one of you is necessary."

"You kidding? We don't feel like no team," a red-haired freckle-faced twenty-something called out.

Xander looked at the crowd, making eye contact as his gaze fanned across the group. "That's what I'm here for. If you hang with me, your life will change. I have big plans, and I don't want to leave any of you behind. This place—" he panned the air with an outstretched hand, "is no place to live. But if we team up, we can do great things. Not just survive better." He paused. "Change the flippin' world."

The audience murmured among themselves. He heard remarks about never wanting to belong to a community again after being in Tranquility. But he also heard a number of REMs talking to each other, who seemed excited about what he'd said. They were giving each other fist-bumps in solidarity. The story and the message, along with his lively performance and persuasion, would easily create a minor-league fan club.

But the performances were only the first phase of his recruitment efforts.

Most of the REMs were bored with their daily lives, so soon after the meeting Xander thought up group activities to energize the camp and train the REMs to fit the plans he dreamed about. Xander's desire for lively conversation and games was a magnetic draw.

"Hey, Jasper," Xander called up through the Swiss cheese ceiling. "Want to play a game?"

"What kinda game?"

"A game I made up. But you could probably beat me . . ."

"Hmmm. Before I come down there, I gotta know more of this game."

Reluctant as always, Xander thought. "It's called 'Rock Masters.' Let's see if you're a Master."

Xander heard a shuffling and rustling from above and then Jasper appeared, jumping down from a rafter with ease.

"C'mon. We can use the quad outside for our game court." Xander gestured with this head toward the front "door." A mortared two-foot wall resembling a square outside the building was his vision of the ideal courtyard.

Like a game-show host, Xander grabbed a stick and spoke into it. "Welcome to Rock Masters! You see these rocks and pebbles? Some are pea-sized, others are small boulders. Each has a point value. We're gonna challenge each other. Starting with the gravel and building up to the 20 pounders, each of us tries to get the rock into the target." Xander pointed to a rusty, open half-barrel. "Whoever has the most points gets to invite someone else into the game for the next day's challenge." Xander put down the stick, now trading his spokesperson persona to that of a competitor.

"Sounds pretty jake. I'll take ya on."

Jasper was no match for Xander. After four straight days of winning, and not selecting anyone other than Jasper to play, he finally chose a new player from a growing group of gawking onlookers. Each time he made certain he welcomed and acknowledged them for an attractive characteristic—their talent, or their friends, or even their jokes. Xander bestowed them with personalized nicknames to the amusement of the crowd.

The number of competitors grew and so did the audience. At first, players played for sport only. But as soon as he had a group of six, Xander opened it up to gambling wagers. He was the real Rock Master, of course. He won items and tokens from others, but since these were in short supply, Xander began asking for services. As additional players came into the game, the more they fell under the spell of the gambler's lure, a daily give and take, objects won and lost. Before long, Rock Masters was an obsession among the REMs. They were soon eating out of Xander's hand, depending on him to set up tournaments.

Unification would be essential, he knew. They had to feel a part of something bigger and special where they were all bonded, a feat that would be new to this motley group.

AFTER A COUPLE OF WEEKS, Xander had solidified his team. He knew who he could trust. There were about a dozen

REMs who always followed him around like he was the Pied Piper. But he had his favorites, his core companions. He hung out, hunted, and played most of his Rock Masters games with them. During those days, Xander had been mulling an idea in his head until it became an obsession. He had to see it through.

"Jasper, Bixby, and Graham . . . we're gonna take a walk today." The three of them had just finished up collecting the rocks, strewn about, from the Rock Masters court.

"A walk? What for?" Graham said. "Is it gonna be far? I'm too tired."

"Where we goin'? There ain't nothin' to see around here, Xander," Bixby drawled.

"We're not sight-seeing, guys. We're gonna go on a quest. I saw a theater about three miles out the last time I went hunting. We're headed there."

"I dunno, Xander. Not sure I want to venture too far from camp. It's not safe. Creatures and all. And what good is an old theater, Xander? There ain't no movies playin' . . ." Jasper said.

"Well, you don't always know what you need until you see why you need it," Xander answered. "You all gonna be a bunch of wimps?" The three guys looked at each other, fear flooding their faces. "I'm headin' out. You coming?" Xander had a hard time not cracking a smile. He knew they'd be unable to resist.

Graham spoke up after a long silence. "Ready if you are." Fist bumps erupted all around.

"Bring your bags of tools and weapons."

The band of REMs had become Xander's good friends. He couldn't remember a time in Tranquility when he had people around him whom he enjoyed so much. Each guy was a little offbeat. They were colorful individuals; he admired their out-of-the-box thinking. Graham, especially, was his favorite. No one in Tranquility had siblings. He had never had a brother. Graham was the closest thing to that. Pretty much, the two were inseparable.

Three hours out into the wilderness, Xander shouted. "There! The theater!" Following his lead, the men ran forward to an abandoned, broken-down building, their weariness and concerns forgotten in the final trek to discover what Xander's mission was.

Knowing how hazardous a dilapidated building could be, the tribe entered warily. As they walked past a wall, halfway torn off the top, a shift in the cracked cement below their feet set them on edge. Xander saw Graham shiver and then shake it off.

"Be careful. Watch for anything that looks fragile," Xander said.

It was the same as most buildings Outside; the theater had no door and only some pieces of what could have been a roof, making the ceiling a mosaic of sky and rough plaster. The elements had ruined the theater seats, leaving the cushions torn or nonexistent, their audiences long-gone ghosts.

An enormous screen, its surface shredded and peeling, stared back at them blankly. Xander's eyes, however, were riveted on the curtains on both sides of the empty screen, dozens of yards of red velvet textile. He approached the plush velour with something like awe. He touched it, examining the material with complete reverence. "Looks like this bottom part has some mold . . ."

"Is that what we came for, Xan? And it's ruined?" Graham ran his fingers through his hair in frustration.

Xander cuffed Graham affectionately on the cheek. "I've got this, Graham Cracker. The middle swath up to the top's in great shape. The portico hanging over it must've protected it." He took a deep breath, his eyes sparkling. "My fellow REMs get out your knives. We're takin' these curtains back to camp."

"What? Why?" Jasper looked at Xander with his mouth agape.

"We're gonna make clothes with it, Jasper. All red, elegant! Classy. Desirable. We've got a fraternal order of REMs to represent. We're stronger together, and we're gonna celebrate it. Get your knives. Start cutting that drapery down!"

Journal Entry #5587

Bringing new members into the Elite is a natural process. It's a pleasure bringing in new Elite. It's quite a feat to be the happiest citizens in the city. Once Elite, the decisions they make must continue to make them happy. So, I'm always impressed with their capacity to love and care for others.

Then they are my counsel—those I trust to help me make decisions. But having too many Elite makes me nervous. Right now, there are only fifty Elite. And this is perfect. Power should remain in the hands of a carefully controlled group. I want only those who see things the way I do.

The biggest threat to me are the Augur Prize winners. They are the perfect citizens. Each of them chosen because of their points and their dedication to their Status's chosen value, they put these values above all. If a value, for instance, is 'Integrity,' they will always act in that manner, when sometimes that value must be sacrificed for the Greater Good. I can't have people that strong as advisors. Who knows what ideas they might have? They could betray me, wanting to become Magistrate themselves. Some, I'm sure, have planned and schemed to enter the Elite for the sole purpose of bringing me down. I've had to carefully control these threats. To keep our city pure, this is a job that needs to be done.

Journal Entry #5587

I've been an excellent Magistrate, unlike any other. Luckily for the citizens, I hold my position until I die. I care deeply about the people here, and they know I have their best interests at heart. I must protect myself at all costs.
—Serpio Magnus, Magistrate

22

Ember's Inquisition

Ember was frantic at the loss of the ring. She knew she had taken it with her. Now it was gone.

Hating the thought, but sure she was right, she couldn't trust Will anymore. His aura appeared dark to her, and his emotions were running all over the place. Finding the ring and discovering the truth about her mother were her top priorities. It would have to be all up to her.

She measured her emotions on her Alt, only to see another drop in points. She'd better find something to get her back in touch with her happiness quotient.

"Alt, turn on the music playlist," she said. A second later her favorite artist crooned a song entitled, "New Birth." The music helped put her mind into a meditative state. She sank down into the plush purple recliner, patting its familiar armrests. Might as well enjoy it. In two short days, she would be leaving the apartment.

She suddenly sensed a presence nearby. A wave of distrust and haughtiness ebbed into her spirit. "Visitor at the door, Ember," the house camera chimed, its soothing voice interrupting the singer.

Ember imagined it was maybe Will. Perhaps he had found

the ring after all! Or maybe he came to apologize for taking her ring. If it was Will, he wasn't feeling warm toward her, so it could be him. The monitor confirmed her feelings. It wasn't Will, but a Sciolist! Fear pierced her as if she had been cut. *Why would a Sciolist be here?* Ember's lip trembled. Her heart beat a rapid tempo. *Happiness is a choice that requires effort.*

Ember opened the door and encountered a straight-faced man in red. His cloak flowed around him.

"Ember Vinata. I'm to take you to City Hall to speak directly with the Magistrate. Punishment or Counseling, if necessary, will be determined after questioning. We leave immediately."

≈

No one to call—no one to call. The words went around and round in her head as she sat in the waiting room at City Hall. If only she had her mom. She would know what to do. The loss hit her again, hard, an ache in her chest.

She wasn't waiting long, however; a different Sciolist, somber and red-robed like the other, escorted her into the inner chamber soon after, where the Magistrate, behind a giant desk, arose from an opening in the floor. If she wasn't already intimidated, this did it. Her empathic radar sensed a weird combination of curiosity and impatience rising from the Magistrate's mental state.

The Magistrate raised his arm, palm out, index finger up. Even here, the gesture of acceptance reigned. Ember returned the salute.

"Step forward and be held responsible. You, Ember Vinata, are being arrested on one major count of disobedience. You have been in possession of a ring belonging to deceased citizen, Talesa Vinata. This ring, an Augur Prize of great value, has been returned by a Plauditor."

Ember gasped.

The Magistrate held up her mother's ring. Like a miniature star, it sparkled under the lights. "What have you to say?" The Magistrate's face wore a painted-on smile. Ember could read his emotions and see his aura. The blue cloud shimmered. He was exasperated, impatient.

Ember looked down at her shoes, knowing that whatever she said was never going to matter. No excuse would get her off the hook. She had deliberately kept the ring and broken the law. One thing was for sure, she was right not to trust Will! He had betrayed her. Taking the ring and then lying about it! Her feelings registered on her Alt, and the Magistrate would easily know she was not in control, much less happy.

Nonetheless, she thought, it was time to stand on her own two feet and take charge. She had to get beyond her self-doubts and shyness, grab onto what courage she had, and represent herself as an empowered female.

"You do not deny the charge, then?" The Magistrate's voice was a cat's purr; he, of course, would never cause a citizen to become alarmed, even one who was under the microscope.

"I was on my way to City Hall to turn in the ring . . . which I found in an odd place . . . when it disappeared. I don't know how it became lost," Ember fibbed.

"But you did have it for an extensive time. You didn't turn it in with the rest of Telesa Vinata's things. Do you know something about this ring you're not telling me?"

"Only that I wanted to keep it because it was my mother's. She earned it, and I'm sure she would want me to have it."

"What Ms. Vinata wanted is irrelevant. It is against the law to keep such an item. Did you wear this ring?"

"No. It didn't fit my finger. I carried it, to keep it safe."

"Safe from whom?"

Ember hesitated. Then an idea instantly formed in her mind, and it was the most logical answer of all. "Well, I thought someone was after it. The living space I shared with my mom was ransacked. I didn't think much about it at the time, but once I found the ring, I decided it needed protection from whoever might be looking for it."

"But you had no proof of this, other than your conjecture."

Ember watched the aura around the Magistrate wane and flare at intervals. "No, but the Plauditors who helped me that day would probably agree. Austel Fidelis and Will Verus have records of the break in. They'll tell you how strange it was." Ember began to feel more poised. Her story was all making sense. She checked her Alt to find that it was showing point growth for confidence.

The Magistrate blinked his hooded eyes several times. His eyelids opened and closed so slowly they seemed weighted. "That... sounds like a plausible reason. I'll see if Will and Austel can back that up, and I'll pull the records. Seems rather a strong coincidence . . . Austel Fidelis was the one who brought us the ring."

Ember felt faint. "What? *Austel* brought you the ring?"

"Why, yes. He said you were in possession of it when you came to the Plauditorium. He wanted to make sure it got to City Hall where it belongs. But no matter. I still have questions about your possession of the ring. Did you have any . . . incidents . . . with the ring? Anything strange that you observed about it?

"I don't think so . . ."

"These rings are special. They become attached to their owners emotionally, like a fingerprint. Someone other than the recipient who's wearing the ring will then have their own Alt assessments register incorrectly on the Continuum. We certainly don't want that for our citizens, especially you, Ember, my dear. Of course, that's the main reason we collect the rings. We want you to have a most joyous life, one that you yourself earn with true points." The Magistrate's voice was sonorous; its vocal cadences could put a baby to sleep.

The Magistrate's comforting words inexplicably relaxed her. Yet she sensed she still needed to be on her guard. Something seemed out of place—something she couldn't put her finger on. But . . .Will. She should have trusted Will. He had been in her corner after all.

Right now, though, it was best to take the high road. What would appease the Magistrate? She had to acknowledge his claims, at least. "I apologize. I see now that I've made a mistake. I should have realized that there was a reason City Hall would want the ring returned."

"I am so *happy* to hear that you understand, Ember. Your peace of mind is critical here."

"Of course."

"Just one more thing, Ember. There will be no punishment or counseling at this time, although we are being lenient with you. The Elders wanted Removal, to send you to The Outside for this rebellion, or at the very least, downgrade your Status to a Level One. However, I understand that you also suffered an unusual physical illness at the Plauditorium. Your health is also of paramount concern to us. You'll be reporting to the Solace Institute in two days for assessment and observation. A Sciolist will arrive to escort you at 9 a.m. Be ready."

A Sciolist? Health assessment? Her mouth went dry. Her stomach dropped. *Would a health assessment uncover her empathic abilities? And, what would happen if it did?*

23

Will's Vindication

Talking to Wee had given Will a boost of
inspiration. He could hardly wait to get back into the
Plauditorium the following morning, knowing that so
much depended on his being the best sleuth he could be.
Under the radar, he would get some solid information about
the ring and Talesa. He would win Ember back.

The Plauditorium was quiet and lightly staffed when he
arrived. Only three people had come in before him, and they
welcomed him with the Tranquility acknowledgement. Austel
was not yet present. All good. He could avoid clocking in until
he gave himself access to files. Disloyalty to City Hall was a
serious crime, and he struggled with how terribly it violated
his moral code. His greatest desire in life was to not only
advance in Status, but to be entirely clean, unblighted.
Already this deception on Ember's behalf ran contrary to his
deepest core values. He was good, pure, and honest. It was his
very nature.

He was risking severe punishment—even banishment to
The Outside—should he get caught. He was already
preparing himself for these dark thoughts to show up in his
Alt readings. But he was also devoted to Ember and had a

million questions whirring in his mind about everything that had happened to her.

His monitor and computer turned on, he began with a general search of the ring ceremony, this time trying to find the recent recipients of the award. There must be a way to find a list other than just the first class. Where to find more recent information? *Hmmm…perhaps…*the obvious answer hit him like a bullet. *There's a History of Tranquility page.* All the victories and successes in the city were glorified for all to see here. His own story was there. He zeroed in on the past events, looking specifically for any Celebration of Life or the Day of the Ring Ceremony from last year when Talesa Vinata received her accolades. He saw no Celebration of Life listings. But there . . . the Day of the Ring . . . he could see a picture of all eighteen beneficiaries, their names listed in bold under each photo. This was not some ancient list from the past; this was recent. Those in the photo would still have their rings, and their home addresses would be in the system.

It would be time consuming to interview them all, so he had to be smart about whom he chose. He would begin with the Level One awardee, Carol Eros. Then choose Level Nine, Lennard Robus. And finally Level Eighteen, Omar Sensus. He could check in on them on the pretext of making sure their quality of life was exceptional. A personal visit from a distinguished Level Twelve officer like himself would applaud their accomplishment. After all, wasn't that part of the Plauditor's duties? To guide and inspire? Who knew what he could find out from just speaking to people? And no one would know what he was up to. He could manage the deception physically and emotionally knowing it was also an acceptable and encouraged Plauditor's business. He was elated. His Alt glowed with happy points.

Not a second past his self-celebration, his Alt chimed. "Call from Ember Vinata." The Alt's voice feature resonated with a sexy, electronically generated voice.

"Hey, Ember," Will said. He tried to keep the nervousness out of his voice and out of his body. Would she be calling to hassle him about the ring?

"Will, I'm calling to . . . apologize." Ember's voice sounded strained, a mirror of his own mood. "I shouldn't have been so defensive yesterday. I panicked and lashed out. I know you didn't take the ring."

"You know I didn't take the ring? How?" Will asked, his apprehensions slipping away. *What a relief. Happiness again.*

"The ring—the ring was turned in to City Hall by *Austel.* He must have found it and knew I was keeping it illegally." Ember's eyes filled up, watery at the memory. She swallowed hard, trying to push out the dark feelings.

Will began to fume, but took deep breaths, allowing his own mantra to calm him down. Several seconds went by.

"Will? Do you forgive me?" Ember's voice was small. A whisper.

"Of course, Ember. I was never upset with you—just worried about you. And I'm gonna get to the bottom of all this, just like I promised. Today I'm going out on visits to some ring recipients from your mother's class from Day of the Ring. Want to come?"

"Yeah!" It was like she couldn't catch the word before it exploded from her lips. Will smiled, his spirits beginning to soar. His lips twitched in amusement as she continued to speak, trying to sound less exited. "Umm . . . thanks. I'd . . . I'd love to see you again."

Will jumped in the air, pulling down a fist pump. *Was this the best day ever?*

But Ember's next words settled him down. "I need to tell you about what happened with the Magistrate." Her voice quivered. "The Sciolist came and collected me. Then I was questioned. By the Magistrate! It was horrid. Traumatic."

Oh Shazz. What was going on? "I'll grab a CommuteCar

after work here today, and I'll see you at your place—probably around 5:00. Sound good?"

"I'll be ready. See you then." Ember clicked off, and Will sat back in his chair. All was right between Ember and himself. But there was more to worry about, she said. *No! No worry.* Now was just the time to make everything alright with the world, the way it should be.

Will looked up to see Austel slide into his seat, his arm raised in a one-fingered flag. "You beat me to work today, Will. I think that's a first," Austel quipped, logging in with his Alt.

"No, just got in a shade before you. Logging in now," Will lied. *Lying's not ethical, and definitely negative.* He brushed the guilt-laden thought away but felt the vibration hit his Alt. With reluctance, he returned Austel's greeting, but now had to navigate the distrust polluting his mind. No matter what Austel had done, he couldn't allow the man to get the best of him. He purged his consciousness with a determination he pulled from that iron-clad spirit that set him apart from most people of the city. Austel would never know, nor would his own Alt reflect the invading distrust. A vapor, and then it was gone. *I wasn't called 'Will' for nothing,* he thought.

"Will, how's your friend, Ember? Any fainting spells today?" Austel pulled up his sector on the monitor and made sure his Alt was in synch with the system. His face looked serious, but his Alt points consistently seemed to register a positive return.

"Ember's fine now." He cleared his throat. "I understand you turned in Ember's ring to City Hall," Will said. "Where'd you find it?" Not taking his eyes from his screen, Will hoped his questions didn't sound like he was starting an argument.

"Between you and me, I found it when she fell asleep in the lounge. Wouldn't you know? I noticed she had her hand over her chest there." Austel put his own hand over his chest to demonstrate.

Will picked up an empty cup from his desk and put it underneath in the cubby for used dishes. It was immediately vacuum sucked from the area to travel down to the Plauditorium's recycling center. He glanced over at Austel, hoping the typical behavior looked nonchalant. "So? What's so odd about that?"

"I was worried that she might have had a heart attack. Or that we might have to call someone for emotional intervention. So, I was checking her out when you left the room."

"Checking her out?" His voice grew loud and gritty. He couldn't help it. Austel's claim sounded far too personal. Too intimate. Looking at her chest, too? What the—!

"Settle down, Will. I saw a bulgy outline in her front pocket. Didn't know it was a ring. Just wondered what it was. So, I pulled it out. Once I saw it was an honorary ring, I sent it through the Vac-U tube directly to City Hall."

Will bristled. Austel actually touched the pocket on her *chest*. He didn't care if Austel was concerned for Ember's health or not, he shouldn't have touched her. "You shouldn't have done that. That was a personal invasion." Will wished his eyes were lasers. His Alt vibrated. He was taking a hit.

"Will . . . Will. I wasn't hitting on her. But she is hot. Too hot for you."

Will began counting in his head. *Slow the breathing. Blow out. Relax.* One . . . two . . . three . . . four . . . five.

Will stood up from his chair, barely aware that he'd already clocked in and should be watching his screen like a hawk. "And you didn't say a word about finding the ring. Even when I asked you if you'd found anything?" Will looked Austel directly in the eyes, the emeralds burning like fire. "Why would you keep it a secret?"

"Decided you might want to keep your job here and your Status intact. I mean, if you knew she had the ring—and I'm not saying you did—you should be making sure it was turned in. You think this girl is pretty special. I didn't want that to cloud your judgment. Just lookin' out for you, Will. And, honestly? I wanted the credit. I never want to miss an opportunity to give my Status a shot in the arm."

Will shook his head in disbelief. Austel had gone behind his back. Been creepy with Ember. Yet, that was the job of a Plauditor, to make sure that everything was in order. It wasn't like they were good friends or anything. But poor Ember. She took the brunt of it.

The hours dragged by, Will not making any conversation with Austel unless it was absolutely necessary. That was one way to keep emotions in check—stay away from the negative influences.

At exactly 4:45, Will welcomed the night shift Plauditor to his station. He was always grateful he was assigned the day shift. He grabbed his jacket and rushed out the door to meet the CommuteCar at the curb. Fifteen minutes later, he knocked on the purple door and waved to the surveillance camera.

Seeing Ember open the door sent his heart racing. "Hi, Ember," he said, trying to sound casual. He leaned against the doorframe for effect.

"Hey. Come in." She ushered him into the Great Room, its orderliness in sharp contrast with the last time he was there. "Do we have time to sit down and talk before we go? I have so much to tell you." Her eyes were cloudy, her brows drawn together in an upside down 'V'. Will felt his heart swell.

He touched her shoulder gently and sat down in the nearest chair. "Definitely. I want to hear all about it."

Ember related each detail of her conversation with the Magistrate. Keeping the ring could have been considered treason. He was so relieved she had no punishment. *She was lucky she didn't get Removed.*

"Ember, you did all the right things. You showed great courage. The Magistrate can be intimidating. But he's capable and unusually fair, an admirable leader. And the health check shouldn't be a problem. In fact, it's a good thing. I want to make sure you're okay, too."

The fainting spell bothered him. Was she sick? Too emotionally unstable? She might be in trouble. Worry began to gnaw away. The incident with Austel was awful. Her questioning session with the Magistrate—that was scary. And he was putting it all on the line himself. For her. Gladly.

Ember gazed back at Will with wide eyes. He always felt she could see right through his soul. It was a weird feeling.

"I know. I don't know why I had that spell, so I should find out. I'm soooo happy he didn't put me in counseling. I'm glad I don't have to go back to see him. And telling you about it makes it all seem okay." She smiled, and it was like her face was lit from within.

Will stood up and walked over to her, and took her by the hand, leading her toward the door. "Let's talk more on the way. Right now we're off to the Level One's White Sands address to see Carol Eros. She's the first one on the list of honorees from your mother's class."

"What do you think someone from White Sands knows?"

"Maybe nothing. Maybe, though, she's going to help put this puzzle together." He sure hoped they'd find an easy answer. In the meantime, he'd stay on the tightrope.

24

Xander's Leadership

Xander wasted no time getting back to Camp with his followers. The next challenge was to get his fellow REMs outfitted to represent a united force. It was the spine of a plan he had been dreaming up; his crew had to feel they were winners.

He wanted them to have long capes—easy to make and symbolic of greatness. Getting cloaks sewn for his crew would require his teaching the REMs how to make something that looked not only decent, but impressive. He would have to train them in yet another skill. He silently thanked his seamstress mother for her insistence that he learn the basics of sewing when he was a young teen. What began as an interest in fashion helped motivate him to create pieces he wore in the city, and he got good at it.

But first they needed scissors. Knives would not do what they would need done. Convinced that the tool shop was the place to begin, Xander identified the best tool workers in the building. He found a couple of REMs willing to take on the project. Rebar, skeleton pieces of the crumbling buildings, lay everywhere in the camp. These could be melted, then flattened and shaped into blades on an anvil. With some heat in the center, a spring could be formed. Once cooled and fired to make them flexible, the new scissors would be functional.

Using thorns of the hawthorn bushes that dotted the landscape, they made needles for sewing. Dead and dried, the thorns had sharp points. The group whittled sticks as well, each REM trying to best the other on how sharp and fine their needles could be. Nettles were stripped for their fibers to use as thread.

Each member of Xander's crew now had the simple tools to make the crimson mantles that would set them apart.

Without any fanfare, Xander worked feverishly to create his own cape, knowing he was always the inspiration to his pack of outcasts. *Well, they won't look better than me, but they'll have some pride.*

Eager to copy Xander's example, the REMs could hardly wait to sew up their own. And, just like that, in less than a week, Xander's gang was looking transformed. He was ready for the next step. It was time to share his vision.

REMs gathered for their Rock Masters game in the courtyard as if it was any other day, joking and threatening each other's upcoming losses. This day, every REM sported a new cape that billowed in the dry, cold wind. Like superheroes of lore, the glorified clothing seemed to empower them, each one becoming a cock-fighting rooster strutting about the court.

Xander's stepped up onto the top of a broken wall, his face infused with a glow rivaling a full moon on a dark night. "Fellow REMs, you're looking royal and like warriors," Xander shouted.

A cheer rippled through the crowd.

"I want you to know, you don't just look good. You're destined for tremendous things. Thank the stars you have me to lead you."

The REMs shuffled about, some sharing some confused looks, others whistling or clapping.

"Tranquility shamed us—only because we want to be

ourselves! We want a full range of choices and emotions. Because we're all human, we had no quality of life without permission to speak our minds and share our hearts. So, we are here. In the land of broken things, wild things. This is wrong." Xander paused a full fifteen seconds, although all eyes were on him. He savored the way the throng hung on his every word.

Jasper interrupted the silence. "Xander, we all know this. We're with you, but we're stuck here."

Xander snickered. "Yeah, you might think so, buddy." He reached out and grabbed Jasper's shoulder. "But we're gonna start taking back our rights. We're gonna take the *city.*" A murmur swelled through the group.

Graham spoke up, turning to the crowd, a cold wind whipping his cape up around his chest. "Xander must have a plan, so let's all listen before we go thinking we're all gonna be dead."

"Graham, you told me that something goes on out here, out to the east, and it isn't your grandma's barbecue. Tranquility's involved. In fact, you warned me not to follow the smoke. We're gonna do exactly that. If they're coming out here, they've got to go back in, and I want to see exactly what they're doing."

Journal Entry #5597

The Elite. They're my family. No matter what, they're sworn to defend the city and myself. Over the years they've accepted that what I tell them is true. When people become overly virtuous, it is suspicious. I have to watch out for citizens in the upper Status levels. We must keep our affairs quiet and secret. To do otherwise would be betraying the confidence of our people and increase unhappiness in our very special world. I'm grateful that my Elite is loyal.

   —Serpio Magnus, Magistrate

25

Ember's Visit

Ember was relieved that Will couldn't read her emotions as she read his. As she rode along in the CommuteCar with him, she was more excited and content than she had been in days. She was with Will and knew he could be trusted. More than that, she finally admitted to herself that he was pretty beautiful. As he looked her way, his deep, vivid green eyes alone left her weak.

I wonder if this is how people feel when they're drunk. I'm giddy! The random thought made her smile. There would be no issues with her Alt points today. She was falling in love! She'd been easily able to discern his feelings for her all along; he was an open book to her, his aura flexing and pulsing. But because of the trauma she had experienced, she'd had no space in her head and heart to acknowledge her own attraction to him until now. She had worked hard to put everything, including her mother's death, into perspective, suppressing the grief and negativity until it was no more than little dust particles hiding in the recesses of her brain.

She still desperately mourned her mother, but she couldn't allow those thoughts to tear her down emotionally. She had to put her sorrow and confusion on hold, no matter how difficult it was.

About ten minutes later, the daffodil yellow CommuteCar pulled up in front of the White Sands' gate. The arch holding the gate, constructed of sand-coated concrete, had "White Sands" etched into its header. The pale half-moon crescent of the entrance looked ghostly, especially as the sun's waning rays tinged its outline with a dull glow. The camera winked at them from both sides of the entrance, and Will made sure the camera saw both of them clearly in spite of the evening shadows. Their visit shouldn't be questionable, but he was taking no chances. Trying to hide something was a real red flag at City Hall.

The community was always last on the list of city priorities for improvement, as the peeling paint on the gate gave testimony. More frustrating, it resisted opening, its hinges rusty, finally voicing its protest in a heavy whine. Will gave Ember a high five once the gate swung wide.

"Carol's house is just inside the gate," Will said. "It's Abode Number Four. You ready to see what Carol can tell us about her ring?"

"If anything. I'm not sure if the ring has anything special about it other than what I've been told."

The white door to Carol's place was wide and looked to be freshly painted, a concession probably due to the lady's honored status. A camera noted their arrival, sending a reverberating chime beyond. Without delay, the door opened to reveal a smiling young lady about Ember's age, who looked angelic in a white floor-length dress, her curly brown hair springing out in divergent directions.

"Hello, fellow Tranks!" Carol raised her arm in customary fashion, flexing her right index finger in what looked like a tiny wave. "How are you doing on this fine day?" she asked. "And you're a Plauditor! I'm so flattered by your visit."

"We're doing great," Will responded, also raising his arm in greeting. "I'm Will Verus, and this is Ember Vinata, a friend. We're out visiting the Augur Prize Honorees of last term's Day of the Ring. If you don't mind, we want to ask you a few questions about how your life has been since you were honored by City Hall."

"Of course, of course. Come on in."

Will and Ember stepped inside an alabaster room. All the furniture, art, and walls were white, and Ember realized in a way Will had gone back home. His parent's place just down the street had to be virtually identical.

"Sit down, please," Carol commanded. With that, she gestured broadly, her right hand decorated with the gleaming honorary ring. Ember was able to see how much Carol's ring looked identical to her mother's. Only the stone was different. This one was a pearl with extraordinary luster set off by tiny diamonds.

"Thanks so much. We won't take too much of your time." Will sat down on the milky sofa, patting the seat next to him for Ember.

"No problem at all. Whatever I can do for our fine city, Mr. Verus." Carol sat directly across from her guests, carefully smoothing her dress to prevent wrinkles.

"Please, call me Will. Congratulations on your recent prestige as the White Sands honoree. I'll bet you're looking forward to moving up soon. It can't be long."

"Yes, I was so thrilled. I've only taken my ring off once, and that was to clean it." She glanced down at her hand and, with a little smile, turned the ring to sit perfectly on her finger.

"My mother, Talesa, was also in your group. She was amazing, but she's since . . . passed away. Have you had any problems since you were inducted?" Ember felt her voice catch on her mother's name. *So much for burying the sadness,* she thought.

"First of all, I'm truly sorry about your mother. I don't

understand why she died. I'm sure it's been a struggle with your Alt." Carol's face wrinkled in sympathy. "But problems for me? Why, no. I've had nothing but happiness." The honoree's face suddenly became radiant. "Everyone in White Sands treats me like a queen, and I seem to be respected everywhere I go in the City. I'm given VIP treatment. I feel as if I'm already a higher Status, when I'm still only a Level One. I know I'll be moving up the Continuum into Level Two in a short time. Happiness is a choice, right?"

Ember couldn't deny Carol's contentment. The smile, the confidence, the exuberance—Carol was, without doubt, the model of a successful "Trank." Her aura glowed pink. But even though Carol was probably Ember's age, Carol was still only a Level One. An accomplished Level One, recognized and given the Augur Prize for Purity. But it had taken her a long time to achieve that level of success. Not even a Level Two yet. Ember suddenly became self-conscious of her own Status. Poor Carol—her assigned clothes all white. All at once, Ember felt uncomfortable in her royal blue cashmere sweater and knit pants.

"So glad to hear. I'm so thrilled that you are such an outstanding example in our fair city. It's been wonderful meeting you." Will flashed her a charming smile, sure to melt the young girl's heart. "Just one more question. Does your ring have a number engraved inside?"

Carol shook her head. "Not that I've seen, unless it's microscopic. The one time I took it off, I cleaned it, and I didn't see anything unusual." She began fidgeting with the ring once more, twirling it around her finger. "You need to check it? I haven't done anything wrong, have I?"

"No, you haven't done anything wrong. I'm not here to put you under the spotlight. I'd love to examine the ring, though. Would that be alright?" Will gently smiled, placing his hand on her shoulder as reassurance.

She nodded. After a slight struggle with the ring, Carol

pulled it off and handed it across to Will. "I feel pretty naked without it. Not that it's as important as my Alt, but I'm totally attached to it."

"I understand."

Ember watched Will turn it over in his hand and look intently at the interior band. Nothing. There was no number, no inscription. Will handed the ring back, dropping it into Carol's outstretched palm.

Ember felt the girl's relief wash over her the second the ring was back in her hand. The emotion almost knocked her over. *That must be some attachment,* Ember concluded.

"Thanks for the visit, Carol. Ember and I wish you continued success." Will stood and headed to the door. Ember followed, knowing her disappointment would register on her Alt.

"Goodbye, Will and Ember. Hope the rest of your visits are pleasurable."

Closing the door to Number Four, Will and Ember looked at each other. The dark had crept in, right on schedule, as if the night was trying to hide all the answers they needed. Yet Will's voice brimmed with optimism. "Well, we didn't find out much there, but we've only just begun. What do you say we go grab dinner together?"

"Yes. Love it. I'm starving." Ember giggled as her stomach rumbled its agreement.

Will gave his Alt the command for the Level Twelve CommuteCar and placed his finger on his Alt's sensor for a reading as well.

Ember could feel and see Will's cheerfulness. It affected every cell in her being, but she couldn't let that show. "Everything okay?" she asked coyly.

"Oh, yeah. Points are high and car's on its way. There's only one thing that would make me happier."

"What's that?"

Will placed his hands on Ember's shoulders and gently turned her to face him. "This." He kissed her. Softly and then urgently. Like wildfire, the kiss burned its way down through her body until her feet melted into the pavement.

26

Xander's Journey

Once the voices died down to a low murmur, Xander began to assemble the REMs into a hierarchy of command. His friends from the beginning, Jasper, Graham, and Bixby would become his lieutenants, each charged with specialized jobs for the venture to come.

"Jasper, you're gonna be in charge of making sure the crew has all their equipment ready to go. No one can lack the basic elements—food, water, rocks, weapons, and tools. Everybody has to have a way to carry everything. Bixby, you're the lineman at the end of the group as we travel, making sure that we all stay together. No one falls behind. Each of the guys pounded each other on the back and shoulders. You'd think they'd just won a lofty prize.

Xander clapped Graham on the shoulder. "And Graham, you're my right-hand man. If anything happens to me, you're in charge."

"Xander, ya better protect yourself. I ain't ready to be in charge." He shuffled his feet as he wandered around gathering rocks for the trip.

"You're ready. The best one to do it." He kept his eye on Graham. The guy was always a surprise. He chuckled to himself as he saw him pick up a sharp stick and examine it before thrusting it out several times in a make-believe fight.

"I can't," he said as he dropped the stick to the dirt. "Why not pick Jasper?"

"Jasper's not my best bud. You are. You'll take care of everyone." Xander jogged over to help Bixby collect a few rocks that had fallen from his hands. *Overambitious with the size of those things,* he thought. "Don't collect so many ya can't carry 'em, Bix." He sprinted back over to where he'd left Graham fighting the losing battle with the stick.

Graham rubbed his dirty hands over a much filthier face. "I dunno. I never led anybody."

"Till lately, me either, Graham."

"Yeah . . . you either? I've seen ya. You got serious skills."

A series of heartbeats marked a moment of silence before Xander walked over to stand directly in front of Graham. "Remember when we found those giant bugs?"

Graham slapped his face with his hand. "Xander. That was bad. Don't wanna think about it."

"No—listen. Every one of 'em was three inches long. I thought they'd be a real feast. We caught those bugs, about thirty of 'em, brought 'em back and cooked 'em up." He looked Graham in the eye, his mouth holding a half-smile.

"Xander, that was your idea, not mine."

"Yeah. But we did it. Together." Xander grabbed Graham's shoulders tightly and gave him a tiny push.

"I didn't eat any of those. You, Jasper, Bixby, and a few other guys all got sick. Puked all night."

"But you helped me when we got sick. Helped the others. Went and got water and made us drink it. Without you, we'd have been miserable a lot longer. And you cheered everyone up. I see what's there. You're a leader."

"I didn't do that much." Graham looked away and shuffled his feet.

"But you took over. That's why you're the choice."

Xander made a fist and held up his arm. Graham grinned before stepping forward, fist bumped him, and said. "Just don't die or nothin'."

I don't plan on it, he thought. *There's nothing I can't handle.*

Xander turned to the entire group of twelve, revitalized. "We're rollin' out today, REMs! Goin' out east to the alleged burn site first." Xander pumped his fists in the air, seeming to stir the dry wind rustling the dead vegetation scattered about. Today the air was cold, its bony fingers grabbing their bodies like a tomb raider. But Xander was hot under his skin, his ambition and unsuppressed resentment igniting his entire being.

Several hours later, the troop assembled and equipped, they left Camp behind.

About two miles out, the group began to drag. The heat was oppressive, the sweat running down their arms and legs. Dirt and sand burned their feet so badly they would scamper quickly, as if hurrying would make it hurt less. With no warning, they'd walk into an icy wind, and then they would shiver. The landscape was not only boring, but the brutal environment of opposites sucked the energy from their bodies.

Xander knew he had to keep their spirits up. If not, they'd want to head back to Camp to veg in the relative safety of their wretched "apartments."

"Hey, Jasper?"

"Yeah."

"You know when you look good?"

"Ah, no . . ."

"You look good when your eyes are closed, but you look the best when *my* eyes are closed!"

Laughter punctured the bleakness. *It's easy to make them laugh, and we all need it.*

One by one, he singled them out for a joke or two.

"Iris! You're lagging behind a bit. But, hey—if I promise to miss ya, will you go far, far away?"

Iris burst out laughing and the others echoed with their guffaws.

"Oh, Bixby, didja ever wonder why there aren't more trees around here? If idiots grew on trees, this place would be an orchard." Xander laughed along with them, adding to their sense of camaraderie.

By the time they had made it another few miles, Xander had sufficiently roasted each member of the clan, and spirits were high. *I almost feel I'm doing a Plauditor's job—keeping my guys in a good mood in this god-forsaken territory. How ironic is that.*

They trudged ahead, scanning the horizon for smoke from the top of a massive hill littered with a pile of what appeared to be incinerated black rocks and massive boulders. The group stopped for a breather, joking about rolling down the hill to get where they were going faster. At the peak's base, yawning ravines and gorges were outlined in craggy stone. They created a deep space for water, but the area held only shadows.

Xander mounted the vast pile of rubble, jumping to the top notch, a boulder the size of a small car. "Hey, hey! The 'Pinnacle of Success,' right REMs?" The monolith provided a great vantage point, but Xander saw no vestige of smoke from their spectacular vantage point. Disappointed, he climbed down. On his way, he found a treasure half buried in the dirt. It was a metal pike, six feet tall, which he decided was far too heavy to carry along in their journey. He looked at it long-ingly, then dramatically kissed it goodbye, to the amusement of the crew. They made the journey down, picking their way carefully among the rough obstacles.

No less than five minutes later, the guys stopped in their tracks. A blood-curdling snarl rippled through the wind. The hair on Xander's arms stood up, his brain echoing with alarm.

"What was that?" A girl toward the back of the group squeaked the question, and it hung, suspended, in silence.

"Shh. Listen and don't move." Xander stood stock still,

only his head whipping around, looking in every direction. Whatever it was, it was close enough to hear, but not near enough to see. "I don't see anything but have your weapons ready and stay close. We move forward." Xander began surveying the geography of the area for a protected space. Vegetation was nonexistent. And it looked as if there had never been a city or anything else there. No structures decorated the landscape.

"Not another word."

The members pulled their best weapons from their knapsacks, most carrying knives, but some boasting square hammers of steel. They were equipped with some fearsome deterrents, but their band was unwieldy and inexperienced. They moved mutely along, their faces creased with abstract fear.

The snarl came again, louder, an evil omen of something vicious. The creatures they knew—those they hunted and ate to survive—were docile and half-witted. None of those growled or revealed their presence; they hid themselves in a desperate effort to survive an already-hostile environment.

The party turned warily in the direction of the rumble, their accelerated, drumming hearts almost audible.

A Greelox raced from the west toward their group. Even from its distance, Xander noted its eyes, alight with a jaundiced glow. Its teeth dripped with saliva, crimson from a recent kill. Bared, jagged fangs, razor-sharp, held the evil promise of ripped flesh. The creature loomed eight feet tall, its body a muscle-bound, fibrous hulk.

Xander had heard about Greelox. But the rumors he had heard about these animals didn't come close to what he was seeing. As the beast drew closer, the scritching of its paws along the uneven terrain emphasized its clawed talons, each several inches long with needle-sharp tips. Ten-to twelve-inch spikes along the top of its head trailed down its neck and shoulders, stopping for a merciful break along its compact back. Smaller spikes protruded from its hindquarters, continuing down to the start of a furless lion-like tail, the tuft at the end it's only softness. Black tiger stripes on its sinewy skin were a promise of the darkness within.

A roar thundered from the cat's deep chest as it landed in front of the group, its final leap a deadly challenge. *Oh my god. Let my team be up to this.* In an ironic answer to his thoughts, all but his three officers, Jasper, Graham, and Bixby, turned back the way they had come, running for dear life. Their screams led their journey to the hill they'd traversed just minutes before.

I can't let my destiny be devoured by this freak of nature. Frikkin' Shazz! Fight! Xander attacked, adrenaline flooding his limbs. He stabbed at the beast with his knife, reaching—stretching— for its leathery chest. A swing, and the blade missed. A plunge of the knife into a skeletal dent under the chest did nothing. The blade seemed like a mere feather in his hands. Xander eyed the spikes along the being's back, realizing that there was no way to penetrate the spine of the animal, even if he could jump high enough.

Meanwhile, Xander saw Jasper, Graham, and Bixby spread out several feet away from the Greelox. They threw rocks from their satchels at the beast's head and flanks. The six-inch rocks hit their target, time after time, repeatedly. The mutant tiger screamed. It was being hurt, and it bled from raw cavities in its flesh, but it did not stop snapping its jaws and lashing its claws. From the corner of his eye, Xander watched Graham bravely recover the REM's rocks, now scattered around the creature. The other two continued their assault, the Rock Masters in the competition of their lives.

It's now or never. Xander knew the plan forming in his mind was risky. For a moment he agonized . . . *I either die right here or try a plan to protect everyone else. I hate like hell leaving my three guys alone. But no time to hesitate. It has to work. This is our only chance to bring this monster down.*

Xander screamed out, "Run to the gorge! Now!" Then he turned and sped as fast as he could to the top of the hill. He felt as if sandbags weighed him down. Damp with terror, he smelled his own sweat. Each step fractured the dust as he sped to the top of the hill. The crest of the hill taunted his efforts, as it seemed to move away rather than rise up to greet him. But finally, he reached the pinnacle, breathing hard, a burn spreading through his chest. The frightened army of eight REMs, who ran for their lives, gathered around him as if he had just returned from the dead. "Xander! You're safe!" one of them cried. He pushed them all away. There was no time for a sentimental reunion.

The view from the top was no longer a welcome one. The scene at the bottom of the hill was grim. Graham's arm was bleeding scarlet. The monster had bitten into his forearm where it hung by thin sinew. The monster pulled it away with another snap of its jaws. The Greelox continued its shredding, now consumed with its goal to destroy and devour its prey. Graham's screams rent the air, earsplitting and agonizing.

"Bixby, go, go, GO!" Jasper screamed. "To the gorge!"

"But Graham . . . !"

"GO! We can't save him!" Jasper bolted toward the hillside. Bixby followed on Jasper's heels, blood dripping from scratches on his arms. Adrenaline seemed to make them superhuman, and the men pushed toward the ravine where they fell into the cleft, exhausted.

The growls grew louder as the monster ripped and tore. Graham's shrieks suddenly went silent. Jasper and Bixby watched in horror as their friend Graham paid the ultimate sacrifice, his body disappearing into pieces.

His bravery spent, Jasper sobbed and wailed. Bixby howled in fear, exposing their whereabouts in the crevasse.

Their safety became uncertain once again. The Greelox turned sharply to pursue Bixby and Jasper. The cat raised and lowered its head as if to judge the distance. It assembled its girth and balanced on its haunches, ready to close the expanse with a calculated leap.

Forcibly grabbing the pike he had regretfully left behind earlier, Xander bellowed orders to his panicked REMs. He jammed the metal bar under a bulky stone, just below the mammoth boulder atop the crest. "Girls—throw rocks from your satchels at that animal! Guys—grab the bar and lift—as hard as you can! The rest of you—pry up this rock!" They pushed and pulled, their sweat and tears dripping salty serum on the rocks. Their combined strength nudged the rock off its space, but it was not enough. "Push—harder!" Xander yelled, desperate.

The second thrust sent the underlying rock free, its release causing a domino effect. Dozens of hefty, misshapen rocks let loose and hurtled down the hillside. The crowning boulder at the top, where Xander had stood earlier, jesting about success, followed. It rolled downward in the path laid out, its descent a force of solid fury, gaining speed in a frantic rush.

The Greelox's pointy ears lay back in defiance as it turned toward the roar from the hillside.

The shower of rocks was followed by the deafening crash of Xander's "Success" boulder, quaking the hillside. A brown, dense cloud permeated the air. The echo was multi-layered thunder, bouncing off the canyon and shattering the grainy terrain. Then silence. The settling powder finally revealed the Greelox, lying dead in the dust.

27

Will's Day Off

After Will had said goodnight to Ember, he returned home in a mood not unlike an airborne balloon. His Alt points were climbing. The only thing bothering him was the mystery of Ember's mom and her ring. When he thought about the problems, his good Alt points seemed to evaporate.

In spite of the threatening losses, he was off the next day and ready to delve deeper. While he would have loved another day with Ember, she had her appointment with the Magistrate for her checkup. He would have to go solo.

He had already found the next ring recipient on the list, Omar Sensus. He was Level Eighteen. After starting with Level One, it seemed logical to next speak with the person who represented the top Status. Will hurried into his yellow pants and threw on his printed tank top—the one with the collar and small images of a lemony sun on a pale goldenrod background. He debated about the windbreaker but decided it would be unnecessary; he'd be back before nightfall.

As Level Eighteen Omar Sensus was Gold, his home would be luxurious. Will was looking forward to seeing what awaited him, too, once he made it to Level Eighteen. He daydreamed about how long it would take to achieve Status Eighteen. If he stayed true, he wondered if he could be at eighteen in less than five years. He could be Elite before he was even twenty-five! Maybe that achievement would be a first. He could make history—again. He smiled broadly. His future was bright.

The sweet daydream made his trip across town go by in no time at all. Will arrived at Number Sixteen Hundred, Golden Circle Drive, in the Gold Coast sector of dwellings. This time the CommuteCar had driven right through the palatial arch, the camera recognizing his badge as he held it up for viewing. The gates, a shimmering metallic gold, opened gently with an orchestral rendering of Bach's Opus Five.

At Number Sixteen Hundred's door, he rang a massive doorbell that chimed a few bars of Tranquility's anthem. He looked directly into the camera at the door, smiled, and gave a little wave.

"Hello, may I help you?" came a woman's voice through a speaker.

"Yeah." He caught himself. His language should be professional. "I mean, yes, I hope so. I'm Will Verus. I'm actually a Plauditor, though I'm not dressed in uniform today." His Level Twelve yellow sportswear was a glaring contradiction to the customary black uniform. "Looking to congratulate Omar Sensus on his achievement. The city wants to make sure he's enjoying his new advantages as a ring recipient. Is he available?"

The metallic door opened from the bottom, sliding up in an electronic whoosh. "I'm his wife, Fennie. Come in." She gave Will the citizen's salute, her golden fluffy sleeve rustling with the movement.

Will returned the gesture and stepped inside an elegant room. Shiny gold frames on the wall. Burnished gilded arms and legs on the chairs and tables. Large glittering vases of mums. Plush gold velvet upholstery. A tea cart with gold-veined swirls accenting the marble. *This place is ridiculous,* Will mused. *Wow.*

"I was just sitting down for my breakfast." She indicated the crisply set table. "Care to join me?"

"Yes. That would be a pleasure." He took the chair offered up to him.

"I'm afraid Omar won't be joining us, though. Omar died. About two months ago. It's still . . . a shock." She picked up a petite gold paper fan lying on the table next to her plate and fanned herself gently. Laying it back down, her hand trembled slightly, but she gave Will a genuine smile. "You're a Plauditor. I'm surprised you didn't know about Omar before coming out here."

Will felt overwhelmed. The news about Omar was sad, but it put him one step closer to unraveling the mystery. Was Omar's death like Talesa's? He wanted to do more, but his compassion for this woman kept him from asking more questions. After all, his life's work was to cheer people up, not cause them to grieve. Probing further might just push her to lose points. Better to reassure her and give her hope.

"You have my deepest sympathies, Mrs. Sensus. I'm truly sorry for your loss and for disturbing you at this difficult time." Will reached out and touched her hand. "Is there anything I can do for you?"

"I wish there was. It seems no one can help me understand what happened with Omar." She poured Will a cup of hot tea from a pot on the table and set it before him. "Help yourself to any of the food, too."

"Thank you. Mrs. Sensus, I can try to help." Will's pulse quickened. If she was going to talk, he was going to listen.

"I doubt you can, but I'll tell you the story. A few days before his death, we talked about how he didn't feel right, but we postponed reporting it, thinking it was an emotional thing. We didn't want to draw attention . . ."

"Of course. But his Alt? Did it show that Omar was in an

emotional crisis? Someone like me could have come." Will wished the man had reached out. Maybe Omar would still be sitting here.

"We weren't sure what to do. And Omar didn't want any fuss. He was a good person and wanted only to help others. His journal, 'Words of Wisdom' was an encouragement to many. That's why he earned the Augur Prize. But he never wished for the attention he received." She stood up and walked across the room, where she picked up a framed picture from a small table. "Here. Here's his picture." She gazed at it longingly. "I only focus on the good memories. Not the loss."

"He was lucky to have you. It seems you were a great couple." He took several sips of the warm tea to give himself a moment. Will thought about his own relationship with Ember. When two people know they're meant to be together, the loss must be terrible. He shivered slightly, thinking of what losing Ember that way would be like.

"Yes. And Omar was only a hundred Alt points away from being designated 'Elite.' But He wasn't sure if he wanted to become part of the government. Now he'll never have to worry about it." Her face brightened a bit, as if she had just found the silver lining.

"Again, I'm so sorry, Mrs. Sensus. I see by your clothes that you're also a Level Eighteen, so you'll be staying in your dwelling. But, please—take care of yourself. Your Alt points depend on it." Will set his cup down and prepared to leave. "Thanks for the tea. Maybe I'll stop in another time to see how you are doing." Will was anxious to leave this place. He could hardly keep from running out the door.

"Certainly. Thanks for stopping by." Fennie tossed her dark hair and walked him to the curb out with a smile. She waved to him as he headed for the safety of his ride, but he barely saw it.

The CommuteCar was waiting for him at the curb, just as he had requested. He jumped in and told the car to head to the Plauditorium. There he could find other ring recipients. The information from Fennie had changed everything. Something was going on, and it was bizarre. At this point, he didn't want to waste time with face-to-face interviews. He decided to make some calls through his Alt; he could even face-time.

The CommuteCar was not even completely stopped when Will jumped out. He vaguely heard the car wishing him a "positive and sparkling day" before his feet hit the sidewalk. From there, he dashed. He was on a mission.

As he opened the door to the Plauditorium, he immediately saw his Alt score post on the overhead screen. As usual, it was extra high, but adrenaline seemed to be escalating it. He noticed his name was at the top of the leaderboard for Alt points. *Great—no one will bat an eye that I'm here.*

He cruised over to his regular station, but of course the weekly Temp occupied it. If not for the Temps, he would never have a day off. He approached the woman at the desk, relieved to find it was someone he knew. Darla was an older Level Fifteen, probably fifty, but she prided herself on her appearance. Will could tell she spent much of her spare time in the youth-restoring shops on Bliss Avenue. Her white hair was adorned with elaborate hair combs, and her indigo-colored clothes set off her rosy complexion.

"Hi, Darla!" Will extended his arm in greeting. "Thanks for being here on my day off."

"Well—hello, Will. What an unexpected surprise! I'd be thinking you'd be out enjoying your day." Darla never took her eyes off her screen but returned the Tranquility salute with enthusiasm.

"Just thought I'd allow you to go to lunch early and have an extended break. It's my Act of Kindness for the week." He'd already done his act of kindness, but this would be an ideal opportunity to slide into his workstation for a while.

"So sweet of you, kid. Rack up those points! It won't be long before you're Orange. And Level Thirteen fits you perfectly. Level Thirteen—Optimism. You've got that nailed already." She talked to him without taking her eyes from her screen. Darla took her work seriously.

"Yeah…thanks. Just settling in to Twelve, but—"

She interrupted, her voice enthusiastic. "I'd be thrilled to take a longer lunch today. Thank you, Will." Darla finally took her eyes briefly off the screen to look him up and down, a provocative appraisal that made Will blush.

"I'll fill your seat for ninety minutes. How's that sound?"

"Why, just wonderful. You really are so . . . special." With that, Darla rose from her chair and caressed Will's face. "See you soon, babe."

Ugh! I shouldn't let her touch me. But the temporary takeover was easy. So glad Austel is off today, too. Perfect. Will flew into the chair, and logged into the history page to find, once again, the picture and names for Talesa's class of ring honorees. He had a sudden deep twinge of conscience as he accessed the database, feeling as if he was completely betraying his city and his grandfather. He had made a promise to his Gramps to follow the laws. Here he was, instead, acquiring information that was classified. He felt hideously corrupt. Sinful. He could be severely disciplined for this if someone found out, and he would not only lose his job and his Status, but he would bring dishonor on his entire family.

He hesitated again, the guilt becoming a monstrous stone in his gut. His Alt vibrated, and the screen above showed a steep dip in his Alt points. The negative thinking was toxic. Will closed his eyes, thinking about the sacrifice he was making on Ember's behalf. The surge of tenderness and compassion instantly resurrected his points.

Accessing the data while keeping an eye on the surveillance screen, he looked again at Omar's name on the list. Everything showed as it was before. He examined more recent newsletters. There was nothing to indicate Omar's death. Or Talesa's, for that matter.

Going back, he quickly zoned in on the Level Fifteen, Sixteen, and Seventeen honorees. Transferring their contact numbers into his Alt with a click of a button, he sighed with a combination of relief and satisfaction. As soon as Darla returned, he could be on his way. He was eager to make the calls. *Were there any more dead "Tranks" out there?*

In the meantime, Will returned his eyes to the monitor. It wouldn't be acceptable if he didn't monitor it closely. Darla was a good person and a first-rate Plauditor. He wasn't willing to mess up her observation record at the station.

No sooner had he focused on the screen when he saw the boxy, tan vehicle again that drew his attention a few days ago. There it was in the corner of the screen, disappearing almost instantly from view. *Shazz. What in the heck is that doing out there? I'm gonna have to make a report.*

He punched his screen and pulled up the report form. He typed quickly, filling it out. There was so much on the form he couldn't answer, other than the description of the thing. He clicked "submit" after making sure that it went in under Darla's account.

He wasn't even supposed to be here, and he wanted no questions. He squirmed in his seat, his thoughts distracted. His chest was tight. He longed to be told he was doing the right thing by doing his investigations. The burden was getting heavy.

He heard the click of heels approaching his station, but his concentration was still on the screen. "Darla, you're back early. You could have taken more time."

"Great compliment, but I'm no Darla."

Will jerked around in his chair. It was Austel who stood there, grinning. "Nothing better to do on your day off, Will? You should be with Ember—at least to watch her. She's up to something."

"Yeah, yeah . . . I'm keeping an eye on her. Can't be sure of her motivations either. I'll keep you informed." Will turned back around in his chair to monitor the screen again, avoiding eye contact with Austel. He thought he sounded more convincing that way.

"Good, good. At least we know why that break-in happened. The Sciolist would never allow someone to keep a ring that didn't belong to them."

"That break-in was Sciolist? How do you know that?"

Austel patted himself on the back. "I've recently made a friend in the Elite, Will. You'd better watch what you do."

Journal Entry #5618

Talesa Vinata had to be eliminated. At first, I thought Talesa was lovely. We became acquainted. I spent some secret time with her last year. We dated for quite some time, unbeknownst to anyone. She even made me wonder if I might marry her. Especially since she was beautiful. I was quite in love with her.

But after a time, I began to feel uneasy in her presence. She began cancelling our dates. She had to be plotting just like others in the higher classes...but, I digress.

And now, the woman's daughter, Ember, has caught my interest. There is something about her that's different. It's not just her beauty, so much more vibrant than her mother's. Perhaps she is poison as well. Or, could she be valuable? I'll be looking deeper.

—Serpio Magnus, Magistrate

28

Ember's Exam

E mber wished she could be with Will. He would be
investigating on his day off, and she would report to the
Solace Institute for her exam. She was nervous. She
had never been to the building before. Her Alt was already
showing distress so, as she sat in the waiting area, she practiced a
4-7-8 breathing technique. The breathing became a tranquilizer:
she exhaled completely through her mouth, making a whooshing
sound, then closed her mouth and inhaled quietly through her
nose to a count of four. She held her breath—seven counts; she
then exhaled through her mouth to a count of eight. Now she
was more relaxed, and her Alt was responding by holding steady.

Her mother came to mind. She still grieved, still felt the
vast loss, especially when she needed her mom, like now. She
held back tears when any little memory was triggered. Would
they be looking for that, too? And when they discovered that
grief that she tried so hard to bury, would they send her to be
counseled?

A medic with the name tag, Carly Spero, called out,
"Ember Vinata." When Ember stood up, Carly gave her the
anticipated Tranquility signal.

Ember appraised Ms. Spero's emotional set as she ushered Ember into a plain, white room. The medic was happy as a child in the Fun Zone, her aura a mottled blue. "How are you doing today, Ember? We received a report about a time when you became weak and faint. We're just going to check your vitals and do some imaging. We'll be able to see if your heart is functioning okay, and if your brain is free of any blockages. These are things your Alt can't measure for us. We hope you can be comfortable during this process. It won't take long."

"Thank you. I wasn't sure what to expect."

The medic quickly pulled a rustling royal blue liner across the table. "Just lie down on the bed here."

Ember climbed up awkwardly, thinking that "bed" was an exaggeration for the thing she lay on. She tried to get comfortable, but the cot wasn't made for pampering. *So much for making people happy,* she thought.

"That's right. All you need to do is relax. The Inscape will do all the analysis." She held up a shiny white box with an olive-green blinking light on the front near the top. It reminded Ember of a cat's eye.

"Okay. Does this hurt?" Ember dreaded this whole thing, but she didn't want to suffer pain, too.

The medic laughed. "No. Not at all. First, we'll scan the front of your body, and then the back. All the data will be uploaded immediately, so we can see exactly what you are experiencing from minute to minute." The practitioner moved the square device back and forth over Ember's five-foot-four frame. The six-inch cube intermittently lit up in various colors depending on where it was being directed. It vibrated with a soft, soothing hum.

Miss Spero stopped moving the instrument in several places. Ember saw her examine the screen on the Inscape. "Are you feeling anything here? No? How about here?" the medic asked. "All right, now you may turn over." Her voice sounded strained.

Ember did as she was told. *What is she finding?* While she couldn't help but be relaxed by the Inscape, paranoid thoughts nagged at her.

A few more passes of the Inscape, and Miss Spero asked Ember to sit up. "Are you sure you're feeling okay today, Ember?"

"Yeah. Other than being a little nervous, I feel great. Why?"

"The Inscape is showing a number of irregularities. I'll need to show this to my supervisor."

"Irregularities? Like what?" Ember asked. Her palms grew moist.

Miss Spero looked as if she was choosing her words carefully. "Your brain scan shows extra activity and spikes. I've never seen these types of brain flashes. Excuse me while I speak into my Alt."

Alarm bells were now going off in Ember's head. She fought the urge to jump off the table and run out the door. "Look, you have to tell me what's going on."

"Ember, please stay calm. It appears you have an uncommon capability. I can't tell you any more than that. Someone else will be in within a moment or two."

After a mere heartbeat, the door opened. Ember gasped. The Magistrate himself strode in, his aura a pulsing deep blue. *Why was he standing by? Was he waiting for this?*

"Ember. I understand you have an abnormal reading." The Magistrate's voice seemed like cold liquid, bathing her from head to toe. His eyes met hers, flashing with fire.

Ember swallowed hard. She tried not to gag.

The Magistrate continued. "You have a rare condition. You can feel and see emotions, correct?"

Panic surged through her. Her whole body quivered. She couldn't even breathe, couldn't even feel her pulse. Then her heart fluttered like a butterfly, and thrummed one long, endless beat. Ember could barely nod, "yes," when all she wanted to do was scream. *Deny! Deny!* But Ember knew it was no use. Her aptitude had been discovered.

The Magistrate's voice trembled with fervor, and his eyes bulged with wonder. "You will be of great service to our city, Ember. An Empath! We've never had someone like you. You will be the Star of Tranquility, and soon we will celebrate!"

29

Xander's Revelation

Xander gathered his troops around him after the dust had cleared, and there were hugs and back pats all around. They had survived! Their relief made them feel like butterflies, finally realizing they had been reborn from their beginnings as lowly caterpillars.

Bixby and Jasper picked their way uphill to cheers from the group. They were filthy and exhausted, their clothes ragged and bloody. Xander greeted them with open arms as they reached the top, his thoughts as crushing as the rocks that killed the Greelox.

"We'll take as much time as we need to remember and honor our fallen comrade. Graham was a wonderful friend to all of us," Xander said. His eyes, already bloodshot from the wind, dust, and battle, teared up, glassy, increasing the redness, in spite of his iron spirit. His heart threatened to explode with grief. He'd never had such a loss—never allowed himself to get close enough to anyone. The moment overwhelmed him, and he swayed on his feet. His breath felt compressed in his chest, like something had sucked it all away. He was authentically sad, and although he'd never had reason to mourn in his life, it was a relief to know that he could do it here in The Outside, where no Alt measured his pain.

"Without his sacrifice and quick thinking, more of us would've perished. Let's each silently stand and remember his friendship and bravery." The moment was thick with emotion as the entire crew suffered, each in his own way. Their group appeared defeated, their shoulders slumped, even though they had won the assault. Jasper and Iris held hands, staring into space. Bixby covered his face with his hands, occasionally sniffing and wiping his nose. Sobs rent the air. A dozen of them joined arms in a show of unity. The rest looked down, their eyes too much a mirror of their hearts.

Xander picked up the pike and wiped his eyes. "Let's go. There's another way to memorialize our loss." Xander took the lead, the others following him to the base of the peak. Next to the pile of rubble, Xander spied a torn and shredded piece of Graham's red cape. Tying it on the end of the pike, Xander drove the spike into the ground. Here would mark the site of Graham's valor.

"Your quick thinking helped us all, Xander. We owe you our lives as well," Jasper said. "Let's hear it for our leader Xander!" The REMs exploded in a cheer, their confidence renewed. Drained, but zealous, they surrounded Xander once again, exchanging high-fives.

"Let's move out. We have places to go," Xander reminded them. "We know, no matter what we face, we're gonna be victorious!"

The crew surged forward, Xander turning one last time in a goodbye glance as the scrap of velvet blew in the wind.

SEVERAL HOURS LATER, the youngest girl in the group, Iris, shouted. "Look! Some trees!"

Sure enough, Xander, too, caught sight of them a split second later. Without a doubt, the trees were dead, but were probably only a half-mile away. He decided then and there to make camp as soon as they arrived at the small woods. With a little luck, they could make a fire from tree branches, a welcome provider of light and warmth, and just in time. The sun had almost finished its descent, leaving only a glowing silver ribbon outlining the horizon. In spite of their weariness, the bedraggled group stepped up their pace. They were ready for a night's rest.

Xander was the first to enter the copse of trees. The trees stood in solid groups, and they were dense as cordwood. Their trunks were thick, but brittle and faded; spindly branches stretched out like spider webs reaching for the sun. *If ever trees could be unhappy, these are,* he said to himself. "C'mon, guys— let's see if this is some sort of enchanted forest." He laughed, his mirth swallowed up by the guffaws of the group. They forged their way behind him through the forlorn woods.

In a matter of minutes, he came to the other side of the thicket and into a clearing. Not much of a forest. There were still a few trees in sight a ways ahead, but they were scattered, almost as if each one had broken away to run for its life. There before him was a mammoth, charred pile of wood. Curiously, the blackened branches were piled high and wide, as if the campfire belonged to that of a giant. *Someone else has been here, and recently.* The logs' fire was out, but the remains still radiated a wispy, frail heat. "Be careful—the fire site's still warm," Xander called out.

He inhaled the scent of stagnant smoke, but his senses wilted at an odd repulsive smell pervading the space. *This must have been quite a camp out. Smells like burnt meat . . . but it's not appetizing. What did someone cook that smells like sulfur and rotting leather?*

Right behind him, the group wound its way past the ashen trees into the glade. Jasper stepped into the clearing. "Shazz! What's goin' on? Smells like rotten dung here."

"Who cares? We can sure make a fire. Look—there's even some cut branches over here that are unused," observed James, a burly thirty-year-old REM.

"Heck, yeah! Let's set up camp," Bixby boomed, with newfound bravado. He ran over to grab a small branch and began to drag it back to the blackened area.

Throwing his hands in the air in a "stop" gesture, Xander interrupted, his brow furrowed. "Listen, everybody. We set up, but we spread out around the outside of the fire. Some of you as far back as the trees." He pointed his finger in that direction. "We want to be alert. One night here will be great, but we've got to be on our guard. Who knows who was here and why?" Xander said. "Pick your spot and have your weapons ready. A few of you help me build a new fire." He bent to pick up a random stick and threw it toward the sooty area. "We're not hunting, so eat the jerky in your knapsacks. Then we sleep. We're outta here at dawn."

A few of the guys dragged wood to the fire site. That was one skill at which they were pros. Within a couple of minutes, the group had piled the wood and lit kindling. As the fire flared up, a fanfare of popping sounds splintered the air. A few of the guys jumped, and then laughter and jokes erupted.

While his group was settling in, Xander took the opportunity to do some scouting around. He was determined to figure out if this was the site he had been expecting to find. It appeared it was regularly used and visited fairly recently.

Since they all had come through the wooded area and saw nothing unusual, he set out toward the singular trees ahead, separated by space between them. Fresh footprints in the dust formed a path to each of the trees. He examined them, puzzled. Following the impressions, he was astonished to find that the first tree had markings. He ran his fingers over the carvings. Someone had deeply etched two, three, or four-digit numbers into the hardwood. *The numbers aren't in sequence, but there are so many here.* He wandered over to the next tree. More numbers. There were five trees spaced out at intervals, and each one he saw had the odd numbers on them. *What do these mean? Numbers. On random trees. What the heck?*

His instincts were warning him that this was a dangerous place to be. Was this the fire he first smelled when entering The Outside? And the rumors. Were they true? Were bodies burned here?

He decided to climb one of the trees. Perhaps he could look across the land. If nothing else, he could see what more was out there. He wanted no more surprises. The ideal tree had branches for footholds, so it was easy to climb. His only concern was the brittleness of the wood and its ability to hold him. Cautious, he scrambled upward, but soon he was at its zenith where he had a 360-degree view.

He gazed about, at first seeing nothing much of interest other than more desolate land with a few random trees. He turned to descend, disappointed and bored. *Wait . . . is that something out on the horizon?* He paused and craned his neck. Wishing he had binoculars for a closer analysis, he would have to wait it out. *Yes, it's something . . . it's moving . . . it's a vehicle . . .* Xander strained his eyes. It was hard to see—the color of the flat, tan earth, but there was no doubt it was a transport of some sort, and it was headed their direction!

This was close to discovering a dinosaur had survived the Ice Age, only to find it was in the room with you. Xander knew this was an opportunity, but a dangerous one. Someone else was indeed out here, and he was hoping the vehicle was gonna be their ride.

He monkeyed his way down the tree and raced back to his crew, who were now relaxing by the fire. "Change of plans, people! We're gonna have company. Retreat to the woods behind us. Flatten yourselves on the ground. Hide as well as you can. Bixby, Jasper, wait for my word. Then get your rocks ready. All of you—be prepared for battle."

The REMs responded uniformly, gathering their things back into their sacks. Once they scrambled into the woods, they seemed to melt away as they silently hid themselves. They didn't know what was coming, but they knew it had to be serious. No one was taking any chances.

The regiment had a thirty-minute lull before a silky rumble caught their ears. A vehicle was indeed arriving, and its shallow motor was certainly no CommuteCar engine. Xander looked through the trees as the transport pulled up just inside the clearing. *No wonder I didn't find tire tracks. The thing is elevated off the ground!*

A strong puff of air, some sort of hydraulic system, lowered the vehicle to the powdery dirt while simultaneously raising automatic doors on each side of the conveyance. A blond man with wide shoulders emerged from one side, and then another guy, bearded with a severe dark crewcut. Their clothing was as tan as the vehicle in which they rode. The garments were bland, having no required Status colors. Xander wondered if they were from Tranquility at all, until he noticed a red "T" embroidered on an arm patch. *They're Tranks, for sure. They're just wearing some sort of odd uniform—all one piece with no imagination.* The men had shotgun weapons over their shoulders. Xander had never seen a shotgun before. Tranquility was a gun-free society. But he knew about guns from his history lessons. The men looked stern. These were not tranquil Tranks.

"What's goin' on here?" the blond man said. He turned to the other, his narrow eyes glittering. "No way this should be lit."

The fire, by this time, was a blaze. Xander cringed. They were bound to be discovered. His skin bristled with fear. *We're gonna have to be on the offensive.*

"Better check it out," the other guy said with a gravelly voice. A more sinister but bulky presence than the other, he began to advance toward the fire, gazing toward the woods, his hands grabbing for the weapon on his right shoulder.

Xander had opened his supply bag and gestured to the others to do the same. For the second time in a day, their rocks came out, and they had them ready. Xander made a quick move, throwing a six inch stone at the advancing male. The remainder of Xander's brigade popped out and began their assault, stones flying through the air like missiles.

The Trank duo had no chance to defend themselves from the unexpected onslaught. Bleeding and battered, each fell to the ground. Screams and moans spilled from their mouths, only energizing the band of REMs.

"Let's go!" Xander shouted. He signaled to his gang to check out the condition of their foes. Within a minute the pack surrounded the men, Jasper jumping on the back of one, while the other guy continued to receive blows from a team of five.

Jasper's man was already dead. His companion, after a final grunt, lay inert, his head a split melon. "Got 'im!" Jasper yelled.

"Congratulations, REMs! You've not only killed these men successfully, but now we have transportation." Xander gazed at the boxy transport as if it was God. He ran over to the thing and ran his hands across the front of it.

"Yeah! No more walking!" Jasper called out. The rest of the group cheered.

"No more walking! But we have more than that! We've got a way back into the city!" Xander thrust his fist into the air. "We're on our way!"

Another cheer rang out, louder than the first. The REMs surrounded the vehicle, pounding on its sides.

"How 'bout we celebrate?" Xander yelled.

Iris yelled out from the back of the group. "Yeah! But how?"

"I'm givin' you all a new name! You're not REMs anymore!"

"Not REMs? We gonna be Xander's Crew?" Bixby cried.

"Flattered . . . but no," Xander said, exaggerating the compliment. Then, he hesitated for dramatic effect, punching emotion into celebratory words. "We have risen from the ashes! From now on, *we are Phoenix!*"

30

Will's Missing Pieces

W ill was unnerved with Austel's warning to watch out. Was Austel planning to report on everything he did?

Austel swatted Will on the back as he turned away, loping across the room to find a spunky thirty-year-old, Aurora, a fast rising Level Eleven, who was closing down her shift.

So, he's got a date, then. No wonder he's here. Didn't plan for that glitch . . .

He finished logging in the transport sighting when Darla tapped on his shoulder. "I'm back, Will. Thanks again for the break."

"No problem. Glad I could do something nice for you, Darla." Will's feet itched to leave. He fairly flew out the door. *Now time for some real answers, I hope.*

A call buzzed through on his Alt. City Hall was calling.

City Hall? That wasn't good.

"Hello, Will," said a silky female computer-generated voice. "Report immediately to City Hall for matters of urgent concern. A.S.P.E.R. will check you in at the front desk." The call ended.

Hmmm. I wonder what this is about.

Apprehension began to creep in, but Will pushed it aside by using a physical technique he'd learned as a younger teen. He swiped an imaginary object (his fear) from the air, balled it up with both hands, tossed it up again and "hit" it with a make-believe bat. "Outta here!" he said aloud. A tiny buzz from his Alt measured both an incoming—and outgoing—fear.

He began walking, close enough to City Hall to get there easily in twenty minutes, allowing his mind to dwell on when he would see Ember again.

∼

SURE ENOUGH, A.S.P.E.R. checked him in with her mechanical efficiency and beauty. City Hall wasn't taking any chances with a real person; they'd have to be totally impartial and close-mouthed. Sensitive work went on here.

Eighteen chairs of various hues lined the wall. He took a seat on the chair meant for him—a pillowy plush yellow chair in the waiting room where upbeat music saturated the air. A tray of cookies, fresh from the oven, sat on the side table for his enjoyment. Having the Status he held had its benefits. He smiled.

A red door to his left opened, and a Sciolist stepped out. "Will Verus, please."

Will's saliva caught in his throat, provoking an embarrassing gurgle. He coughed. *A Sciolist! Why?* His brain raced with all kinds of thoughts, but his heart seemed to stop. A bleep from his Alt registered a drop in points. He jetted to his feet, hoping he at least appeared cheerful and confident. He took a deep breath, pulling his own mood up with the force of a tsunami. He had to be at least stable. Glancing at his Alt, he saw the points edge up.

Silent as a sleepwalker, he followed the Sciolist through the door.

Better to not say a word until I know what this is about.

The Sciolist, a male with frizzy hair in what Will imagined was his forties, said, "Sit, please. A counselor will be with you soon."

"A Counselor? I'm being *counseled?*"

"Yes, Mr. Verus. We *care* about you. Have a splendid day." He exited through a door in the back.

Will started counting his breaths, quieting his mind. "...55, 56..."

The back door opened, and a gold-clad gentleman entered. A Level Eighteen, no less. *An Elite.* Will allowed his awe free rein.

"Winslow Liberalis—you can call me 'Win.'" The man gave a tight Tranquility salute, to which Will responded. "Have a seat, Will."

Will's knees were a trifle weak, so he fell into the chair. He bit back a thousand questions.

"Congratulations to you for your amazing Status change, Will. And on your appointment to the Plauditorium. Excellent." The man smiled.

Will nodded. *Shazz!* He was gripping the arms of the chair too tightly. In spite of Winslow's words, this didn't seem like a congratulatory meeting—not one bit.

Win continued. "As you know, Tranquility requires strict adherence to the Accords."

"Of course. I'm dedicated to the laws," he told Win.

"You're in violation."

The words sunk in like a brick through water.

"What? How?" *Had they caught him up information? Had Austel found out and reported it? Were they tracking the searches?* He would have to come up with an explanation and fast, or he could be looking at more than just counseling.

"Will, you know that you can't be developing a relationship with a Level Eight. Ember Vinata is a Level Eight."

Ah. They've noticed his calls and paired it with his extreme Alt highs. They know I've been with her—and they have her on it, too, no doubt. Shazz! Not good. He forced his mind into thinking about HER instead of the violation. He needed to keep his Alt points up.

"Sir, please," Will said. "Ember is a friend, and I've had to help her through some difficult times. She's—she's a good person. I'll admit she's beautiful, but a *relationship*? I do think she's beneath me, Sir." His voice quaked with a put-on arrogance. He hoped his lies would convince Winslow. The one thing the Alt couldn't do was measure a truth against a lie. That is, unless his emotions betrayed him. As he distorted the facts, his mind chanted "Traitor, traitor!"

"Yes, yes, of course," Winslow replied. "I understand you want to help. But we have to be sure, you know. You cannot see this girl again, Will. If you do, you'll have an in-depth counseling next time. This could be a Purge-worthy offense. Or more."

"I take my vows as a Plauditor very seriously, Mr. Liberalis. I would never let my city down."

"You are a good citizen indeed, Will. Here's looking to a bright future for you." With that, he showed Will to the door where, as he left, Will felt the man's eyes boring into the back of his head.

Will's stomach soured. He knew the threat of further action was real, and he meant what he said to Winslow. His deepest desire had always been to be a devoted citizen. He wanted to rise up in society. He wanted to prove himself. He desperately wanted to elevate his parents' Status through efforts in the government. But he also loved Ember. She moved his heart in ways he had never known. The choice was torturous. Who would he betray?

∾

HE WASN'T ABOUT to make his Augur Prize investigative calls near the vicinity of City Hall. He would need privacy. He grabbed a yellow CommuteCar that just happened to be leaving the curb and asked the C-Car to drop him near the Solace Institute. First of all, he knew Ember was there. But the grounds at Solace, thick with vegetation, were also designed for impenetrable silence. The work conducted in the building was sensitive. Emotionally unstable people were examined and treated there. An interruption could derail an analysis or therapy. He could stand just outside the fence to make his calls.

His call to Level Fifteen's honoree, Andrea Noxa, rang through. He stared at his Alt as he heard a series of beeps, followed by a message. A crisp automated voice intoned, "This Alt is no longer registered to a user." *Okay...there's a problem.*

Next up, number Sixteen. "Alt, call James Candidus." Again, the call generated a recorded response. *No James...*

One more to go with Jordan Pietas, number Seventeen. Will remembered meeting Jordan at a public meeting not long ago. He had been impressed with his gracious personality and his sharp wit. Although Jordan, age fifty-two, was considerably older than he was, Will loved talking to him about the city and looked forward to seeing him again. Jordan had great ideas about improvements he was hoping the Elite would approve.

Will tried to be prepared as he spoke Jordan's name into the Alt. This time it went to voicemail. "Hello, this is Jordan Pietas. Please leave a caring message, and I will happily return your call as soon as possible. Have a beautiful day." Thank the stars—the Alt was still active. Will felt hopeful again. "Hello, Jordan! This is Will Ver—" An automated voice cut him off. "This message box is full, and messages have not been retrieved for seven days." *Seven days? No one had messages for seven days! Unless...*

Will couldn't wrap his head around this discovery. The ring recipients were either missing or dead. *But why? Why would these promising Tranks—so distinguished—be gone before their time? Why was there no news of this, no acknowledgement?*

Will was confused about what to do next. He, of course, would tell Ember what he had found. *Her mother was not the only one, but where to go from there?*

Journal Entry #2805

Today I am angry. There seem to be more and more shadows following me. Once I'm able to send more conspirators to The Outside to be burned into cinders, I'll have a new outlook on life. That will happen today. Once again, I will feel safe.

To tell the truth, other people just never measure up. They are full of excuses. The city needs me as Magistrate. What would become of them if I weren't here?

—Serpio Magnus, Magistrate

31

Ember's New Assignment

E mber, feeling like a wild bird that had just had a cage descend over it, stood before the Magistrate. She wanted to flap her wings and make noise, but she knew it would do no good—the cage was secure. There was nothing to do but find out what would be happening next.

"Celebrate?" Ember asked.

"Of course! You are the ultimate emotional control for our people, Ember. For the good of our city, I want to help change and influence all our people to make correct decisions. Detecting their true emotional state is the first step. You are my new right hand, and the symbol of all we uphold. You will work with me, making sure that all decisions are perfect."

"Magistrate . . . I don't even have good personal emotional control. And, I know nothing about government decisions." Ember shuffled her feet and looked down, unwilling to meet the man's eyes.

The Magistrate reached out and took her hand. He patted it. "Not yet. Your ability will be developed. Soon you will be psychic."

Her skin crawled at Serpio's touch. She desperately wanted to free her hand, but he held it tightly. "I can't . . . be that. I only feel emotions. That's all." *At least he doesn't know about the dreams. He could take that to the next level. Although I don't understand them myself...*

"Ah, Ember, my dear. You can see a threat—and feel it— among the masses. With your power and my leadership, nothing evil or threatening can ever endanger our city." He began to rub her hand, and his eyes penetrated hers.

Ember felt Serpio's zeal like a force field. His deep ambition unnerved her. But more than that, the physical contact between his hand and hers caused an immediate change in his aura. The murky red that surrounded Serpio most of the time morphed into a bright red. *Oh my god. He's feeling* **desire.** Disgust surged through her, enough to cause a sour sickness in her stomach.

Somehow, she'd have to convince him that she wasn't able to do what he thought she could. And, honestly, she couldn't. She'd never had abilities like that. "I . . . umm . . . isn't that what the Alts are for? To root out people who don't fit here?"

Serpio dropped her hand, but instead, put his arm around her shoulders. "It's not enough, my dear. With you, we'll never have to worry about Alts being hacked. Or lies. You can easily detect those."

She squirmed inside; internally she seemed to be screaming. "Don't you think I'd love to see lies if I could? Believe me, I'd have had a use for—"

"Ember, Ember . . . You can't do this alone. You need help. And that's where I come in. I have big plans." He removed his arm from her shoulders only to turn her to face him. He put his hands on her shoulders and looked directly into her eyes, as if this act would make her accept what he had to say.

Ember felt she was a true prisoner. *I'm going to be in service to the Magistrate? I don't want this! I should feel honored, but I don't. I'm being used, and nothing will ever be the same.*

"But first, we introduce you to the entire city as our new

superpower. Tomorrow morning, from the Plauditorium, we we'll broadcast the good news to all of Tranquility. On every screen. On every street corner."

One more try... "Magistrate. That's quite an honor. But I don't like attention. I'm shy. With my . . . handicap, I can't have a lot of people around me."

"Nonsense. You're a gift. Time to let the world know." His words stirred with excitement. He smiled broadly, revealing some tiny age-related lines around his eyes. He panned the air with his hands. "You will need uniquely special clothing— something that sets you apart from every other citizen." He looked her up and down and then turned her around, akin to examining an unusual specimen under the microscope. "A golden gown with glittering shoes, yes. And then, a cloak of all the colors of Tranquility in velvets and satin. You will be above all in exquisite finery." The Magistrate's aura flared into green. Ember felt it fill her very lungs. Green was a serious warning sign. He was feeling excessive power. So scary.

"Pardon me, Magistrate, but this is too much. I—I'm concerned I'll disappoint you. Already I can see my Alt is showing my distress." Indeed, it was true, but Ember had to do more to talk the Magistrate out of his crazy idea. *If only I could use my abilities that way.* "I'd like to go home now, if I may. It's been an exhausting day."

"Ember. Of *course*. You'll need to go home to a well-deserved rest. I am aware all of your possessions are packed up already for your imminent move from Purple Vale. Tomorrow you'll return, and we'll move you into my official residence. I can't have you far from my side. My personal CommuteCar awaits outside to take you home. Nothing but the best for you from now on."

Ember felt like she was going to puke. *I must talk to Will! He needs to know what's happening!* "I appreciate your kindness, Magistrate. You are truly good. But I'd prefer one last oppor-tunity to be a part of my normal life. I need time for this to sink in. It would make me happiest if I could walk for a ways and then catch a CommuteCar of my own."

"As you wish, for now. Happiness is the most important thing. Tomorrow my private car will be at your abode to pick you up at ten. We have much to do." The Magistrate spoke to his Alt, and the door to the chamber opened. "Oh, by the way . . . after today your Alt will be a thing of the past." A Sciolist, who seemed to appear like magic, offered Ember his arm and escorted her to the exit.

Oh. Oh. Oh. Her head felt a rush as she stepped outside into the fresh air. The compressed quiet of the Solace Institute was her only comfort.

32

Xander's Plan

The flurry of another fight had energized Xander's group. Their new identity seemed to transform them as well. They were eager to get on with their adventure.

"Guys—let's get these uniforms off the Tranks. I'm gonna wear one, and Jasper, you wear the other." Never one for modesty, Xander stripped off his clothes, smiling in pleasure as he caught the eye of a few of the girls. He teased Jasper when he darted behind a tree to make the switch.

"Okay, Phoenix. Gather around. We need a plan." The group surrounded Xander, their respect evident in their acute attention. "We're goin' into the city. I don't know where this transport goes when it gets there. We take it to where we can get out, and then we've got to hide. We're outlaws and we'll be easily spotted once we arrive. This is gonna be a big gamble. We could be imprisoned or killed. So if you wanna leave, you know the way back to Camp."

A breeze blew through, stirring the dust. The crew stood firm.

"Once we have a proper hiding place, and we know we've been undetected, we're gonna try to get into the Plauditorium. Our goal is to take over the pulse of the city. Thanks to those stupid Tranks, we now have guns. No one will be expecting any intruders—we know that. But we have to take it one step at a time, and plot as we go. We've got no other options or anyone on whom we can depend on the inside."

Xander fielded a few questions, mostly concerning their ability to stay hidden. He tried to reassure his team, but it was going to be a crapshoot.

"Time to get in the back of the transport, folks. You're gonna be packed in there, but the journey shouldn't be long. Get your gear and say goodbye to The Outside. Our lives are gonna change, one way or the other."

The group picked up their things, talking animatedly among themselves and joking about the body odor they would create inside the vehicle, some threatening to fart on purpose. One of the crew, Gabriel, boasted he would be the first to board. Dropping his sack of supplies, he found an electronic panel that had a button. One touch and the door in the back of the carrier released and scrolled up. Immediately it was clear that the vehicle was not empty.

"Xander—we gotta take stuff out," he yelled.

"Well, do it. We need to get rolling," Xander called from up front.

Gabriel grabbed onto the end of a cylindrical package. The dark, opaque plastic was warm and moist to the touch, but was easy to grip. What gave him trouble was the weight. "C'mon, you all. I ain't doin' this by myself. Damn thing is like stone."

A few guys jumped up onto the platform and hauled out the first bundle, dropping it to the ground and going for another. There were two bales left, so they set to work.

Xander wanted them to hurry up. They needed to get back to Tranquility before the sunset. He knew the gates wouldn't open to them after dark. Suddenly, the thumping and grunting he heard a minute before was extinguished by a blunt silence. A woman's scream rang out. *Was there an attack? Another Trank? A Greelox?* Scurrying to the back, Xander pushed through the group gathered in a sloppy semicircle. His eyes fell on a waxy corpse, laying on the ground, its plastic cocoon unraveled.

"Get 'em all out," Xander directed with a slight shudder. "So we now know for sure. They were here to burn bodies. Tranquility is not at all what it claims to be, and we're gonna turn it upside down."

33

Will's Silver Lining

W ill craned his neck to see the door to the Solace Institute from his position outside the fence. He was hoping it wouldn't be long until Ember emerged. It was driving him crazy. *What is going on in there?* He gritted his teeth, wishing he could be doing something for her. A physical exam at Solace frequently did not end well. And after making the calls, he was now concerned about the city's safety—more than a Plauditor should. He would need to get answers but told himself that there had to be a reasonable explanation for each of his calls reaching a dead end—he just couldn't think of what it could be. And Ember was so innocent. He would have to figure out at least how to spin this inexplicable and appalling news in an upbeat way. His Alt and hers depended on finding the silver lining, no matter what. And he'd have to do all this without putting them in danger. Because the city was targeting him for the relationship, they would have to be extra careful. No one could know any of their meetings, and he decided to keep his visit to City Hall a secret from her. She had enough to worry about.

At last he saw her emerge from the building. She stood there for a moment as if she were lost, trying to get her bearings, and then stepped off the stoop. He whistled to get her attention, hoping it would penetrate the corral of silence, but her head didn't turn in his direction. Time to get within eyesight. He looked around and hoped for camouflage. He loped over to where the gate would let her out. As she saw him waiting there, she stumbled a bit before unlatching the gate. "Oh, Will! You're here!"

Will hugged her tightly. "Are you kidding? It's been so difficult not to worry! How are you? What'd they say?" The words spilled out in a rush.

Will felt Ember wilt in his arms. She broke away and met his eyes. "I'll tell you, but when I do, you need to be prepared. You're going to be shocked."

"Shocked? You're not dying, are you?" His heart leaped to his throat, the pulse threatening to push out his neck.

"No, no Will." She hugged him again, quickly, before continuing. "I—I have a . . . condition. I've had it all my life. I've kept it hidden. It's weird. Baffling. I've always felt freakish. I didn't think it was wise to tell anyone. Not even my mom knew."

Will listened as Ember then revealed her secret and what she experienced every day. *An Empath? I've never heard of something so bizarre. No wonder she didn't want anyone to know! She's amazing, though, to be able to keep that private. That takes real strength. I wonder if being an Empath is what caused her fainting spell at the Plauditorium . . .*

". . . and now that they know, I'm to be some sort of mascot or secret weapon. I have to live with the Magistrate, starting tomorrow!" Her face was flushed, and her brows knitted in a knot of dread.

Will felt as if he was on an airplane spinning out of control, ready to implode upon impact. *Live with the Magistrate!* His Alt vibrated and lit up, signaling a major emotional dive. Severe enough, and he could be suspended as a Plauditor. *Think. Concentrate.* He compelled himself to think only about Ember. His sympathy and compassion would bring his Alt back into line.

"Ember, I'm so sorry." Will grabbed Ember's shoulders and turned her to face him. "You are stronger than you know, and I'm already thinking about ways I can help." There was always a silver lining.

"I'm going to be a prisoner, Will! This can't be good in any way."

"Shh. Don't say that out loud! The Magistrate will expect your loyalty, and his decision not to punish you hangs in the balance. And, listen. Because of what I found out today, this can be an advantage."

Will described the Alt calls briefly, watching Ember's eyes grow wide with astonishment. She said, "It's . . . bizarre. No one else seems to be poking around like we are, either. It—it—seems death's just been accepted, and that's it. Otherwise, their Alt scores would be at stake."

"Yeah. We gotta find out what's going on! But now, you're going to be *inside*. You can find out everything we need to know."

Ember squared her shoulders. He had been amazed that she had shed no tears, and now she looked resolute. He could see raw grit in her eyes. Secret weapon, indeed.

Journal Entry #5592

Nothing sensitive about our citizens is ever transmitted electronically. So when I receive a note delivered by a Sciolist I take it seriously. An anonymous source placed it on the Elite's docket for review. They have determined some allegations to be a real concern. I have been furious about it all day. One of our most esteemed Plauditors has been visiting Augur Prize recipients. The reason for these visits is unknown, but not for long. Will Verus will need more counseling or Purging. He has already been corrected for his relationship with Ember Vinata and now he looks like a traitor to the City. Will Verus has become a problem.

— Serpio Magnus, Magistrate

34

Ember's Dilemma

E mber was afraid. She couldn't imagine what she would have to give up or do. Would she still be able to see Will? Her biggest concern was about her privacy. Would she have her own bedroom or . . .? She shivered, and Will put his arm around her.

She knew Will was right. It put her in the perfect position to find out what was going on. She had to look on the bright side.

Will asked, "How long do you have before you have to report in?"

"Tomorrow, I go."

"We're gonna be together every minute until then, Ember. We have all night. And you probably know how I'm feeling about that, right?" Will winked at her, and Ember's blood turned to lava. *Good thing he can't read* my *emotions. He might very well catch on fire.* She laughed softly and smiled at him, dreaming about the possibilities.

"I'd love to just go somewhere and be alone with you, Will. I want you to know that." She reached out and put her hands on his arms. "But I'll probably be cut off from you after today. We should spend our time as detectives instead—get a game plan." Disappointment streamed through her. And she didn't need her empathic ability to know how Will would be feeling at her remark.

He clasped his hands tightly over his head and then released them "Okay. Ugh! So bummed! Just hoping to make today about us. But, you're right." Will glanced down at his Alt and then shook his head in disgust. He had taken a hit.

"Let's talk. Plan. And then, maybe . . . ?" She caught his eye and gave him a meaningful look.

"Yeah. We better get planning then." He winked at her and then looked away. He put his hands in his pockets, as if to keep himself from touching her. Taking a deep breath, he began to pace in short steps. "We've got to figure this out. Before you're incommunicado. And before someone else dies. It's life or death. And us . . . well, you and I . . . we're together, no matter what."

Ember smiled up at him, his words settling into her heart like a downy blanket. She was still tempted to just push everything aside and just be with Will. Suddenly Ember's eyes went wide. "Shazz! The Magistrate asked me in my first interview if I felt anything weird happened to me when I had my mom's ring. I didn't—not until I was at the Plauditorium and I felt faint. I had the ring with me! The exam today didn't uncover anything about that, but what if it was the ring making me feel sick? It was in my pocket . . ."

"Right. Next. To. Your. Heart." Will's voice quavered as a troublesome possibility hit him. "The rings have something wrong with them! They're causing illness—and death—and City Hall wants to cover it all up."

"But why cover it up? Why not recall the rings if they're harmful?" Ember felt more confused than ever. This had to be an accident, of course. But dread wound its way through her throat like a python, squeezing the air from her lungs. "They're supposed to protect all of us here, but this isn't protection—it's murder! Oh, Will! My mother was killed because she wore her ring!" She grabbed onto Will, her nails digging pits into his arms. "My mother was trying to talk to me at the end. She was telling me not to wear something! It has to be the ring she was talking about. How could we not see this before?"

Will said, "Slow down. Let's not think the worst. This has got to be a mistake—a coincidence. A murder—much less more than one—would never happen here, Ember!" He paced back and forth, his Alt vibrating with every step.

"You're right, Will. I'm overreacting." She reached out and grabbed his arm, pulling him to a standstill.

"Someone who makes these rings is using something toxic, and they don't even know it! The city is probably investigating it, and that's why you didn't get any answers. That's got to be it." Will's loyalty to the city was still true blue, and right now, that's how his aura looked. "We could figure out the problem, and the Magistrate will be so grateful!"

"Shoot, Will. We can help fix the problem." She licked her lips nervously. "But, babe, I don't know where the rings are made, do you?"

"Yeah, I do. South side of the city in the manufacturing district. Right nearby where the Level Two's live." Will tilted his Alt to speak into its face. "Give me the name and address of the jeweler on the South Side."

"That would be Nemo Enterprises, Will," the Alt replied. "1500 Amity Avenue. Shall I call a CommuteCar?"

"Yes, thanks," Will said. He turned to Ember. "For, um, appearances, you might want to take a Level Eight."

Ember shot him a dubious look, seeing a wave of his unease flaring out in a shadowy curve around his head. *I hope he knows what he's doing.* "We're taking separate cars?"

"It's going to seem more normal, our not being in the same car," he replied.

"But we're going to the same place," she argued.

"Appearances are everything, Ember. Trust me."

She shrugged her shoulders. "Okay, but I don't understand why we can't just go there together."

"You'll arrive after me, of course. I'll wait for you outside."

She nodded her head, forcing a smile. Will was acting weird. She absorbed his nervousness, and it caused a mirror reaction in her. A rush of jitters rippled down her spine and seemed to detonate in her tailbone.

Two seconds later, the CommuteCars pulled up and there was no more time for conversation.

⁓

THE SIGN for Nemo Enterprises rose up on the left, its candy pink neon letters lit in a flashy display.

She wished she felt as confident as Will looked as she joined him at a medieval-looking ivory-colored door. The shop was definitely a Level Two establishment. Ember commented aloud. "The Elite must want to keep this low-key. A Level Two neighborhood? For these rings?"

The sign in the beveled glass window advertised jewelry, trophies, and Status accessories, but no one of any higher Status would ever come into this neighborhood to shop.

Will appeared suddenly his old self. "Now I can be an All-Star Plauditor. See how well the rings are made," Will joked. "It shouldn't be a stretch for them to show me around." He opened the door, a computerized chime announcing their entry.

Inside, the foyer sparkled with rhinestone walls. A marble desk of white and gray almost completely hid a dwarfish man behind it. With his white hair and scraggly beard, her reminded Ember of a gnome.

"Hello! Renner Fide, here. How may I help you today?" The pint-sized proprietor raised his arm in greeting.

Will returned the customary greeting. "Hello. I'm Will Verus. I'm a Plauditor. This is my friend, Ember."

Across the desk, Will whispered in Renner's ear. "Look, I'm hoping you can help me impress this girl. You know how it is."

"Oh, well . . . sure . . . we just have to be secure," Renner whispered back.

"Just checking up to see if the city can help you in any way," Will said, his voice now full of a confident authority.

"I'm doing well here—busy as I can possibly be. Between the orders for the city and personal items for Status, I'm afraid I don't have time for a tour. But I can answer any questions you might have."

"Ah, well. I'm disappointed, but perhaps we can just see your most important commission. You make the rings here for the city, is that right? Perhaps we could just have a look at the ones for the next ceremony?"

The clerk seemed to puff up with pride. "Our very special requisition. Of course. And since you work for the city, I could give you a little sneak peek. We're proud of our rings. And, it just so happens, it's no trouble. I have the latest ones right here." Renner leaned down just a bit and pulled out a tray from behind the desk. The rings sparkled as if they had divine light.

"Those are beautiful!" Ember gushed. "What a thrill to see them all together!"

"Incredible workmanship," Will agreed as his eyes scanned the tray. He hesitated and then said, "But there are only thirteen rings here. Are you still making the other five?"

"No. All the rings are complete. We always send the higher-level rings right out to the city since they're priceless. The Elite don't want the rings for those levels at risk—they're more valuable so they go to be kept in the safe at City Hall. Once they go, no one else sees them again until the ceremony."

"Ah. So they go straight to a safe, then?"

"Yes, and these other rings will follow, closer to the ceremony."

"Thank you, Renner. You seem to have an understanding of how important your work is. I appreciate your sharing and talking with me today. If I can ever be at your service . . ."

"Are you sure I can't interest you in any other rings today?" Renner said, a twinkle in his eye.

Will chuckled and glanced at Ember, returning his attention to Renner, whose expectant look was quite comical under the circumstances. "No, sir. I don't think my girlfriend here is quite ready for a commitment."

The man's face fell. "Well, remember me when you need something special."

Ember observed that a camera filmed and recorded the entire conversation in case of any security breach. An electronic bell signaled their exit from the shop.

Once outside, Ember asked, "Will, won't City Hall know we visited the store? You know better than anyone—Plauditors are watching our every move."

"City Hall won't receive any reports unless some Plauditor wonders why I was visiting the jeweler. Just like Renner, they're gonna think we were shopping for engagement rings or something." He gave her a wink.

For Ember, the wink delivered a warm, fuzzy buzz. "Good."

Will's aura shifted. Ember picked up underlying emotional pain. It hurt her. *He's struggling with something, but it's not the cameras. Change the subject.* "Weren't the rings beautiful? All the different stones and craftsmanship! Amazing!"

"Agree—but the upper Status rings weren't there. Remember, the people who are dying have been wearing *those*. Something is happening to those rings *after* they've left Nemo Enterprises."

Ah, maybe that's what he's grappling with. It's really affecting him, she mused.

Ember said, "I'll bet they're in a safe. But they're in that safe because they have a poison or a drug or something."

"When you get close to the Magistrate, you need to find out. Then we should get hold of one of the rings. That's the only way we'll know for certain."

"Whatever I need to do, I'll do." Her inner core seemed to tighten with a single-minded determination. She would do more than try. She would make a mark.

35

Will's Choice

The uncomfortable meeting with Winslow had been weighing heavily on Will's mind. Even as he investigated the rings, he was torn. City Hall would *never* approve of his illicit relationship with Ember. It was doomed. Plus, if he continued to date her, all he had built —all his goodness—could be brought to an end. He would certainly be removed as a Plauditor if he continued to see her. From there, he would be counseled and then even sent to the Outside for his defiance.

Bottom line—he would have to break it off. His insides turned upside down as he thought about the pain this would cause them both. The struggle to stay happy about it would be a Herculean challenge, but in the long run, he was doing the right thing. The secret quest they had been on together was nothing Ember was in a position to fix, especially now that she was under the Magistrate's control. It would have to be him, and he would need to do it alone.

His eyes suddenly glistened with spontaneous, careless tears. Unacceptable. He checked his Alt. *Shazz!* The downward flashing arrows were pulsing, and the dive would continue if he couldn't put a positive spin on all this! *Hmm. Okay, new mindset: I'll be doing both of us a favor,* he thought. *In fact, I'm doing the heroic, chivalrous thing for her, and also keeping myself in the game. Good. I **can** be happy about this—the relationship is just too complicated.* He let the positive thoughts wash over him from the inside out, until an actual smile lit on his lips. It would be all right.

Winslow was right to have talked to him. This relationship was poison—would definitely lead to unhappiness. It had taken him a while to look at the big picture, so blinded had he been by his attraction to her and by all the events that had happened since, but now he realized the obvious.

It was an easy "out." Ember would be taken away, and it would keep him whole. He'd have to just forget about her, and yet still somehow solve the mysteries of the rings. She had become far too dependent on him; she needed to develop her inner strength. Because of this alone, he should no longer be involved with her. He would have to tell her that today would be the last time they could be together.

"Sorry about the separate CommuteCars, Ember. I know you can't really understand."

"What? You don't think I know how dangerous this is?" She threw her arms out to emphasize her words. "Someone at City Hall discovering our investigations? That's all I can think about!"

"Stay calm. We have to be *cheerful,* Ember, no matter what. Already I know our concern triggers low readings of our Alts. It will be noticed and logged. We're nervous about being discovered and we're freaked out over the rings. We have to put it all in proper perspective, or we're gonna be on the radar." He wanted to sound positive, but his voice squeaked out, strained.

Ember said, "Tomorrow I'll be with the Magistrate, so I don't think my mood matters. He's interested in my abilities, not my happiness."

Her shoulders slumped, and her face seemed to gray in

the afternoon light. He wanted to scream from the frustration of the challenges, the alien emotions, and the injustice.

"Your happiness does matter!" He impulsively put his arm around her shoulders and squeezed. "What do you say we go somewhere private? In all this crap we've been through—you've been through—we need to have some time just for ourselves. First the plan, and then us, right?"

He watched her face color pink and then transform as if it were illuminated from within. "I would love that," she said. Her words came out sounding like a summer breeze.

It was hard to resist her. He reached up to touch the hair that had fallen across her face. *Stop. Not now. Not here.*

Where to go? he thought. They couldn't go to his place or hers. They needed to go somewhere the all-seeing cameras wouldn't easily pick them up, a populated place where they were just random people in a crowd.

Maybe at one of the Maglev Monorail stops. The epiphany made sense. Known as the "M," the public high-speed elevated train ran on massive magnets. It generated an electromagnetic field to hold the monorail on its tracks. Dense, flowery hedges near the rails surrounded it. Not exactly the most romantic place, which was optimal. And, no one would find it odd if they were both discovered in the same general vicinity. Often the magnetic fields threw the Alt's GPS off entirely without disturbing the collection of happiness points.

Afterward, it would be easy to melt into the crowd. They could both take the "M" home. They would board separately. His more luxurious Status Twelve area in the front of the train and her simpler Level Eight toward the back would further disconnect them. Nothing would look abnormal.

"Ember, call up your CommuteCar again and meet me at the M's Cloud Nine stop."

"The 'M'?" Her eyes searched his face, as if looking for a more sensible answer.

"No one can track us when we're there, Ember."

"Of course. You're right. Good call." She winked at him and patted his arm playfully. He groaned inwardly.

Like before, when they met at Nemo's, Will waited until Ember's car picked her up before ordering up his own. It gave him time to pull his mood up further and distance himself from her physically so no one would question a simultaneous arrival. Now, just to stay the course.

ON HIS WAY TO THE "M" Will's mind whirred. He used everything in his power—all his training—to elevate his mood. He was seldom, if ever, unable to bring up his points. He could do it. This time was no exception. He thought about how lucky he was and concentrated on happier moments.

The "M" was one of those moments. When he was last at the "M" was the very reason why he had been promoted to Level Twelve. He let his memory fall back to that day . . .

IT HAD BEEN JUST an ordinary day, a day he took a simple walking shortcut home when he became an unexpected hero. Always hyper-aware of his surroundings, he gasped as he rounded the bend. What he saw about ten feet away from the walking path seized the breath in his chest. A fair-skinned, dark-haired boy about twelve was poised to throw a Frisbee from the top of the Bird's Eye Pass Bridge to a group of kids standing beneath.

The "M" system ran along this ridge at a high speed, and signs were posted to warn pedestrians anywhere near the tracks.

*How did that kid get **up** there? Will thought. A feeling of dread overwhelmed him, the tingle going down through his toes. As he watched the young boy dance on top of the bridge, Will realized that the kid had probably used the bridge's abutment sculptures to climb up there. Tranquility prided itself on artistic structures, and the bridge was no excep-*

tion. *A series of steel, colorful shapes arranged in a vertical pattern, rose up on either side of the bridge. Climbing the shapes like a jungle gym would be an intriguing challenge for a boy trying to prove himself. It was a risky escapade, most likely fueled by his friends' encouragement. The boy was too busy proving himself to understand how much he was putting his life at risk.*

"Hey, stop, kid! Stop! Get down!" Will yelled. *Will looked at his Alt: 2:10 p.m. The monorail would be flying by in mere minutes.*

Without any acknowledgement of Will, the boy shouted, teasing, "Who's gonna catch it? Successful catch—big Alt numbers!"

With glee, the children below screamed as the Frisbee was released and sailed down through the air to the lucky one who could jump the highest to capture it.

What sounded like an earthquake suddenly caught the attention of the little show-off on the bridge. He instantly froze. Will heard it, too—the unmistakable rumble of the Monorail making its way down the track from the south. There was nowhere for the kid to go; jumping off the bridge was out of the question. He saw the lights of the train; its horn blared. Will's mind whirred. Less than three minutes and the kid would be dead.

Will shoved through the now-screaming kids, rushing over to the northern end of the bridge's concrete support pillar. Grab the first structure. Climb. No . . . he slipped! Refocus. Climb faster! Grab the guardrail —pull up! Run!

The Monorail was in sight. Its horn blared. Eighteen seconds. The kid shrieked. Will jerked the boy off his feet by his waist. "Got ya!" *Dropping the boy over the guardrail, he commanded,* "Hold on to that square, kid!"

Eight seconds. . . the train would be upon him, too. Will vaulted over a two-foot divider on the parapet and hung on with his arms once again to the outside guardrail of the bridge. The monorail raced by, out of sight in the blink of an eye.

A deep breath, and Will carefully lowered himself down to where the boy was still hanging on, white-knuckled, to a decorative yellow square sculpture. Crying tears of terror and remorse, the boy grabbed onto

Will's shirt and put his face into his chest. "Oooooh," *the youngster moaned.*

"You okay, kid?" *Will asked in a strained voice.*

"I'm okay . . . yeah . . ." *He blinked, still in shock.*

"C'mon. I know you're shook up, but we've got to get back down."

Will helped the boy, step by step, cautiously navigate down the geometric gauntlet to the concrete sidewalk below.

Simultaneously now jabbering, the kid's audience of friends erupted, jumping all over them, finally forming a haphazard circle around the victim and his savior.

A trio of male friends high-fived the boy, their faces unwinding like the release of a too-tight spring. Two highly hysterical girls were crying—tears of joy or fear, Will couldn't tell.

"Hey, now. We're all safe. But, what's your name, Frisbee King?"

"I'm Jesse. I live in Orange Glen. Who are you, mister?"

"I'm Will. So glad I was nearby. We were both lucky today. But now, I'm going to make sure you get home. And, I'm going to tell your parents about what happened here today." *Will wiped the sweat off his brow with his hand. Realizing it too late, Will looked at his hands, dirty from the ordeal, and knew his face was now streaked with grime. His shirt, too, was torn. Will imagined he looked like a filthy rag doll that had seen better days.*

Jesse shook his head. "Thanks for coming to get me." *Another tear leaked out of Jesse's eye.*

"Yeah, well . . . let's go. You need some rest—after your parents' lecture, that is." *Will winked.*

As they walked away down the path, leaving Jesse's friends behind, Will felt his Alt vibrate. Glancing down, he saw it reflect a powerful upturn in points. The Alt's numbers registered like a casino's slot jackpot. The Alt was posting points that dramatically exceeded his current status! He wryly smiled at the Alt's acknowledgement of his emotional outpouring of strength today but had no complete idea what the leveling up entailed.

It wasn't that Will didn't appreciate the points, but what made him feel on top of the world was the opportunity to unselfishly help another person in distress. He felt amazing in spite of what he had been through. Exhausted, but also totally euphoric, he felt more fulfilled than by anything he had ever done in his life.

As if in answer, his Alt actually began to glow. A dim light within the face of his Alt increasingly became brighter and brighter. Looking down, Will gasped. The Alt's luminescence was radiant. This was new and mysterious, but certainly something significant had happened to his Status.

Will walked the rest of the way to Jesse's house, where he gave him up to a relieved and thankful set of parents.

~

A DAY later the story hit the Tranquility News, and the rest was history. The memory brought a broad smile to his face. What an opportunity he'd been given. He was sure he was doing the right thing by letting Ember go. He needed to be on his own and follow the laws of his city. Too much depended on it.

36

Ember's Rendezvous

Ember arrived at the jam-packed Cloud Nine station as the late afternoon sun dropped behind the horizon. Her attention, though, was drawn to the colorful surroundings of the site. This was where the Bird's Eye Pass Bridge rose up from the park trails below. The "M" whooshed by, fifty feet from the waiting area at the top of the bridge. Sections of brightly hued chairs lined the perimeter of the area, grouped by color, so those with higher Status sat furthest away from the Maglev. Ember stood in the center. The plaza was a monument to color; the abundance of vines, flowers, and fluffy hedges beckoned with their beauty. Blooms perfumed the air. It would be at least a beautiful place to meet Will. Not only gorgeous, but romantic as well, especially as the sunset streaked the sky with color.

Her eyes scanned the crowd for him. It was a while before she saw his yellow CommuteCar pull up to the curb, where she saw Will exit his ride. Her insides always responded like a wax candle, both burning brightly and melting at the same time. The real joy in her life. Her Alt buzzed, and she checked its face. Her points were soaring in her anticipation of spending time alone with Will.

Even from a distance, she observed that his aura had changed since she had seen him just minutes earlier. Puzzling. It appeared in rainbow waves, but some flashed murky, some vibrant. She thought maybe he was just nervous about a private time alone. After all, they had never had the opportunity. She nourished a growing eagerness in her own heart. Her pupils widened as he approached, and her breath came in short bursts. Warmth spread through her body. The place wasn't secluded enough for what she longed for, but at least the flora would provide a partial privacy screen.

Will approached, and again, his aura changed. His feelings were up, then down—a random bouquet. She gathered up his emotions—concern first, then the typical welcoming ardor and kindness. Yet, Will was nervous, too. He approached her, and quickly grabbed her arm without even a "hello."

"Will, are we in a hurry?" She didn't know what else to think. This was going strangely.

"We're in a hurry to find some camouflage."

"Oh. Sure. I'm just thrilled we can spend some time together," Ember replied.

"Me too. C'mon," he urged.

Am I blushing? She put her hands up to her face and felt its heat. *I **am** blushing!* she thought.

She noticed a little twitch in the corner of his right eye, proof of the jittery energy emanating from him.

His aura now glittered with determined tones of red. She smiled, knowing now, for sure, he was anxious to wrap his arms around her. Wherever and whenever they were together, her happiness would soar.

He pulled her along, dodging people milling about the area. Some Tranks waiting in line to board the "M" glanced their way and wished them a "good day" to score more Alt points, and some, immersed in their own daily routine or examining their Alts, were like tangible ghosts. They'd never remember ever seeing them. Some faces lit up with recognition as Will walked by, obviously recognizing him from his recent heroics. Several turned their way, as if to flag him down. Will kept striding through the crowd, where they could disappear in an anonymous gulf. Blending in was the best way to disguise their whereabouts.

They headed over close to the bridge. Ember looked down in awe.

"Isn't this where you saved that kid?"

"The very place."

"Can you show me how you climbed up?"

"Sometime. Not today. Today I have an agenda." His voice was thick.

Will is sure impatient, she thought. She didn't know whether to be excited or not. He was intense.

"When we leave, we both take the 'M' home, okay? We need to separate," Will said.

"Got it."

In a couple of minutes, Will guided Ember toward the station's most lushly landscaped area. Night-blooming Jasmine and nine-foot lush, tropical hibiscus made it a garden paradise. He parted some bushes, pulling Ember inside. It seemed suddenly they were in their own mini room, cut off from the rest of the world. The rumble of the Monorail streaking by and the murmur of the crowd outside the zone were the only reminders that they were not completely alone. The space seemed made just for them. About four by four, it was shaded from the sun, save one narrow shaft of sunlight that illuminated Will's face and shimmered in his hair.

Just as Ember had hoped, Will immediately gathered her to him in a tight embrace. She felt consumed by his emotions; love and contentment streamed from his inner soul, infecting her. He leaned in and kissed her—a deep and urgent kiss. She buzzed from head to toe, her legs threatening to give out from under her.

He broke the kiss when both of their Alts vibrated at once. A cascade of electronic bells signaled an upsurge in points. First Ember, and then Will, burst out laughing. Ember had never been so happy.

"So that's how you make extra points, then?" Ember asked when her giggles subsided. "Those are the easiest points I ever made!"

"Yeah," Will said, still breathless.

Ember reached out to Will to draw him close to her again, but Will gently pushed her back. He gazed down at her, his face suddenly somber. His green eyes were mesmerizing as always, but there was something odd in them, like a cloud that had passed in front of the sun. They brimmed with conflict. His aura, so dynamic a minute ago, waned and changed from a vibrant blue to a fish-scale gray. He bit his lip, and shuffled his feet, as if he was balancing on a ship at high sea.

"Will?" Ember felt a quiver in her fingers that echoed her worry. "Something's wrong. I see it and feel it." She drew in a ragged breath.

Dropping his gaze, he stepped even further apart from her. "Look, Ember." He made eye contact again, but she could tell it was an effort. "You know I care for you . . . deeply." *His vocal tones are guarded, odd.* "You've meant so much to me. But, we have to stop seeing each other. Especially now with these strong feelings. And what we know about—everything. It's a massive risk for me—and for you. I have to protect you."

"I know it seems impossible, this thing with the Magistrate. But I think we'll find an answer. *You'll* find a way out. I've been trusting you, I—"

"Ember! *There is no way out!*" Will's voice split the air. "Not right now. What's happening is bigger than we are, and I don't know how to solve any of it. Or if we can. We *have* to break up, Ember."

Ember gasped, her mouth dropping in shock. *I can't believe what I'm hearing.* Her knees buckled and she swayed. Reaching for his arm, she grabbed it to steady herself. She opened her mouth to protest further, but her throat constricted, as if trying to grip the lump that was forming there. She swallowed hard and pushed her voice to the surface. "Will! No! There's got to be something we can do."

"Our relationship's *forbidden*, Ember, and it's gonna lead to real, legit sorrow. I never should have invited you out . . . or anything. That was my mistake. My weakness. And now that you'll be with the Magistrate, and I can't even see you . . . well, it's coming to a natural end anyway." He forced a smile, but it was feeble, joyless. "But I needed to see you alone—just the two of us—one last time."

He can't be serious about this. He CAN'T!

"And what about my mom? The rings? Everything we've found out? You're giving up?" Her words were demanding, pointed, like the edges of broken glass. She hardly knew what to do. Frustration and despair formed a bomb, blowing her heart apart. Her Alt vibrated and chimed again, but this time she knew it was crashing.

Will ran his hands through his hair, as if her questions exasperated him. "No, I'm not giving up, but I'll solve it on my own. It's going to take time, though. A long time. That's why I have to let you go. I'm so sorry, Ember. I really am. You have to believe me. This is for the best."

Don't cry. Don't! But she couldn't help herself. One tear glimmered on her lashes and then the rest broke free like the downpour of a summer storm. Will reached out to wipe them away. She jerked her head away, avoiding his touch.

"Be happy, Ember." Will's voice cracked. "That's what I want."

He spun around and tore through the foliage. Leaving Ember behind. Alone.

37

Xander's Decisions

Xander didn't know quite what to do with the bound-up bodies from the transport. The men who had driven the truck had to be disposed of as well. Should they just leave them lying out in the open? Should they burn them? Bury them? The crew was waiting. He had to make a decision.

"Throw the death-driver Tranks on the fire, gang. We want no trace of those guys left at all. As for the other corpses, leave 'em. We want no part of doing body disposal for the city. We know only too well there are Greelox out here. Leave 'em for them."

Last to board the vehicle, Gabriel and Bixby together tossed the men's bodies on the fire, standing there a moment more to watch the flames wrap around the ill-fated forms. They jumped into the back, pressed the button on the inside to lower the door, and the death wagon rolled away from the scene.

A couple of hours later, their conscripted "bus" arrived at the back entrance of the city.

A Level Ten attendant outside the gate gave a Tranquility salute to Xander and pressed the button allowing the electronic gate to open. Xander drove through. Too easy. So far, the transport had navigated its way back to the city gates on its own. There was no reason why it wouldn't continue all the way back to its original destination.

"Look. There's a small road off to the left in those trees. We're probably headed there." They veered to the left, taking a tiny street that looked as if it were an alley, but after a tenth of a mile it led into an area so thick with vegetation it created a feeling of night. They rode deeper into the enclave. They finally passed a sign that said, "Authorized Access."

Xander's adrenaline was kicking in. Getting back into the city was a bona fide victory, and he was excited. And nervous. The whole mission would rest on whether they could pull this off without being discovered, especially with the others in the back. If they were stopped or discovered, he knew there would be no more banishment to The Outside. They would be executed.

Up ahead he saw a building the same color as the truck— a dusty tan. Foliage partly hid the structure, but it was obviously a type of garage. Their vehicle pulled up to the front and the mega door opened, revealing a spot for the transport, right next to an identical carrier.

Their vehicle's doors opened.

"Jasper, stay calm. Act like this is no big deal." Xander whispered before exiting. He then moved with an affected laziness, even stretching once his feet were outside the vehicle.

Jasper followed suit. "Glad to be back. Another successful trip." Xander looked around the garage. It appeared that not only was this area for the vehicles to park, there was a large, sturdy table standing in the "third car" space. On the walls hung rolls of tape, rope, and spools of plastic sheeting. Zip ties lay in a plastic tray. Colorful and diverse in length, they appeared weirdly festive in the morbid environment. *So, this is where they get the bodies ready…right before they put them in the truck. These supplies are gonna be perfect for what we need.*

They both looked around. There seemed to be no one there to welcome them. Xander imagined there would be surveillance cameras, but had no idea where they would be or who would be monitoring this bizarre type of activity. It wouldn't be the Plauditors' responsibility—not this kind of top-secret operation.

Nothing to do but try to be quiet; he had to let his team out of the back. It was already dark outside. The interior of the garage was not yet lit, but he knew it was only a matter of time until some lights went on for nighttime security.

"Jasper, we've gotta open the back. Now." Xander scurried around the vehicle and discharged the door's mechanism. The door rolled up.

"Hey. You all get out—fast." Xander kept his voice to a whisper. "No noise. Hurry." Xander said.

One by one, the REMs dropped down and lined up behind the truck. *So far, so good.*

A squeak and a rustle. *Shazz!* Xander's ears would have stood up had he been a dog. He strode back to the front of the transport to be ready for anything.

A female voice cracked their comfort zone. "You're back early. Wasn't expecting you 'til nine. You must be gettin' good at this."

Xander leaned nonchalantly against the hood. "Well, it doesn't take long to do the job," he quipped. He radiated his most charming smile. "Happy to be working for our fine city."

The blonde sashayed to within three feet of him and narrowed her eyes. "I don't recognize you. You new?"

"Yeah, yeah. Just started. Guess I'm gonna be able to handle this just fine."

"You think so? An hour early will be questionable at City Hall. I'm Shelly, by the way." She gave him the Tranquility salute.

"Xander." He threw his arm up with his finger extended to respond correctly. Jasper walked around from the back.

"And this is Jasper. Look, Shelly, can we just keep this early arrival between us? I just started this job, and I don't want to get questioned. I can trust you, right?"

If he wasn't mistaken, he thought he caught a flirtatious wink aimed Jasper's way. He felt a little deflated.

"Hope so. Have a good night."

One of the REMs hidden behind the vehicle shifted, creating a light scuffle. She stopped again as she was halfway to the door and turned. "Is there something going on here?"

Jasper affected a forward faint on the hood. "Ah…you caught me," he said with his face to the metal. "I saw that wink, you know. Sort of bowled me over."

She laughed. "Keep that emotion, and your Alt will thank you. Catch you later." She was out the door with a sassy wave.

"Shazz!" Xander wiped his brow. "Good work, Jasper. She was into you. Sorry it won't work out." Xander grinned.

"Up yours, Xander."

"C'mon, guys. We need to leave. We can't risk being in here if another Trank comes in. Once we get outside, the bushes and trees'll camouflage us. We sleep for a while and get up before dawn. It has to be totally dark when we make our way to the interior of the city."

Xander looked around the garage. "Jasper—help me grab a couple rolls of tape and rope. Bixby—grab most of those zip ties, and zip tie them together. Put them in your bags. It's a jackpot."

One of the girls, who was always crushing on Xander, pressed up against him as they maneuvered outside. "What's the plan, Xan?" she whispered.

"We're goin' to the Plauditorium. That's where everything that City Hall wants its citizens to know gets broadcast. Our citizens need to know what we discovered, don't you think?"

38

Will's Disclosure

William knew he was walking a thin line. His emotions were all over the place, like a pinball machine gone mad. He had to get a handle on himself. The guilt alone was eating him alive. Soon his Alt would be his enemy, sucking him down into an endless drain. City Hall would be questioning him, counseling him. He had to act.

Will headed to the Fun Zone. By then it was getting late—past ten—but he had to get his thoughts off all he had discovered about the rings and his permanent separation from Ember. In spite of his iron core, his Alt numbers had been slipping, point by point, since they said goodbye. He had to get his mind and heart back in the right gear.

He called Wee and asked him to meet him at the Sugar Shack inside the park. He needed to update his buddy about all that had happened, and Wee always was the best one to give advice. He grinned as he saw his friend round the corner.

"Wee—buddy! Glad you could be here!"

"Yeah. Where you been keepin' yourself?" Wee ran up and gave Will a bro hug.

"Still sorting some things out. You won't believe what's

been goin' on." Will hoped his eyes didn't look as wild as he felt.

"You got the girl still? Or was the apology too late?"

"A lot's happened. We were good. We had something. Something great. But, I'm not gonna get to see her anymore. City Hall knows about us. I broke it off tonight." Will ran his fingers through his hair.

"Whoa, Will. I'm sorry." Wee reached out and gave Will's arm a pat.

"And that's not all. The Magistrate's taking her. She has to go live in his mansion."

"Shazz! Why?"

"It's a long, complicated story. Most of it you won't believe. I'll give you the highlights. But I have to get straight. I've got an Alt crisis going on."

Wee put his hand on Will's shoulder. "You? In an Alt crisis? Man—I didn't expect that. I'm here to listen. But, I'm gonna lighten you up, too. I imagine that's why we're here?"

Will shook his head emphatically. "Thanks, brother."

The lights in the park twinkled against the night sky. A slight drizzle—the start of the nightly rain—caused Wee's hair to crinkle into even tighter curls, a side effect he good-naturedly joked about with Will. The easy banter already soothed Will's broken spirit as they wandered to the most popular ride in the park, the Turbo Tunnel, where a spinning tube with music, images, and scents, gave visitors a rush of pleasurable endorphins.

They took their spin, although Will's ride was eight minutes longer and more thrilling due to his Status. Both tumbled out, laughing, at the end. They compared their Alt readings, where Will's Alt bested Wee's by ten points. *I'm back up—at least for the hour ahead.*

They grabbed some Jarnish and frosty lemonade at the food stand where Will gave his friend all the harsh details since their last visit.

"So, you actually think people are being killed—on purpose?" Wee stopped between bites. "I mean, c'mon, man!"

"I didn't believe it either, but it's all pointing that way. Why else would all those people be gone? And, more than that, I don't want something to happen to Ember. I just know she's in danger."

"Is she able to find out anything from being with the Magistrate?"

"I told her to, but she'll be watched closely. And, it doesn't matter. I can't see her anyway."

"Look. It's good you're not seeing her anymore. You can't be doing that. But even if you've ended the relationship, you have to get her out—somehow. Who else is gonna do that? And you've got to have help. That would be where I come in." Wee puffed out his chest and pointed to himself, as if he'd just decided to become Superman.

"Yeah. I know. But it's too risky. They're already watching me. That's one reason I broke things off. That, and I don't want to lose my job. I'm a *Plauditor*, ya know? I need to focus on just getting over her and then try to work through the other stuff."

"The *other* stuff? Frik, Will. Getting her freed from the Magistrate is the right thing to do. And, yeah, you're a Plauditor. But aren't you some sort of *hero*? You're good at saving people, remember? Happiness is about doing the ultimate good. Ya don't have to *date* her, but you do have to *save* her."

Will put interlaced hands on his head, his eyes wide. *Of course he couldn't leave Ember to fend for herself! What kind of lowlife was he becoming?* "Shazz! You're right. I needed to hear that, Wee. Guess I'm failing everyone, including myself."

Wee jumped in, almost cutting him off. His voice, now raised, vibrated with energy. "We'll have to take her, and then . . . hide her somewhere, right? You come up with a plan— you're the smart one."

"Meet tomorrow at my work? Lunch?"

"Yeah! Let's do it." Then he clapped his hand on his head. "Shazz. Can't meet you tomorrow. I'm scheduled for a working lunch meeting with my department."

"Crap. Really? Tomorrow Ember's already with the Magistrate. I can't wait too long to make plans. Who knows what he'll be doing with her?"

"Man. So sorry. But, come up with a plan, will ya? I'll think too. Meet you on Thursday for lunch. Plauditorium."

"You sure you're ready for this, Wee? This is dangerous. Really dangerous. We could be sent to The Outside—or worse."

"With all that you've told me, there's a lot at stake here. I don't want to believe it, but I trust you. And you're gonna need me in order to do something about it—you can't do it on your own. You're my best friend, Will. We're in this together."

THE NEXT MORNING, Will was a few minutes late arriving at the Plauditorium. He suddenly did not care, realizing that his lack of punctuality shouldn't be a reason for his now-sunny disposition to take a dive. Austel was already seated and checked in, involved in surveillance.

"Hey, what's up?" Will asked, sliding into his seat.

"Nothing new, as usual. I'm always secretly wishing that something crazy would happen, either on the screen or in an emergency. We still on for some competition with our Alt points today?" As usual, Austel looked at Will with hooded eyes, impossible to read.

"Of course. I've been waiting all morning. Yesterday you prevailed by a couple of points. Not gonna let that happen today." Will smiled, disguising his ulterior plan for an unnerving conversation with Austel.

"Oh, yeah? With all due respect, my dear friend, in spite of your talent, I can make it a streak, I'm sure."

Will let some minutes go by without saying any more. He glanced over at Austel, measuring the impact his next words would have. *I'm going to drop this news like a bomb.* He turned on the city's radio, OptiStation, enjoying the programmed gaiety of the Top Ten. Waiting just a moment so the music would mask their voices . . .

Will whispered. "So . . . Ember's sickness came from a ring."

Austel blinked twice. "Cut it out."

"I'm dead serious."

"How do you know?"

"Ember and I figured it out. The ring made her mother sick too, and then she died. Other people with rings are dead. Lots of them."

Although Austel didn't shift his position, Will knew he had Austel's full attention now. Austel spoke through gritted teeth. "I'm not sure why you're telling me this. I should report you for treason."

"You do, and you're gonna have to tell them what I told you. Then *you'll* be in the hot seat, no matter what your Alt readings are."

Will glanced up at the screen on the wall. Austel's Alt readings showed a keen fall. Tedman, the supervisor, would be alerted. The conversation had created the desired effect.

Will watched his colleague shift nervously in his seat before he became a stone sphinx, his eyes on the screen ahead of him. Time stretched out.

Finally, Austel spoke. "If you're sure about this, you're a bigger hero than everyone thought. Or a delusional fool. You've got balls, that's for sure. I'm just gonna keep my mouth shut and keep to myself. And, for the record, you've won the competition. I'm asking you kindly—please don't involve me in this for even one more second." Austel turned away and pushed the comm button signaling he was taking a break, calling a Temp to fill his spot. Then he abruptly got up from his chair, slamming it against his work desk.

Will smiled broadly, accidentally making eye contact with another Plauditor across the room. The woman, a young twenty-something, smiled back, and blushing, smoothed down her hair. He'd brought a few moments of happiness to someone, and he hadn't even tried.

But it was the quiet revenge with Austel that made his own morning. He was never the type to intentionally cause anyone unnecessary pain. He prided himself on it. But, in spite of the unkindness, his Alt rewarded him with points. Funny how sometimes the Alt could misread things. The pleasure he'd gotten from doing something devious had actually helped him.

He swiveled in his chair, full circle, in an act of pure joy, before engaging with his screen. As he locked himself into the mind-numbing position at the monitor, it was the perfect time to scheme and lay out a plan to rescue Ember.

As he mentally dreamed of rushing into the Magistrate's mansion on a white horse, sweeping Ember off her feet and carrying her away, excited voices from near the broadcast booth distracted him from his fantasy. Tedman emerged from the broadcast room, accompanied by the main anchor. Something had them pumped up. Will was twenty feet away, but he heard occasional words repeated and stressed, as if the words were popcorn under heat. "Magistrate." "Tomorrow." "Important!" "Critical." "Special!" And then . . . "Ember." A flush of heat spread through his chest.

A Temp slid into Austel's chair, filling the spot. He didn't know the Temp, but the Level Fourteen gave him a smile and the Tranquility salute as he settled in. Tedman's group continued to jabber and gush as they walked along the wall toward the lavatory.

"Mind watching my monitor for just one minute? Bathroom trip! Quick." Will didn't wait for a reply from the Temp, but dashed across the room, looking like a guy on an emergency sprint to the restroom.

Will practically slid into Tedman, as if he was trying to make home plate. The news anchor scrambled out of the way, a frightened look on his face. "Whoa, buddy!" he cried out. Then, as he turned to walk away, he added, "Tedman, thanks for the heads up. We'll be prepared."

"So! Will! Letting it go a little too long, son?" Tedman asked, chuckling.

"Ah, yeah. But I think it was a false alarm. Just gas, I guess. And . . . sorry." A fake apologetic smile touched his lips, as he fanned the area with his hand.

Tedman guffawed. "So glad to know you're human, kid. Was beginning to wonder."

Will laughed. "Human for sure. Umm . . . why all the excitement over here?"

"So, curious, huh? That's a good trait for a Plauditor. Magistrate's bringing in a special guest for tomorrow morning's broadcast."

"Oh, yeah? A new agent?" Will used all his self-control to keep his voice level.

Tedman's eyes sparkled. "No. But not sure why exactly. No real details. He's introducing a girl for some reason. She's some kind of special. We won't know everything 'til he goes on air."

"Huh. Hope whoever it is takes the spotlight for a while."

"So, yes. Maybe a new hero." He put his hand on Will's shoulder and looked at him with sympathy. "Fame is fleeting, right?"

"Guess so." He motioned toward the bathroom door. "Think I'll make a stop in here after all."

"Got your station covered?"

"Long enough."

Tedman chuckled again before calling out an order to stay focused on his way to another Plauditor's workstation.

Will ducked into the restroom just to compose himself and think. Leaning against the wall, his adrenaline was pumping. *Ember will be in the Plauditorium tomorrow morning.* He would have to act then. He paced back and forth a few times to dispel the nervousness he felt. Then he took some calming, deep breaths, used the toilet for relief, and left, ready to return to his station.

As he approached, he said to the Temp, "Sorry. Took me a little longer than I thought. You know how it is."

The Temp waved off the apology. "No worries. It's amazing how our bodies process all that. Have you ever thought about it? Why is pee even yellow? I mean, it's a full-scale chemical reaction in there."

Chemical reaction. The words were like a bolt from the blue. *Wee works at City Hall as a chemical engineer. He has access to chemicals.*

". . . don't you think?" The Temp had continued to talk, his newly uttered words disappearing into space, unheard by Will.

"Oh. Sorry. Yeah. Crazy."

Austel stood behind the Temp. "Thanks, Rob. You can go." Austel waited patiently for his replacement to exit the chair and settled back in. Austel did everything he could to erect an imaginary wall between them.

Will's heart raced as a plan began to form in his mind. As much as he hated to involve his friend, Wee was the key. The plan was perfect.

Will could hardly wait until he could clock out. When 5:00 came, he raced from the building. Thirty feet out, in an area without people, he made the call. He tapped his foot impatiently until he heard Weeford's voice come through his Alt. "Will, hey. How's things?"

"Got news. Ember's coming to the Plaud tomorrow. For a broadcast."

"No way."

"Yep. I've got a plan. But you're gonna have to help. And it's dangerous . . ."

"Shut up. Just . . .what."

"Can you get a knock-out chemical?"

Silence. "Yeah, probably. What're you thinking?"

"We can bomb the broadcast room when Magnus and Ember are in there. Just somethin' to put 'em out."

Weeford whistled. "Yeah. I can see it. And then?"

"We go in and take Ember out. For medical reasons, of course. We'd come to her aid." He could feel a smile growing wide.

"Wow. It could work. It'll be tricky gettin' that stuff, though. It'll have to be tomorrow. I'm already off."

"Can you come in the morning first thing?"

"Don't know if I'll have it by then. I'll try . . ."

"If you can't, just come as soon as you can. We'll maybe have to think on our feet. Delay."

"We'll need masks, too. No good if you or I pass out."

"Good thought. See you tomorrow?"

"Yeah."

"Wee?"

"Yeah, Will?"

"Thanks."

"No worries, Bro. Just hope I can get there in time."

Will hung up, not sure whether the buzz he was feeling was anxiety or exultation. Only his Alt knew for sure.

Journal Entry #5599

Her name is Ember. Such an unfortunate name. Who names their child for what's left over after a fire? Did her mother possibly have a premonition? But no matter. She'll be protected and encouraged to grow the talent she has within her. She's not yet explored her potential. Ember must develop her cognitive empathic abilities. She can then predict outcomes, distinguish truth from lies, and see the causes of emotions. She must be isolated from everyone, especially Will Verus. She is far too valuable to become emotionally attached to anyone, unless, of course, it is me. I already feel a connection to her.

    —Serpio Magnus, Magistrate

39

Ember's Challenge

The morning after the breakup, Ember found the Magistrate's limousine standing by at number Twenty-five in Purple Vale. She had been waiting, her palms sweating. Now, as she stepped out of her home, she turned one last time toward the place where she had so many memories with her mom. She threw a kiss to the wind, hoping that her mother could somehow feel her love.

She was like the walking dead after last night with Will, her heart shattered in a million pieces. Now this. Her march toward an unknown, but certainly bleak future. Losing Will. Leaving home. Living with the Magistrate. It was all too much.

Her Alt measured extreme distress as she trudged down the sidewalk. Blinking and vibrating. *Who cares? My Alt will be no longer used anyway. I won't be treated the same as everyone else ever again.* No felon going to the guillotine could have felt worse.

The door to the elite car opened with its customary electronic sigh. Inside, the Magistrate himself smiled with self-confident joy, like a kid blowing out birthday candles.

"Ember . . . so glad to see you." His arm went up in the familiar gesture. "Welcome to your new life."

Ember returned the salute and settled hesitantly into the polished leather seat. The scent of chocolate saturated the limo's interior, a reminder that even fragrances could control feelings of well-being.

"Thank you, Magistrate." She stepped into the idling car, her legs quivering.

"Once we're to the mansion, I'll dispose of your Alt properly. Then you'll see your new bedroom and meet the rest of the staff. You'll have your own attendant, too. And your new wardrobe is already in your closet, so you'll want to change immediately."

"Sounds . . . wonderful." Ember tried to muster up a convincing enthusiasm.

"I'm so glad you'll be part of the family, Ember. You're going to be the daughter I never had, my dear, and nothing is too good for you."

She suppressed an urge to vomit.

EMBER'S ROOM was indeed amazing. Beautifully decorated in all the metallic shades of the upper Status levels—copper, silver, and gold, it had every convenience and comfort anyone would ever want. Her wardrobe, too, impressive—fit for a queen. The latest styles arranged neatly in her closet, were gorgeous. The Magistrate assured her that no one else had clothes this color—a metallic tint of pale grayish-white that resembled the metal, platinum. Yet nothing compared to the cloak. It was breathtaking. Silks, satins, velvets, and metallics in Status colors overlapped in inch-wide vertical stripes from top to bottom.

"Your cloak is your signature piece, Ember. You'll be wearing it every day." The Magistrate's eyes sparkled when he pulled it out specially to show her. "Tomorrow you'll be introduced on the Tranquility daily broadcast wearing your cloak

of many colors. We'll introduce you as our ultimate achievement in Emotional Management—the ability to see and experience what others are feeling."

Ember sought a shred of courage. This moment was a
perfect opportunity to find out more about the rings. "Magistrate, with all due respect, I don't feel special, even with all the
glittering clothes and the cloak. What's missing is a ring. How
can I go about being at the top of Tranquility's Status when I
don't have an Augur Prize?"

The Magistrate tilted his head as if thinking. "Ember, my
dear. You certainly deserve that—you're right. And, of course,
if that makes you happier, we'll want to make one especially
for you." The Magistrate paused, looked around the room,
and then put his hands up in the air, drawing an imaginary
box, as if to frame an idea. "Yours will have to be platinum.
Gold and silver—no. Those will not do. As for the stone . . .
there's a rare gem that changes color—an Alexandrite. It will
be perfect. Of course, the style will still be the Augur Prize
design." His excitement showed itself in a tangible aura—
intense pink and green.

*This is going well. Now, to get the Magistrate to talk about the other
rings.* "You know, my mother had a ring? Remember
her? Talesa Vinata?"

The Magistrate let out a slow breath. He put his hand on
her shoulder. His face became doleful.

"I'm so very sorry about your mother's passing. Such a
shame—so unexpected! But, yet, here you are, a star in your
own right."

Ember noted the sudden insecurity ebbing from the
Magistrate's psyche. If she could continue to press . . . She
gathered up her nerve. *What do I have to lose? I'm in a position of
power—he put me here. I can't imagine he would deny me anything at
this point.* Still, she trembled a bit as she pushed on.

"Yes. I've put all the sadness and negativity from that time
behind me. But I wonder if I could see some of the rings? If

it's not too much trouble, of course." She felt a rush of achievement once she said the words. This was uncharted territory. Ember looked squarely into the Magistrate's eyes. The blackness there seemed infinite. She looked into their depths, daring her own courage to become a counterforce. She boldly held his gaze.

The Magistrate blinked as if he had just awakened, and then, to her surprise, chuckled. "You're more ambitious than I thought you'd be. But, you're Elite now. Just looking at the rings for a minute should be alright. We will keep it brief, though. You need to settle in. There's much you will learn, and plenty of time to learn it."

"Of course. I'm just beyond excited about having my own ring. I've admired them so much."

"Then right this way." The Magistrate stiffened with importance as he turned to lead her out.

Ember wondered why this quest was all so easy, but she was still filled with trepidation. She followed the Magistrate through the residence to an interior entrance to City Hall. Who knew there was a way to City Hall by just going through a simple door? Once inside the lobby, they walked across the room, passing A.S.P.E.R. at a desk along the way. She felt the memory of her encounter there acutely—a sad steppingstone to a widening mystery. She heard A.S.P.E.R. greet them with a chirpy "hello," after which the robot added, "Esteemed Magistrate. Have a perfect day."

Opening another door on the opposite wall, the Magistrate took her into a paneled library. The books on the walls were bound in colors indicating Status, each color on its own shelf, creating a leathery rainbow across the room. She bit back questions about why hard-bound books were there in such an official capacity when technology made informational books obsolete.

The Magistrate strode over to a section of the wall that held no books. Instead, a wooden panel carved with a dozen different faces of humans, all smiling, protruded several inches into space. The Magistrate touched something—Ember could not tell what—and the disturbing façade opened to become an entryway.

Inside were crystal cases. Interior lights glowed in each, setting off each ring's stunning gems. Sure enough, the higher levels of rings were there. A ring identical to her mother's Level Fourteen winked at her with its amethyst purple stone, while the male Level Fifteen ring next to it, a sapphire, glowed like a dark star. The next ring's Goldstone gem had a glittery metallic flash, made from copper oxide crystals, the epitome of Level Sixteen. A slightly grayed clear stone was the ideal stone for "Silver" Level Seventeen, and the last ring's gem, for Level Eighteen, glinted gold.

The Magistrate spoke. "Each ring embodies the spirit of the stone and the level's core value. See the stone for Level Seventeen? That's Phenakite. It balances energy. It comforts and stabilizes. It offers energy protection and relieves and alleviates despair and fear. The Level Seventeen core value is 'Enlightenment,' so I think the stone captures that well, don't you?"

"Yes. And they're beautiful!" she said. *Beautiful and deadly.* "Could I try one on?" She gave the Magistrate an innocent smile, hoping he would be straight with her about the real reason they were under lock and key.

"No, no, no, my *dear* Ember. Your ring will come to you in time. For now, we are letting these retain their energy fields until they're ready for the next group of honorees. And, now, we must go. We've spent enough time dreaming."

Ember felt relief at not having to put any of the rings on her finger. But frustration surged inside like boiled soup. Even though he considered her to be Elite, he wouldn't admit to the poisons buried in the rings. She scanned his emotions, knowing his affectionate words were camouflage for a coiled viper.

40

Ember's Deja Vu

A s she lay in the king-size bed that night, her mind raced. She thought about the rings again, their beauty a sparkling disguise for whatever poison they held. At some point, could she warn the people who would receive them? Could she tell someone in the Elite what she knew? She couldn't even tell Will. Her stomach dropped. Some way, somehow, the truth had to come out. Were there more answers to be found in City Hall?

Finally, she got up out of bed. It was impossible to sleep. Nor did she welcome her sinister dreams. She had to make use of her time when the Magistrate and others weren't around. She slid her fingers along the soft fabric of a silky nightgown. This would never do. She'd need an outfit suited to exploring. After switching on a tiny light inside the closet, she pulled out a pair of tight pants and a loose velveteen tunic that hit her mid-thigh. Comfortable and warm, the clothes were perfect. She threw off her nightgown and dressed quickly, deciding against shoes. They would be far too noisy as she walked.

Her bedroom door had an interior bolt for privacy, although the Magistrate had assured her that she would never need to lock it—she was protected here. She put her finger on the latch where it picked up fingerprint permission. She winced and then froze when she heard its answering "click." It slid open with barely a sigh. After a moment of suspended effort, she guardedly poked her head out of the doorway. No one could know she was up roaming the mansion. Who knows what the Magistrate would do? Perhaps then the lock would be on the outside.

The hallway beyond was inky, a shroud of security for her midnight probe. As she went along, her bare feet made tiny impressions in the fleecy carpet, but no noise at all. It was as if she were a ghost floating along the floor. She even controlled her breathing, making sure her adrenaline didn't cause an audible rush of air.

She stood at the end of the hallway, mentally tracing the route she remembered. The interior entry to City Hall was on the opposite wall. The moonlight from an adjacent window pearlized the raindrops on the glass and illuminated the metallic shine on the door to City Hall. She scampered across the room, not knowing if she would discover an accessible entrance or a secured one.

She was instantly rewarded when the electronic knob turned with no resistance, and the door slid open, but her heart pounded when A.S.P.E.R. greeted her from the front desk, blinking her eyes and moving stiffly, apparently "awakened" by Ember's intrusion. Ember hesitated, frozen in place, worrying about further alarms, but when A.S.P.E.R. settled back into a fixed pose, she advanced toward the library. *I guess even artificial intelligence needs to sleep,* she mused.

The library also had easy access. She imagined that the Magistrate had no need to lock the inner doors. He alone would be inside at night. Even the servants were gone.

Wishing she had a whisper of light, she took a moment to adjust to the gloom there. Her eyes scanned the room, stopping on the panel with the carved smiling faces, now appearing eerie in the shadows. She could perhaps steal a ring, but she remembered the rings were under lock and key. Something else . . .

Her eyes settled on the books lining the shelves. She pulled a yellow one out at random and flipped it open. The book held handwritten pages. What secrets did it hold? She stopped at an entry, straining her eyes to read it. A few words were in bold, and she could pick those out. "Happiness," "monitoring" and "hope," but the darkness made it impossible to read more. She slid it back and pulled another, this one's cover a kelly green. But, just like the other, the book was thin, possibly containing about a hundred pages, and hopelessly indecipherable in the dimness. *I'll have to take one with me*, she thought, *but which one?*

In the gloom, she backed up into a chunky desk, hitting her left heel on a broad, heavy leg. Vibrating pain tore through her foot. "Shazz!" she yelled out. Putting her hand over her mouth, she froze. She desperately hoped the Magistrate was a sound sleeper or that the walls of the place were solid. *So clumsy.*

After a minute, she heard nothing and began to relax again. But it was time to go. The longer she stayed, the more vulnerable she was. *Now, grab a book and—*

The library door slid open. Her heart skipped a beat.

She dropped to all fours and scrambled around the desk's solid hulk, finding the desk's chair well, a perfect cubby for hiding. She didn't dare breathe as she wedged herself into the space, silently thanking the chair for being pushed aside.

It has to be the Magistrate. Frik! She wanted to melt into the floor.

She could see nothing from her vantage point—it was both protection and a blind spot. She heard soft footsteps trolling the room. Exasperation and puzzlement flowed her way, hitting her like a fuzzy cloud. The person seemed to pace for several interminable minutes before stopping; then a shallow beacon of light swept the room, stopping here and there. She held her breath when the pinpoint beam finally settled on the top of the desk. Then, as if the final illumination was satisfactory, Ember heard the person soft shoe his way back out the door, its "whoosh" of sound a balm to her panic.

She exhaled in relief and gradually crawled out. Grabbing the desktop's edge, she pulled herself up. Her fingers hit on a flat object on the desk. It was another book, this one a dark color. She wouldn't have seen it in the gloom, but this seemed meant to be—the book she'd "take home" to read. She picked it up, turning it over in her hand. Her mind was a mush of emotions and conflicting ideas. If she could see her own aura, which was a gift she didn't have, it wouldn't have been a pretty sight.

It had been a close call, but she was still safe. She had no idea who had investigated the library in the murky darkness. Was it the Magistrate? Or a servant? The cover of night was a security blanket, but it also yielded no answers.

The best payout was the mysterious book. She craved its explanations. Something she could use against the Magistrate or the Elite? Inanimate objects had no auras, but she felt the book's presence as strongly if it were a real person. She pulled up her shirt and firmly tucked the five-by-seven-inch tome into her underwear. It lay perfectly flat, tight against her skin. She dared anyone, even on the Magistrate's turf, to search her private parts.

She could return to her quarters and settle down to peruse the book. She sighed. No. She'd get out of here somehow and find Will. No matter what he said, no matter why he was distancing himself, she knew he would help her read and analyze the book. He had to. He was her one singular hope.

She tiptoed her way to the library door, daring the surveillance cameras whirring away in the dark to find her. At this point, the electronic supervision didn't matter. As instrumental as she was to his vile plans, she knew in her head, even if she were caught, the Magistrate would never damage her. In spite of it all, she shivered. Her mouth went deathly dry.

She broke out in a fresh sweat. She was going to charge to the front door of City Hall and flee. She could see no other way.

Her anxiety fueled her sprint, each step seeming faster than the last, the door looming large before her. Her white knuckles shone brightly in the silvery moonbeams sliding down from the promontory windows as she grabbed the massive lock and turned. Gears clicked. Then the door opened with a purr before a piercing siren ripped through the air.

Shazz!

Ember bolted out the door, running as fast as she could. She prayed for wings—for gazelle legs—for invisibility—anything—yet knowing that she was merely mortal and that she must prevail on her own. Adrenaline was her gasoline, her footsteps slapping the cobblestone pavement as she barreled along with full scale abandon.

Oh, no! The rain had begun in earnest for the night. Already there were shallow puddles forming. The rain was a steady shower as she catapulted herself down the pathway.

Behind her, low-beam spotlights from outside City Hall abruptly flared into the blackness, illuminating her flight path and electrifying her panic. Bare. Exposed. She trekked on, willing herself to go faster and faster. She heard heavy footfalls trailing her, their scuffed sound powdery, consistent with distance. With them came more flashes of light. In that instant she could see everything around her, as if a strobe punctuated the landscape. Just to her right, the Solace Institute loomed brightly and then waned in shadow. She jetted past the trees lining the avenue, their limbs normally welcoming, like arms stretched out. Tonight in the dark they harbored ghoulish shadows that pressed in on her. The rain became a deluge, and her feet slipped miserably on the unforgiving pavement.

Her breath came in ragged gasps as she struggled to keep sprinting at high speed, each step more demanding than the last. She had never been much of an athlete, and echoes of her mother's advice on keeping fit polluted her mind. A sense of failure gripped her. She put her hands to her head. *Keep going. Keep going.* She was going to win. To make it. She'd had enough of a head start. She'd find a place to hide and then contact Will—her Alt now more of a friend than foe.

Suddenly, a sense of déjà vu enveloped her. She had already been here, done this . . . *Oh stars. My dream! I'm in my dream.* The books. The flight to escape. And, if she was right, there was more to come. The sweat on her forehead dripped its salty sting into her eyes. She ached in every joint. But she couldn't give up. She urged herself to keep running, but it was as if she now struggled against some invisible force, pushing against her with dynamic strength. Her feet were leaden stumps. The harder she pushed, the less progress she made.

Still hearing the rapid, thudding footfalls of assailants, she glanced back. Several figures were narrowing the space between them. *Shazz! SHAZZ!!* She heaved desperate breaths.

Although she took her eyes off her path for a mere fractured second, a chunky, loose stone materialized out of nowhere in front of her. She dodged, but not in time. She stumbled, grabbing at the air, diving headlong toward the slick flagstone, where she lay flat on her stomach.

A rusty taste. Blood. She had bitten her tongue in the fall and split her upper lip. Her Alt blinked alternating screens of black and red, something she had never seen before. With dismay, she noticed a tiny crack in its upper left corner. *Ugh!* She pushed herself up on her elbows, scrambling to rise.

Ah! She was up! She shook out her limbs, stiff and scraped from the slide, and began to propel forward once again. But the remnants of the recurring nightmare flushed her brain.

Her battered legs, thick with pain, kept her momentum to a lope, not a run.

Footfalls thundered behind her, growing closer and more insistent. The percussive rumble of pursuit accelerated like the "M" train at high speed. She knew her aggressors were close; to her horror, their auras engulfed her, penetrating her mind and spirit. *RUN!*

Powerful hands grabbed her by the arms. She jerked and tried to pull away, her remaining strength targeted toward a final, desperate escape. Her vision blurred. She saw pure red until she was able to focus. A Sciolist. She was in the control of a Sciolist, his lean physique, an athlete's build. He was barely out of breath while she was still heaving.

A clomping of more feet approached. *The rest of the troops,* she concluded. From the noise and the abundance of emotions seeping through the air, there had to be a mob of them. Her eyes closed in weariness. Never had she wished for her mother's love or Will's strength quite so much.

"You thought you'd escape, Ember?" The Magistrate's voice penetrated like a blade. "Impossible. Where do you think you could go where we wouldn't find you?"

He approached and turned her around to face him. "You —!" she cried. She knew then that her dreams were true premonitions. The Magistrate was her assailant. It had always been his face in her dreams.

Two Sciolists flanked his sides. Four people. But it was enough to shatter her hopes of an escape. Her arms tucked into the vise-like grips of the Sciolists, they walked back to City Hall, their footsteps the only sound in the silence.

41

Ember's Debut

The Magistrate insisted he return Ember to her quarters, his arm possessively tight around her shoulders. They walked down a dimly lit hallway where the overhead vents sent out a chilly blast. She trembled, but not merely from the crisp air. Anger ebbed from Serpio like liquid. She felt its sting as it wrapped itself around her. His voice was tight, his words clipped. "Ember, understand. You're not a prisoner, *but you are mine.* Don't ever forget."

"Yours?" Ember looked into his eyes, and a shiver went up her spine. She didn't want to hear anymore, didn't want him to reveal what was in his mind. She could already see the color surrounding him, true colors that revealed the danger she was in.

He drew closer and whispered in her ear. "Your life here is an honor. And we'll be *together.* Nothing will separate us anymore. Not space. Not events. And not Will Verus."

At the sound of Will's name, Ember felt a deep ache in her chest. "You can't cut me off from everything I love!" Ember's tone was like a whip. Sadness at her powerless situation overwhelmed her. She jerked away, Serpio's arm dropping from her shoulder like a lead weight.

"If you don't think you can be happy here, I'll have to do some . . . unpleasant things." The Magistrate grabbed her wrist and yanked her further down the hall to the door of her room.

She cried out and lowered her head. Totally helpless. And no one could save her. A fragment of her nightmare flashed through her mind. She'd seen who chased her. But there was blood in the dream, too. Was the blood the Magistrate's? Or would it be her own?

Serpio released his grip. His words became contrite, silky. "We'll put this behind us and work, instead, on your happiness. You can and will be happy."

Ember shook her head up and down, tears glittering in her eyes. She blinked them away, set on keeping her emotions to herself.

"Now, dear Ember. You need medical attention for that cut." He reached out and touched her mouth. "Those beautiful lips need care. I can send a medic to you."

Ugh. She forcefully shook her head. "No! No. I'll just take a hot bath. I'm not bleeding anymore." She touched her lip gently, and her fingertip glistened with blood. Ember winced at the lie, but the last thing she wanted was to see more people. It was already after midnight.

"Very well. You'll have a servant coming to assist you in the morning, anyway. Sweet dreams, Ember." The Magistrate patted her on the shoulder, pushing her gently into her room before turning away. He strode down the hallway, twisting once to make sure the door had actually shut. She made a point of waiting to see him disappear around the corner before allowing the door to hiss its way closed.

Weariness settled over her. Her shoulders sagged. Her eyes bulged, strained and bloodshot, but she wouldn't allow herself to rest. A new determination fueled her. If she was ever going to get out of here, she had work to do. She reached into her pants and grinned. The book she stole

TANYA ROSS

earlier hadn't been discovered. There was something to be said for tight lingerie.

She ran a bath like she had promised, taking the book with her into the tub. Her cuts and bruises seem to sigh with relief in the hot water. She tenderly held the book in her hands above the water, taking care not to get it wet, and began to read. With each page she read, her eyes widened. The leather-bound volume was a diary. She was inside Serpio's mind, each entry more disturbing than the last. Although her bath water was warm, she shivered, goosebumps marching across her arms. Her mother's name suddenly jumped out at her from the page, and every muscle in her body seized up like a vise. No! Her mother was romantically involved with the Magistrate? And then her own name; she'd been under the microscope all along! Before she'd been examined at Solace! She threw the book over the side of the tub as if it were on fire.

Closing her eyes, she tried to calm her fluttering heart. But as awful as it all was, this was the information she and Will needed to take the Magistrate down. And only Will could help her. She must get this to Will at all costs.

∽

After her dream-like, terrifying night of little sleep, an assigned personal servant awakened her early. The sun was not yet up.

"Good morning, Ember. My name is Padgett. I'll be helping you bathe and dress this morning." The maid's face, round and bright, reminded Ember of a full moon. Her eyes were a watery blue and deep set. *Kind of like little pools*, Ember thought with some amusement. Ember's eyes took in her stiff, pressed uniform, a tangerine orange. Pretty high Status for a servant. But this was the Magistrate's home, after all.

Ember thought about resisting. But she was weary, and her

spirit was wounded. Better to just suck it up. She had to get dressed, after all.

"I don't need a shower, Padgett. I—I had one late last night."

To Ember's relief, Padgett smiled. "I was hoping you'd say that. I can't wait to see you put on your outfit for today." The clothes were laid out on the bed. She giggled, and then held up pieces of Ember's clothing ensemble, one piece at a time. "Bodysuit . . . skirt . . . ." She laid them back on the bed. "Shoes." She picked each up, one at a time, admiring them. "And your cloak."

"Great," Ember said, with untypical sarcasm. "I need to slip into the bathroom."

Remembering the book, Ember knew she couldn't trust leaving it where it was. She'd no real good place to hide it; in a good search it would be easily found. She'd need to keep it with her.

"Sure. Let me know if I can do anything to help."

Once she'd closed the door on Padgett, she pressed a button under the sink, triggering the cabinet door underneath to open. She pulled the journal from the interior back wall where she'd tried to hide it behind some cleaning supplies. Again, she placed it in her underwear, this time in the back.

Ember cracked the bathroom door. "Padgett? Can you pass the bodysuit to me? I'd rather put it on in here."

"No need to be shy, but okay. If it makes you happy." After some rustling in the bedroom, the bodysuit snaked its way through the crack in the door.

"Thanks—really appreciate it." Ember donned the body-suit, taking care to smooth it over her torso like a second skin. The book made a flat lump across the small of her back, but she would have to take a chance it wouldn't be detected under all her outer garments. She came back into the bedroom, feeling triumphant, ready for the rest of her outfit.

Minutes later, Ember looked at her image in the

mirror. She'd never worn anything like this before. Her floor-length flowing skirt had two layers. The underskirt was a rich, deep platinum metallic covered by a translucent layer of shimmering pearl organza that opened all the way to her waist and parted, completely showing off her legs. Underneath, a metallic body suit tightly hugged every curve, sparkling in the morning light, to melt into short boots of gold. The top of the suit was sleeveless, designed to be more comfortable under the cloak she would be wearing over the top. A wide belt made of diamonds accented her waist, its buckle resembling an open butterfly. The cloak of many colors went on top.

After she was dressed, her female assistant removed Ember's Alt. "Oh dear. You have a deep crack in your Alt. What happened?" Her eyes showed her surprise and concern.

Ember shook her head and looked down at the floor. She wasn't going to explain anything.

Padgett placed the Alt in a metal box she had brought with her. "I'll be taking care of this. I know it's devastating to give it up, but what the Magistrate wishes, he gets."

"Sure—okay." *Get **rid** of it.*

A FEW MOMENTS LATER, a quick knock on the door announced the Magistrate. He personally ushered her to the limousine. "On our way to the Plauditorium," the Magistrate said. "It's early, but I want to get you on this morning's city-wide broadcast."

At least I'm going where Will may be. Oh, Will. She needed to get him to share her discovery. And she was feeling his absence like a withdrawal. She was dying to see him. Grabbing an opportunity would be difficult, but she would find a way. The Magistrate patted her knee. Her stomach turned over. *Ugh.*

The Plauditorium, as usual, was pulsing with life, despite the ungodly hour. But the hum of the monitors was strangely soothing, and Ember allowed the collective positive emotions of the room to saturate her. Plauditors were always cheerful.

The Plauditors instantly acknowledged the Magistrate the moment he walked in, although she was the recipient of some gaping, curious stares. But the Plauditors quickly turned back to their screens. No one wanted to be slacking off. Points could be instantly lost. Ember immediately saw Will at his station, but just as she thought, there was no opportunity to even make eye contact. *Nor would he probably want to,* she thought miserably.

Near the door, an older gentleman greeted them—a Level Seventeen, Ember realized with awe. She suppressed a giggle so she wouldn't be rude. He was shorter than she was.

"Tedman Adoravi, at your service," the man said as he gave the Tranquility salute to Ember and the Magistrate. "So. This is your special visitor today. We're ready to do whatever you need."

The Magistrate returned his salute. Putting his arm possessively around Ember, he said, "I have a very special announcement to make today. My visitor will be coming with me into the broadcast space. She'll be on the broadcast."

Tedman nodded enthusiastically, and just like that, whisked them into the communications room, adjacent to the surveillance room, to record the broadcast. In addition to Tedman, there was a crew of five at their posts. They all stopped to acknowledge the Magistrate with awestruck faces, showering him with the proper arm greeting. But she could tell they didn't know what to make of her. They would know better than to give her their attention unless the Magistrate dictated it. One of the news producers who sported a purple suit and tie was the first to speak.

"How are you today, Magistrate? You're looking quite distinguished and powerful today, sir. Can I get you something special this morning?"

"No, thanks, James. We plan to get right to work. Listen,

this will be a significant broadcast. All of you will witness history in the making today. You'll want to make everything even more perfect and jubilant than usual, as we are introducing Ember here, a girl who outshines the best of us."

The broadcasters murmured in excitement, taking on the characteristics of a coyote pack discovering its prey. Now they had an invitation to assess her. *Most days they must dream of something dramatic to share, and it's a rare thing. So, today, it is me. Shazz.*

The crew busied themselves with their equipment. The Level Fourteen purple guy attached tiny, round, clear jewels to their clothing with a magnetic click. Lights on the opposite wall blinked green.

Ember listened to a Level Fifteen woman announce, "Sound on. We're set to go. And, three, two, one . . ."

The Magistrate stood next to her. She cringed as he put his arm around her and coaxed her to look directly into the camera.

"Citizens of Tranquility. Today we have a very special person to introduce to you—Ember Vinata, a real Queen of Hearts. As fortune would have it, we have discovered Ember's secret talent. Yes, a talent she has kept hidden. She has risen above what an ordinary citizen can do with emotional control. She is an Empath who feels the emotions of people around her."

He paused to gaze at her admiringly, his black eyes shining like polished beads. With his right hand, he touched the top of her head; then his hand traveled down the length of it, caressing her hair. Withdrawing his hand, he splayed out his palm as if beckoning his listeners. "Empaths have the ability to sense others on many different levels. From observing what another person is saying, feeling, and thinking, they totally understand that person. Empaths can read body language and energy like no one else, and do not tolerate lies and deception. Please grant her the respect you would give any of the Elite class. With her skills and empathy, she'll be of great assistance to me and to the Elite. I'm excited about the possibilities this will bring to our community. Thank you—and have a spectacular day."

The Magistrate and Ember stepped aside as the camera switched to the main anchor for the day. He continued the broadcast, but now the Tranquility News became the focus. As Ember wondered what was going to happen to her next, she vaguely heard the commentator announcement, "A stunning performance of Tranquility's Town Players will take place tomorrow at the Paradiso Amphitheater. Tickets are available first to those of higher Status . . ." The words seemed so trivial, so stupid. Entertainment happening like nothing was wrong. When the world was completely upside down.

The screen dimmed, while a male voice said, "That's a wrap."

The Magistrate turned to Ember. "You'll be such an inspiration to the citizens. A help to them, perhaps. But a weapon against negativity as well. To develop your talents, we'll work closely together."

Ember managed to squeak, "You're my . . . teacher?"

The Magistrate smiled at her apparent wariness. "Yes, but not just me." He put his hand on her shoulder and gave her a pat he meant to be reassuring. "Elite will be involved. Our counselor, Winslow. Some staff at Solace. Maybe others." He shrugged his shoulders.

"How about Plauditors?" she asked, hope in every syllable.

Serpio pressed his lips together and sighed in exasperation. "Dear Ember. We won't need them. They're agents of a different kind."

Ember's throat tightened, catching an unwise response on the tip of her tongue. *I'm trying hard to get to you, Will.*

"In the meantime, you'll assess all the servants first, just for fun. Can't wait to see how you 'read' everyone's emotions. It'll be kind of like a game, for now. Some entertainment." He put his hand on her arm, propelling her forward toward the door.

"Let's get back to your new home—our home—where we can begin."

She lowered her face as if to watch her step, gathering her skirt and cloak around her. Without her Alt, if she managed her facial expressions, she could keep her emotions hidden. Serpio might use her to determine the emotions of others, but she refused to allow him to see her own. She straightened her spine. Everything now lay on her shoulders. And she could not let down her guard.

42

Xander's Surprise

In the dark of that same night, Xander was awake. He had slept fitfully, knowing the next day could make them or break them. They had no time to hide around the city. They had to act.

He was hungry, famished, really, and knew his REMs would be, too, but the siege was more important than having a meal. There was no way to get food at this point. They would have to wait until they had accomplished their goal. *If we all die, food won't matter much anyway...*

He roused the rest of the team, still slumbering among the foliage. The bushes barely protected them from the nightly rain, now beginning to slow to a drizzle.

"Up, up . . . up! Get up! Time to move!" Xander's voice was thick with urgency, but quiet. He went around rousing his team, shaking each one before moving on.

Each member responded as if already prepared to run or fight. Spirits were high, as they slapped each other's faces in fun and dusted off their damp, filthy clothing with their hands. Bixby did a few jumping jacks before whacking a bush with a stick he'd found on the ground.

"Guys! Pay attention," Iris called out, the female pitch high enough to get everyone's notice. "Xander's speaking!"

The group quickly assembled around Xander in a semicircle, their eyes riveted on his face.

"This is the plan, Phoenix. We're goin' into the Plauditorium today. There are more Plauditors in there than people we have here, but we have weapons—our rocks, knives, the two guns, and the element of surprise. No one will be expecting an attack, least of all from us. The key'll be using the cameras and tricking the people watching the screens. We just have to fool them."

Gabriel chimed in. "How's that possible, Xander? There are cameras everywhere! We'll be captured before we take five steps from here." His voice cracked with worry.

"Ah. You forget. In our uniforms, Jasper and I look like official Tranks. Other than missing our Alts—which is a good thing to keep us undetected—we look like we belong here. You all have your long capes. Pull 'em around you. You'll become fake Sciolists if you walk with authority. No one's gonna look twice at anyone in red, especially in the dark. We act like we *belong* instead of hiding. If you're desperate, flip your cloak up. Cover your heads and faces."

"We gonna stick together?" Jasper called out.

"No. We separate in teams of two. A large number'll draw attention. Each group takes a different direction toward the Plauditorium. Avoid City Hall but take the streets. No citizens will be out. Way past curfew, and it's dark."

One of the women spoke up. "What're we gonna do when we get there?"

"Before we split up, each team of two gets rope, zip ties, and tape. You get there and wait, maybe fifty feet out. You can safely maintain your position as long as you act official. Jasper and I are going to be outside. As soon as the sun comes up and the day officially starts for the Plauditors, we'll go in.

When you hear my whistle, run straight through the front door. Plauditors'll be seated. Surround 'em. Throw your rocks or slash when you face resistance. Use your rope, zip ties, and tape to tie 'em up. We'll be ready to take it from there. Any questions?"

∿

XANDER AND JASPER formed a team and found positions in some thick shrubbery around the side of the Plauditorium. Kneeling on their knees, they peeped out through gaps in the leaves.

Xander handed one of the rifles over to Jasper, his expression serious. "Jasper, what kind of gun do bees use?"

Jasper reached out for the gun, a puzzled look on his face. "What? Bees! I dunno . . ."

"A beebee gun." Xander grinned and cuffed Jasper on the arm.

A bird sang sweetly in the nearby trees. The sun's rays finally emerged, lighting up Tranquility's dome like a transparent buttery glaze. They'd no way to tell the time, but as the sun rose, noises from the streets nearby of CommuteCars and pedestrians chatting were their signals curfew had been lifted. Now, to wait until the Plauditors arrived at the Plauditorium. First a Level Seventeen guy who looked more like a kid because of his size unlocked the door to the place.

"We go in, Xan?" Jasper said.

"No. We wait till all the staff is there. We need hostages to keep Sciolists away from the Plauditorium once we're inside."

"Right."

Some Plauditors arrived alone. Others in twos or threes. Xander began to count. He knew from his schooling the city employed fifty of them. He tapped his foot impatiently, partly from nervous energy, and partly because it was falling asleep.

They were frozen in place, their position outside perilously discoverable. Finally, Xander pulled his arm down in a victory fist pump. "Yes! Number fifty," he whispered. "Jasper, you ready for action?"

"Yeah. Good thing we have the guns."

"Remember—if we have to shoot, we shoot. Otherwise, we're just holding the Plauditors until Phoenix gets in there with us. From there, we go to the broadcast room to make the announcement."

"Roger that."

After a heavy fist-bump, they jumped to their feet. They rounded the corner in a flash. Bounding up the stairs, Xander said, "Stop!" in a muted voice, throwing out his arm against Jasper. He gave a loud, explosive whistle, his signal to Phoenix.

"We got this, Jasper," Xander whispered. He clapped Jasper on the back, twisted the doorknob. He grinned and whispered, "It's unlocked," and then, with a mighty kick, forced the door open. It shuddered and made a cracking sound as it hit the inside wall.

Xander's voice rang out, confident and commanding. "Everybody here! Stay right where you are. If you move, we will shoot! Jaz, lock down the door." A massive six-inch-wide metal bolt shot out from the wall and slid into place.

Screams and yells engulfed the space. Hands went up in the air. The faces of the Plauditors faded to colorless masks. A few Plauditors jumped up in alarm. Some shut their eyes and put their hands in the air, while others looked dazed, gazing back with electrified eyes. *These people are jellyfish. Will they even fight?*

No sooner had his mind captured those thoughts than a Plauditor dropped to the floor. He quickly crawled, scrambling toward the door. A futile attempt. Jasper drew a rock from his satchel, hitting the escapee in the head. The Level Twelve victim fell flat in a "thump." Blood rushed from his head. Screams scorched the air.

A compressed second later, the Phoenix crew stampeded in, bursting from the entrance like a crazed horde of Huns.

From the broadcast booth, five communication agents spilled into the room, yelling for order and quiet. They stood frozen in shock as they realized the noise was a siege.

One broadcaster scrambled back inside the booth. Xander wondered if he was protecting someone or something valuable inside other than himself. No matter. They would be in there soon enough. Exactly where they needed to be to shake up the city.

A moment later, a young woman broke out from the newscast chamber, her face flushed pink. Yells of "Stop!" from behind didn't faze her. She fought against arms trying to pull her back, thrashing to free herself from the announcer's booth. She ran to face the unknown crisis instead of remaining safely tucked inside. At the commotion, Xander immediately swiveled around. He aimed his rifle, ready to shoot.

As he zeroed in, Xander's eyes popped open in surprise. The girl was dazzling, but her face was . . . familiar. Her cloak alone shone with a richness he'd never seen before, and her garments glittered. Her showy clothes, ridiculous! Like hoping to improve an Angel of Light's brilliance. Then it dawned on him. This was Ember—the girl he had bullied so badly as a boy! He'd never forgotten the incident or Win's lesson. *What is she doing here?*

"Ember?" He hadn't seen Ember for years, and now she was every guy's fantasy. He felt his blood surge; fire spread through him. His face flushed and sparkled with a moist sheen. *What's happening to me?*

He was flustered, but still in charge. Phoenix needed his orders and encouragement. "Great work, everyone! Put 'em all against the wall and tie 'em together with rope."

A Plauditor who stood warily in the middle of the room abruptly turned toward Xander, charging him like a bull on speed. The rifle discharged, the burst deafening—and lethal. The Plauditor fell to the floor. Blood gushed from the wound on his chest. A crimson puddle on the floor grew around him.

Ember looked at Xander with dawning recognition, her eyes orbs of horror. "Oh, my—! You shot Will!"

43

Ember's Power

Ember gasped. She ran across the room and dropped to the travertine tile, smearing the blood pooling on the floor and gathering Will's face in her hands. No, no, NO! It couldn't be! Will wasn't moving. Or breathing. Her stomach churned, bile rising up her throat. She put her hand over her mouth to stop herself from heaving. Her body shook in uncontrollable tremors. Then she felt a physical pain in her chest so severe she cried out. *Was it possible she was feeling Will's bullet wound?* It was the first time she had ever sensed someone's physical suffering. It was unbearable, overpowering. Worse, she felt no emotion coming from Will at all. She, too, felt lifeless. Her blood seemed to quit circulating, and her eyes blurred enough to distort the images around her. *Is my very soul being sucked out?*

Will was dead. She knew it. She staggered to her feet and scanned the room. The Plauditors were under attack, and it looked as if this crazy Xander was the instigator. The Plauditors exuded terror; she watched their auras twist and turn like tornados, their rainbow colors fading and flaring. Her heart wailed with sadness, totally broken.

And yet, other than Will, weren't these officers involved in a system of control and death? Her head was filled with unchecked, divergent thoughts. Escape, for one. Escape from the Magistrate while she had the chance. He was evil. Wanted to use her. He probably had her mother killed. In the broadcasting room, he was merely feet away from her. He'd take her again. Yet, she couldn't leave Will lying there.

She squeezed her eyes shut. The fear, the anger, the mistrust, and the desire to subdue—all the emotions in the room—took on a life of their own. The powder keg built inside her. A time bomb, these emotions she was too weak to control. This time, she wouldn't resist its invasion. She embraced all the feelings. Took them in like the air she breathed. She wrapped her arms around herself. "Enough!" she screamed.

Without warning, a power she had never known surged through her. Raw. Explosive. She threw her hands up. A burst of energy coursed through her arms and electrified the air. Continuous quakes rippled throughout her head, chest, and torso. Then everything around her froze in a still-life tableau. People became statues. Nothing moved. No sound. No anything. It was like all the energy had been sucked out of the room. Ember moved her head in slow motion, looking around the room in bewilderment. Xander still stood with his rifle pointed, his face angry and fearful. Plauditors stood up by their stations with hands up. Many around the room had their hands over their faces. Mouths were agape, the look of horror etched there. Wide eyes. Theirs. Hers. Trembling, her knees threatened to buckle. She took in the red-clad REMs. They were crouched, or in the middle of throwing rocks. Some simply gawked at Xander, and others were caught immobilized in a run toward Plauditors sitting at their stations.

Shazz! She put her hand to her head to steady herself and gasped. *She* had done this. Pulled all the emotions from the room together inside herself. On purpose. Something she'd never done before. And this—this thing—happened. But what genuinely startled her was seeing the vast rainbow of colors. The auras of every person in the room still pulsed with life, yet their bodies were totally immobile. She could feel every emotion in the room. But were they breathing? Did they have heartbeats? She didn't know. All she could think about now was Will.

She drew a deep breath and raced over to him. **No aura.** Completely lifeless. No breath. Sobbing, she threw herself on him and gazed at his face—the face that allowed her to get through everything—the face she loved more than life."Will! I can't lose you! What will become of me?" she cried. She put her arms around him and hugged him with all her might.

A fresh bloom of warmth, like liquid honey, flowed through her veins. Suddenly, she felt movement. To her amazement, she saw Will's eyelids flutter. *He's alive!*

"Will! You're back! Oh, my stars!" She sighed and hugged Will even harder.

"Ember . . .What happened? Did someone knock me down?"

She put a hand to her face, wiping away tears. "Yes—yes! You got knocked down. But you can get up. I'm right here. You're safe for now." Will was alive, but there had been blood. Lots of it. She felt around his chest. Nothing. And no blood on the floor either. It was like she had somehow taken a slice out of time. She shook her head as if to bring herself back to reality and wondered if this was all a dream.

And was it? The images of her dreams juxtaposed themselves in her mind. The Prince—the blood. She shook her head, trying to dislodge the wisps of nightmare. Yet, she knew the truth. She had found the Prince and destroyed the blood.

Will struggled to sit up. The scrape of chairs. A unified breath in the room. Movement. Voices. The scene slipped back prior to the shotgun's blast. She felt everyone's confusion, distress, and aggression return to them as they suddenly became responsive again.

Ember whispered quickly, "Take it easy, Will. Go slow. Remember, there's a takeover going on here."

"Shazz! Yes—invasion! Got to help."

"Be careful getting up." She lowered her voice to a whisper. "And when you get up, make sure you talk to Xander immediately. He's the one in charge."

"Okay." Will stood up, unsteady. He reminded Ember of a newborn calf trying out his legs for the first time.

Relief and thankfulness swept over her. She couldn't believe what had happened. All she could figure out was that she had gathered all the emotions in the room, and they gave her the ability to do something impossible.

I guess I AM a secret weapon, after all. I have power! Real power! I'm confused but feel reborn. I don't understand how all this works, but I'm not going to hide from it anymore.

"Ember." Her name came out of Will's mouth in a shaky sigh. "So glad to see you. I'm sorry—"

"I know. It's—it's okay. We're going to survive this—all of it."

Xander's voice rang out. "Great work, everyone! Put 'em all against the wall and tie 'em together with rope." Members of Phoenix scattered through the room grabbed Plauditors, one by one, pulling them out of their chairs. The soft hiss of zip ties lassoing hands and feet was a welcome sound.

Xander raised his rifle and aimed it at Will, his finger touching the trigger. Xander hesitated, puzzled, as he wondered what he was doing, especially when Ember stepped out in front of Will.

"Listen, Xander, please," she urged. "Will here," she gestured in his direction, "can maybe help you." She put her hands up in the air and stepped slowly away.

Xander said, "Help me? I doubt it. Tranquility sucks. It's goin' down. I'll burn it to the ground if I have to."

Ember said, "Don't burn it to the ground. But Will and I aren't happy here either. We're trying to expose awful things. Maybe we're on the same side."

"Okay. Talk," he said to Will. "I'm only listening to you because of her." The rifle quavered a little bit in his hands, but he kept it directed at Will.

Will put his hands up. "Look, don't shoot, okay? Please. My name's Will. I just want to know who you are and what all this is about." His voice was calm, warm.

Xander's gaze swept over Will from head to toe. Then he slowly lowered the gun. "Yeah? You're Will? *Special.* More special is you've met *me.* There's a reason I've brought my crew in here. We have rights. No one tells us how we have to live."

Will returned his arms to his sides. "Okay, okay. Just settle down. Don't hurt anybody. What's the reason you're here?"

Xander turned to address the people in the room. "Everybody here!" he shouted. "We're REMs—but we now call ourselves Phoenix. We know things—things everyone in this city should know. We're gonna broadcast that stuff, and then we're gonna add to our team. This city is no longer going to repress how you feel! Or throw us away like trash. And they're no longer gonna terminate people who've done nothing wrong!"

"Terminate? You know people are being killed?" Will's eyes filled with wonder.

Across the room where he was being tied up against the wall, Austel screamed out, "You're all crazy! Hate and lies! You're traitors!"

One of the REM girls, Iris, plastered a long strip of silvery tape across Austel's mouth. He continued to thrash until Jasper aimed his rifle at him. Ember felt Austel's resentment hit her head-on. He was loyal to the hilt.

Xander walked with deliberate steps over to Will. He stopped an inch from his face. "Tell me what you know," he demanded. His face was alight, as if he had discovered gold at the end of the rainbow.

Journal Entry #55101

Trying to write in my journal today but find it has disappeared! Always on my desk, it's no more than a ghost. I have torn the library apart. I questioned the servants throughout the morning. They all say they know nothing. But someone has been here. Someone has stolen my very thoughts. And someone is lying.

I heard a disturbance last night and checked it out. Nothing seemed amiss as I walked through. I shone a light directly onto my desktop, and my diary was there. This loss is beyond disturbing. Especially when our fair city is threatened. Threatened by chaos.

Unthinkable! An insurrection! I am in hiding. All along, I have suspected groups of individuals, and I've been able to successfully eliminate them. I was not prepared for a revolution like the one I saw today. They were the *rejects* of society—the ones sent to The Outside for a *reason*. This very reason. Undisciplined sociopaths! How this happened, I do not know. They had the only weapons we keep here in Tranquility. I will remain in hiding but will meet with my Elite. From there these REMs will be apprehended and put up as examples of shame for all in our great city. We will do whatever we have to do. We will put down this insurgence and be ready to continue living in Tranquility. Peace.

And so, I continue my diary in a new volume. It could be a sign I must make changes to our life as we know it.

—Serpio Magnus, Magistrate

44

Will's Pledge

Will told Xander of the death of Ember's mom and summarized the events the two of them had discovered. Xander listened with interest, but prompted Will to share their story quickly.

"Please—don't rush me too much. The details are important." To Will's satisfaction, Xander nodded, so he left nothing out.

"So," said Xander. "Whose side are you on, then? I need to know. We're hell-bent on getting the word out. You in, or not?" Xander looked from Will to Ember, his gaze lingering on Ember's face.

Will figured this guy might still be suspicious of him and tried to reassure Xander. "Yeah . . . I'm with you, but you have to promise that Ember's going to be kept safe. She's got a lot at stake here."

"I'd never hurt *her*." His eyes seem to soften as he turned her way. He turned back in a split second. "You, though, better pledge your loyalty to become part of Phoenix, for better or worse."

Will suddenly remembered himself as a child, sitting on his grandpa's lap. The promise he made so long ago haunted him: *"You must promise to always follow the laws we have here in Tranquility. We never want to suffer again. Promise me, Will. Promise me! No matter what, you will never betray your family or your government."* He had *promised*! His spirits sank, but he knew he had seen things causing suffering, not preventing it. This was where a decision had to be made.

"I'm in."

Will shook Xander's hand but wondered how much he would have to kowtow to this peculiar leader. For now, he would use the opportunity to unveil Tranquility's dark side.

"C'mon. To the broadcast room. Ember—stay by my side." Xander barked the order as if he was born for command. It made Will's stomach curl to see Xander appoint himself as Ember's protector.

"Jasper—bring some guys and come into the broadcast suite. We've got work to do in there." Once inside, Xander's men took control of the announcers, an easy feat; the rifle in Xander's hands frightened them. Will had never been in the presence of a gun before. The weapon made him quiver, but he boosted his courage by remembering he was not on the receiving end of the bullets.

"Where's the Magistrate?" Ember blurted.

One of the newscasters splayed out his empty hands. "Gone, of course. Got him out of here before your crew put him in danger."

"But how?" Ember's voice wavered.

His response was swift. "You—traitors—you think you can breach our whole system? We have the ultimate security for the Magistrate and every member of the Elite. You'll never take them down. Or find them."

Xander snickered. "It doesn't matter. Our mission is to shake things up. We'll deal with 'security' later. Seize the day! This broadcast gets made right now."

The Phoenix group ushered the broadcasters into the main room, where they bound them the same way as the others. The main anchor was restrained to a chair in the broadcast room, save for his hands. Xander directed him to cue up the system.

"Get ready to go live," Xander said.

The inside of the broadcast room was crowded and uncharacteristically hot. Will wiped the sweat off his brow. *This is gonna shake things up, all right. Perfect. Our discoveries must have things in common with what Xander knows.*

"How can I help?" Will said.

"Be ready to share what you know. You're on first—then me, representing Phoenix. And make sure you introduce yourself as a Plauditor. The citizens might not believe me, but they'll believe you. You're an official." Xander's eyes smoldered. He pushed Will forward and trained his rifle on the newscaster. "Get that camera rolling."

Will resented the push but tamped it down. He was still someone in control of his emotions. He wasn't going to let any two-bit REM bully him into being barbaric.

"Citizens of Tranquility," Will began. "I come before you today to share news of vital importance. The trust we have put in our Magistrate and the Elite of this city is misplaced. A good friend of mine—Ember Vinata—suffered the untimely death of her mother, only to find the other recipients of the Augur Prize have been dying as well. Do you know any friends or family who have received this award? If so, they are in danger." Will leaned forward and looked boldly at the camera. "The leaders of this city have chosen to eliminate any ring honorees of at least Level Fourteen and above. What starts as an honor becomes a death warrant. We've yet to determine the motive for this atrocity . . ."

Ember, on the sidelines, interrupted. "Wait! I know why!" She dashed to Will's side. "May I?" she asked Will. Without hesitation, he stepped aside. "Hi everyone. You know my name—Ember. The Magistrate introduced me this morning. I'm also the one Will is telling you about. I've been in the

Magistrate's mansion for merely a day, but I discovered a journal in his library."

Will's eyebrows were tents of surprise. *This is incredible news.* Ember scored a break-through discovery. He felt such pride in her.

Ember continued, "I read a journal. It has entries describing the Magistrate's doubts and apprehensions about many of our citizens. He trusts his existing Elite, but not those who are ready to become part of it." She paused, knowing that the words she dropped now would be like bombs. "He murders those Augur Prizes winners who are on the verge of becoming Elite. Your Magistrate has emotional management issues—narcissism and paranoia."

Ember stepped back and gestured to Will to take over. He smiled at Ember and gave her a "thumbs up," but wasted no time picking up where Ember left off. "Your government is a group of assassins." He paused to let the statement lay heavily in the air space. "A full-scale investigation is needed. Be aware. Life is not what it seems in your city. Now, I introduce Xander, leader of a new group, Phoenix. He has information about his own discoveries." Will stepped aside to allow Xander full access to the mic.

"Hello, Tranks. I'm Xander, and I'm a REM. That's right. Cast out of the city. I lived as an outlaw doing crazy things to survive. No human deserves to live Outside. Now I've returned because Tranquility is messed up. Not just for us, the REMs, but for others. We've seen evidence of dead bodies from Tranquility being burned. Murder victims. And numbers are scratched into tree bark. These numbers had no meaning to us, but Will, here, thinks they're numbers on the victims' Augur Prize rings."

Will didn't know how Xander and his crew got back into the city. But he had to give them some respect for what they'd risked doing it. Standing next to Xander, he spoke up. "It's a miracle Xander's back in the city. And at great risk."

Xander nodded to Will, his face serious. "I know I could be arrested and taken back to the Outside. But I think you all need me here . . ." He broke into a rueful smile. ". . . as few of us know the truth. I'm fighting for Tranquility's real peace and happiness. I won't quit 'til it's made right." The two of them gazed into the camera. They turned to one another and shook hands.

"Fellow citizens stay happy. We're going to make everything what it should be. Have an excellent day." Will signed off with the Tranquility salute.

A raucous clamor from the other room stole their attention. Will cried, "What the—"

Xander sprung to life, not wasting a single second on words. He and Will exploded into the main room to discover the Plauditor's monitor screens flashing on and off. A soothing, but loud commanding emergency message blared from the Prismic Sonare, the octagonal white units mounted on the walls around the room. "Citizens of Tranquility. We have a Psychiatric Overhaul going on at our Plauditorium. This is temporary until our Plauditors recalibrate the Life Points Continuum. Please employ your mantras and breathing techniques. Remain where you are until we give you updates. Have a wonderful day."

Plauditors drowned out the message as they demanded to be released to man their stations. "We can't have chaos out there!" one man shouted, his face one second a snapshot of fear, the next of surprise, as he remembered his panic and outrage was against the law.

Will's Plauditor friend, Darla, begged, "Our city! Please— we have to know the citizens are all right. Will, make them understand!"

Will said, "What we did here today will help our city."

Xander said, "The citizens are fine. They've had a shock, but they'll get over it. It's time they see their city leaders through clear eyes."

A series of bangs on the Plauditorium's door echoed into the room. Voices cried out in fear. *Sciolists?* Will thought, his pulse quickening.

Knowing the surveillance system like he did, he barked an order. "Sector Nine! Report."

"Some Level Four Samkhat at the door." The response took the stiffness out of Will's entire body in a second. "Unlock the door," he commanded. "It's a friend."

Jasper pushed the release button, and the bolt slid back. He abruptly pulled the door open, and Wee burst in, lowering his head and ducking under the top of the doorframe. Xander and Jasper swiveled, facing him down with their rifles.

"Whoa—whoa! What's goin' on here?" Wee put his arms in the air, but then crossed them around his body to instinctively protect himself. "I saw the broadcast, but I wasn't prepared for this!"

Xander said to Jasper, "Lock the door," and the bolt again dropped into place. "Who are you?" Xander asked, staring Wee down.

"I'm a friend. A friend of Will's." He pointed. "That guy riiiiight there. Just stoppin' by to meet him for lunch. And find out what's goin' on." Wee put his hands back up.

Will stepped forward. "Had an invasion here. It's okay." He gestured across the room. "They're REMs who came back into the city. We're sharing what we know. Joining forces."

A shout rang out. "Hey! You! New guy! Go get *help*! Raise the Elite! The Elite!" It was Austel yelling from where he was tied to his chair.

Xander shook his head. "Who took the tape off that stupid guy's mouth? *Iris*?"

Standing next to Austel, Iris looked humbled. "Sorry. I thought he was gonna behave."

Jasper walked over and pointed his gun at Austel's head. "Be quiet. You don't know jack."

Will looked at Xander and said, "Leave him be. He thinks

he knows some Elite, but I've never confirmed it. He's harmless."

Wee stood there, still looking confused. He clearly didn't know what to do. Will walked over and gave him a bro hug. Their smiles lit up the room. "Glad you're here. We can use your help."

Ember stepped forward. "Hi. I'm Ember. Will's . . . friend."

Will said, "Finally, you get to meet the girl I've been telling you about." He blushed a little and put his hand on Ember's arm.

Will noticed a frown on Xander's face. "Something wrong?" he asked Xander.

"Nothing I can't handle. Thanks." Xander smirked before turning his face away.

Wee gave Ember the Tranquility signal. "Glad to finally meet you! Wish it was under more normal circumstances." He turned back to Will. "Yeah. So I went lookin', hoping to find the rings you told me about," Wee said.

"Let's step back in the broadcast booth, then. Xander and Ember...you'll need to know this, too." Will was still having doubts about Xander. He seemed to be focused on doing the right thing, but he couldn't trust him completely. He didn't know enough about the guy. Still, it was better that Wee shared what he knew with Xander if it was important. It could represent the next step in a bigger plan.

Xander yelled to Jasper. "You're in charge out here now. I can trust you to keep these Plauditors in line." Will was surprised to hear Xander laugh as he said it. Strangely, the guy now seemed to be having a great time.

"Now I can do without this," Ember said. She untied a petite satin bow at her throat and tossed her rainbow-striped robe on the floor where it lay in a crumpled heap.

The four disappeared into the booth.

"So, I did some poking around at City Hall yesterday," Wee said. "I saw unmarked black doors everywhere."

Xander said, "How're you allowed to walk around City Hall?"

Wee said, "I'm a chemical engineer for the city. I go in and out of those hallways every day. Some doors down an adjacent hallway I can open with my badge. But there are a couple of red doors in City Hall. I don't have clearance for those. Sciolists goin' in and out. You think the rings are in there?"

"Maybe," Will replied. "But if we can't get in there . . . ."

Ember said, "The rings are in a secret room behind the library."

Xander said, "Who cares? We don't have time for getting some stupid rings. We gotta get people on our side. Find the Magistrate. Crush the Elite."

"The thing is, if you're gonna do that, we'll need weapons," Wee said to Xander. "I can get into the chemical storage room with my badge. All kinds of chemicals in there. Like the one I brought today." He looked at Will. "It's Calsanac."

"The knock-out chemical?"

"Yep. Sorry it's a little late." He looked at Will sheepishly. "I tried."

"Wouldn't have mattered anyway, bro."

"I also grabbed a vial of Phenol."

"What's Phenol?" Will said.

Wee pulled a vile out of his pocket and brandished it, grinning. "In case I got caught snoopin' around, I took a vial of it. Causes severe burns. A systemic toxin, too. Kills people with just a few drops."

Xander whistled and looked at Wee with cautious respect. "A weapon like that? Could be the best news all day."

Will said, "Wee! You could be sent to the Outside for stealing! Or worse!" He looked at his Alt, vibrating a warning. All the fear, the anger, and the apprehension during the takeover had been draining points. He felt the guilt of the low readings. Then he grinned. He'd crossed over to the other side. The points were worthless to him. "And be careful with that thing!"

Wee chuckled and slid the vial back in his pocket. He put his hand on Will's shoulder. "Thought we probably'd need the Phenol to get Ember out, too. When we made our plans."

Will turned to Ember and smiled as he took her hand. "I couldn't leave you with the Magistrate. Wee and I were making plans today. But it looks like Xander ruined our effort," he joked.

Xander sneered. "My pleasure. And we're taking down this city even with procrastinating Pretty Boy on our team."

45

Will's Stand

N
o sooner did the words drop from Xander's lips, but a shout from the Plauditorium's interior went up. "Sciolists!" From the broadcast room, the four rushed back into the main room. Wee hung back, worry written on his face.

A REM posted by the door gestured wildly, pointing to the front window, its broad, five-foot expanse partly obscured by tilted shutter slats.

Xander shouted to the four REMs standing guard at the Plauditorium's entrance. "Get right behind the door. Away from the window!"

Will flew over to the Sector Nine monitor, where the same camera that caught Weeford at the entry spanned the inner courtyard. At the workstation for Sector Nine, a Plauditor tied to the chair opened his eyes wide. Will lightly pushed the chair out of the way, where Will slid into the space himself. He watched as the menacing red cars pulled up, one by one, their unusual speed an unexpected wonder. Facing the front of the building, they parked in a perfect semi-circle. Sciolists jumped out of the cars, wielding pole-type devices. They began advancing, but slowly. *Why were they so unsure of themselves? Were*

they waiting for some kind of signal? He watched the Sciolists'
every move, worried they had some way to breach the
building.

As if their red robes weren't intimidating enough, they
wore their hoods, their faces shadowed in the late morning
sunshine. The darkness inside their cowls made them look
faceless, as if they were no longer human. Their weapons
gleamed as they held them aloft. At first, Will thought it was
the sun's reflection, but soon realized the poles crackled with
an electric charge. A blue glow lit up the top end.

"How many?" Xander cried.

"Maybe twenty?" Will answered.

They walked slowly, almost in step, in a sort of robotic
parade. Will heard no words being exchanged among them,
but the Sciolists were not known for their conversational skills.

Ember ran to Will's side. "Guns? Do they have guns?"

"No. Not that I see. And, they wouldn't—shouldn't. Tranquility's a gun-free city."

Walking their way, Wee said, "And you trust that?"

Xander strode over to join them at the monitor. "This," he
patted the rifle, "is for the Tranks going Outside. To be
protected from the *evil* REMs. And Greelox."

"What's Greelox?" Ember asked, her voice worried.

"Never mind. Just—what are they up to?"

A half-dozen Sciolists broke away from the group. They
marched up to the door outside. A high-pitched buzz followed
by a rumble abruptly shook the door. The vibration trembled
with a crackling noise. Pulsing lightning lit up the doorframe.

"They've got those frikkin' rods electrifying the door." Will
said, "I'm on it." He flipped a switch and spoke into a micro-
phone positioned to the right of the monitor. "Sciolists! This is
Will Verus, a Plauditor. The Plauditorium is locked down.
Locked down. Armed REMs are holding Plauditors hostage. I
repeat, *they are armed with guns.* If you breach the building, they
will shoot. If you attempt entry, Plauditors will die. Please.

Stand down. I repeat. Stand down." Will's transmission sent to the speakers outside the building roared with authority.

At the announcement, the advancing Sciolists stopped moving. They stood stock-still, not looking anywhere but forward. Those at the door held firm for a full minute, and then they stepped back, their rods disengaged.

Suddenly, monitors within the Plauditorium flickered. The Magistrate stared back at them from the screen, his face filling the monitor's space. Ember gasped. Will put his hands on his head. Xander spat on the floor. And the room at large answered the image with yells from REMs and muted "hmmms" coming from the taped mouths of Plauditors.

"Plauditors. This is your *beloved* Magistrate. I am aware of your situation. I am surveilling you from a secluded location in City Hall. As you can see, our cameras go both ways. What you can see on the outside, I can see on the inside. I am working hard to make sure all Plauditors can remain safe."

Xander snickered, placing himself fully in front of the camera's scope. He, too, filled the screen with his face. "Can you hear *me*? I'm in charge here."

"Ah. Xander Noble. You *think* you're in charge. There's no escape. You will be arrested. If you turn yourself in now, I promise you a speedy trial, and a quick return to The Outside. Resist? It will result in your immediate death."

Will shook his head, as if the Magistrate could see him. Then he gently pushed Xander aside. "Magistrate. REMs hold all the cards here. If you don't keep the Sciolists at bay, the Plauditors die."

The screen flickered again. The Magistrate was gone. Sector Nine's front exterior shot showed the Sciolist team, still in position.

Ember said, "Now what? If they don't leave, we're actually prisoners."

Will put his arm around her shoulders. "We wait and see.

Remember, Wee's got some chemicals. We have guns. If we have to fight, we battle it out."

"Will. Ember—look." Xander pointed to the screen. Sciolists were retreating, a few speaking into their Alts on their wrists. "He actually called 'em off. Good boy, Serpio."

"I'll be damned. But I don't trust him. He'll be plotting. And when that transport gets here, we'd better have a gun ready."

46

Ember's Assurance

Ember turned to Will. "What are we going to do with all these Plauditors? We can't just leave them here. They're either gonna be a great help or a dangerous foe. I say we give them a chance to commit one way or another."

Will jumped in before Xander could speak. "You're right, Ember. Time to close rank. Since I'm a member here, I'll put it up to them."

Xander said, "Plauditor, you should. But don't go easy." Ember noticed his grudging consent. For a guy who was an Outsider, he was overly self-assured, like he was the master, not the nonperson Tranquility set him up to be. His appearance was scruffy in his rumpled tan jumpsuit. His hair, tousled and long, dipped into his face. A dark stubble that threatened to become an outright beard hid a face marked with dirt. His appearance was so appalling, she couldn't believe this was the same guy she knew as a kid. Back then his arrogant swagger was accented by illegal but highly fashionable clothing, clean, polished skin, and hair made perfect by product and style. She wanted nothing more than to keep the grimy guy at arm's length.

But Ember keenly felt Xander's moods. His emotions were super-charged. Xander's aura glowed green, with a layer of silver close to his skin. Different from the others, its mix of satisfaction and eagerness was so strong she could barely free herself. When she made eye contact, though, the emotional torrent shifted. His aura shifted from green to red the instant their eyes met.

His eyes were loaded with acute sensuality and desire. A laser couldn't have been more intense. The intensity made her uncomfortable, yet she felt herself respond . . .

She ripped her eyes away, diverting them to Will, who was already moving ahead with a plan for the Plauditors.

Will called out to the room at large. "In case you all didn't hear our broadcast, this is a takeover for all the right reasons. Xander and his crew belong here. Tranquility claims to be a place where we can all be happy. But people have disappeared and are dead. This is Ember Vinata." He put his hand on Ember's shoulder. "Her mother was murdered with a simple ring meant to show honor to her. Your City Halld, your Magistrate, your Elite—they do this. We don't know why, but we'll find out. In the meantime, you have a choice to make. You can pledge your loyalty to us—to Phoenix—and we can make our city a true place of hope and love. Or we will have to put you where you can't interfere."

Xander chimed in during Will's momentary pause. "Those who don't join? We'll load you up and take you out of the city. We have the means to transport all of you. Believe me, though, you won't tolerate it out there. Make no mistake, there's no coming back." Xander turned to Jasper. "We need the transport vehicle—at least one. You still have your Trank uniform on, so make your way to the garage and get those wheels over here."

"Right, Xan. I'll keep just off the streets, like before." He clenched the rifle in his hands and was out the door before the clock pushed twenty seconds. Ember wondered where he was going and if he would be able to get across the city. She admired his courage, self-sacrifice, and determination. *He has more positive emotions than some regular Tranks,* she thought.

"Now, who's with us?" Xander shouted. "If you're with us, you're gonna be untied, but you'll remain here with Phoenix. This is now *our* headquarters. We'll be using the monitors and your knowledge to plan activities. No one leaves except my crew. Or those of you who, like idiots, want to go to The Outside. Understand?"

The room buzzed with murmurs and protests, the Plauditors without gags trying to confer with others around them. Ember tried to push back the jangle of confusion, including all the auras. They overwhelmed her.

Her thoughts were snarled after the whole incident with Will. She not only didn't understand it, she wasn't ready to share her bizarre power with Phoenix. No one—not even Will—knew what had happened earlier, and now was not the time to have a conversation about it. The secret had to be saved for another day. But, one thing was for sure. She'd never repress what she could feel from herself and others. Never deny the power within her. Even if she had to make sacrifices, she was ready to start trusting herself and leave herself open to the unknown.

Will made the rounds questioning Plauditors, one by one. Some who agreed to join their cause also circled the room to get decisions. Will directed others agreeing to join Phoenix back to their stations. Ember was the ultimate definer; she could read their emotions better than their Alts could, so she followed behind, making sure the decisions were strong.

"Will, this Plauditor here isn't dedicated enough." She raised a man's arm as a signal. Several of Xander's crew escorted the faithless Plauditor to the broadcast booth, his objections ringing with defiance.

She continued to assess each case and at last was satisfied; the remaining group would be loyal. With some REM help,

Xander corralled eight uncooperative Plauditors into a group. Bound with their zip ties, they continued to protest as Xander shoved them into the broadcast booth, where they would await the transport vehicle.

Ember couldn't imagine why they'd choose the bleak uncertainty of The Outside over a reborn Tranquility. She understood their loyalty to the only government they knew. But she realized that unlike her, they hadn't seen the depth of the Magistrate's crimes.

47

Will Rises Up

Xander grouped Ember, Will, and Wee in a huddle. "We all go to The Outside with our passengers to show you everything we discovered out there. I've no worries about leaving Phoenix in charge here. What do you say?"

Will replied, "Yeah. You think it's safe enough?" Will realized as soon as the words were out of his mouth that he sounded weak in front of his best friend and his girl—and yes, she was *his girl*—but especially in front of this guy who was so full of himself.

Xander chuckled. "If you're afraid of a little ride, you'd better stay here where it's protected. For me—I'm not worried. I can handle anything."

"Just making sure we don't get ourselves in an irreversible situation. Forewarned is forearmed. But, yeah. I'll be going along."

Xander smirked at him, and Will barely resisted the urge to boost him across the room. Tranquility's conduct code and his own morals kept him from acting it out.

Ember looked from one to the other. Her eyes flashed a warning. "We have to stick together—all of us. For

better or worse. We do this right or . . . or die trying.
I'm in."

Wee said, "What if we're stopped?"

Xander said, "Still have a rifle." He ran his hands along
the shaft.

Wee gave a fist pump. "Ready."

Ember grabbed Will's hand once the decision was made.
At the touch of her hand, he felt a rush, like an electric
current. He longed to take her in his arms and let the world
fall away. As if she heard his thoughts as well as felt his
emotions, she led him off to a corner of the Plauditorium.
She gazed at him, her eyes full of . . . what? Wishfulness?
Sadness? Desire? They hadn't yet spoken about their breakup.

Ember squeezed Will's hand. "I need to show you the
Magistrate's journal. It's terrifying. I have it hidden away in a
cabinet in the Plauditoriums's lounge. I can't get it out yet. But
we can read it together. When there's time."

"Yeah. You did good, getting that. You're amazing. And,
as soon as we have a chance, we'll read it. Keep it safe." He
felt his palms getting sweaty, and he dropped his hand from
hers. His confusion at the awkward moment made him want
to become invisible. Instead, he stepped away. "Have to go.
I'm watching Sector Nine."

He returned to Sector Nine like it was a long-lost friend.
He exclusively commandeered Sector Nine himself, keeping
his eyes glued to the screen as only a dedicated Plauditor knew
how to do. With the passing minutes, the hope Jasper could
return with the city vehicle was dimming, even with his
customary optimistic spirit. His forehead gleamed with perspi-
ration, and he felt drained of energy. As the minutes ticked by,
Will began to doubt the calm which had settled on the Plauditorium. Other than the Plauditors who'd resisted joining the
cause, he and his friends were in a holding pattern. Yet there
were still no signs of Sciolists outside the building.

Viewing the exterior of the building was essential. But at

what cost? The Magistrate could use cameras against them if it worked like a two-way mirror. Who knows what he'd seen them do already? He sighed. Better to cut the cord.

The shutdown would become a nightmare if he didn't work it right. Tedman Adoravi, their supervisor, was bound up and ready to go to the Outside, along with every broadcaster in the building. But one other guy named "Banks" knew tech well. Banks had pledged his loyalty to Phoenix, and Ember had verified it. Will would turn the system over to him.

"Banks," Will said as he approached. "Shut down the monitors."

The Plauditor was still rubbing his wrists from the chafing the zip ties had made. But he stopped abruptly, and scrutinized Will for a good ten seconds. "We're all playing with fire here. You sure shutting down's a good idea? We won't be able to see what's going on in the city."

"We can't have the Magistrate spying on us. And we can't let him get any broadcasts up. Or let him talk to us via those cameras. It has to be done."

Banks shook his head up and down slowly. "I hear ya. I'll take it from here."

"Thanks." Will turned away. "And thanks for seeing the truth."

Banks looked as if he were about to reply when shouts went up. The transport vehicle was pulling up mere steps from the front door.

Will turned and bolted to the front interior of the building. REMs—no, Phoenix, he corrected himself—were opening the deadbolt on the Plauditorium's door. Xander ran right behind Will, his rifle at the ready, in case of an ambush after the door opened. As if on cue, Xander's crew brought the identified resistors—Tedman, five broadcasters, and eight Plauditors, including Austel, to the door. A quick exodus would buy them more security.

Jasper grinned as he hopped out of the vehicle. "Got

stopped once by Sciolists not far from here. Told 'em I was headed to pick up dead REMs at the Plauditorium." He shrugged his shoulders. "They didn't believe me. Had to shoot 'em."

Will shivered. Blood was being shed. Then he remembered; this was no game. Good innocent people were already dead. It was wartime.

"That's right—get right up in there. Death Wagon at your service," Will said. The disloyal Plauditors stepped up into the van, their bodies jerking and kicking in futile rebellion. Will regretted having to free up their ankles, but they had to get them into the van somehow. Jasper watched for any threats while Xander, Ember, and Wee helped to secure them in the back of the transport by binding their zip-tied bodies to large hooks attached to the van's steel walls.

Xander jumped up into the back once the last one had been fully boarded and secured. "Hello, fellow passengers," Xander said. "Your luxury vacation awaits, far, far away." His voice dripped with mockery.

Will smiled wryly. This guy's sarcasm was a real trademark.

Wee bolted to the front seat of the vehicle. "I call shotgun!" Wee's shoulders looked tight as he slid into the passenger seat. Will remembered Wee's fear of the dark. No way could he have survived a ride in the cargo hold.

Xander whistled something totally tuneless, his body relaxed as an unbound scarecrow; he climbed into the transport's command seat as if he was born to it. Will turned to Ember. "You okay being in the back?" Will knew it would be like a coffin in there—pitch black and stifling.

"Yeah. I'll be happy to." Her voice was a melodious chirp; he cautiously put his arm around her. Her bravado was endearing.

"We'll be there together. Let me help you up." He jumped into the cargo hold, and extended his arm, helping to pull her aboard. They sat opposite the prisoners whose eyes shot invisible bullets. He was amazed how little time had passed before they completely gave up their emotional self-control.

Except for Xander, he realized, none of them had ever been to The Outside—not even the Plauditors. What would it be like? Were they crazy to go out there? Would the transport vehicle still take them back? Salty beads of sweat prickled his forehead. Maybe they would all die out there somewhere, and everything would be for nothing. Blood pounded in his head. He couldn't let Ember see how vulnerable he felt. Then he realized, for the first time, she felt it anyway.

He felt a familiar vibration and looked at his Alt for a typical reading. It lit up, flooding his face with light, its gauge showing a catastrophic drop in points. He sucked in a breath, flushed with panic, only to suddenly realize that, if they were successful, no one's Alt would matter anymore.

He turned to find Ember gazing at him with soft doe eyes. "The Alt's showing your true colors, Will."

"I know. And you've seen them all along."

"Yes."

Will took Ember's hand, and they fell silent. The Plauditors' sudden fidgeting, scratching against the van's inner wall, filled the lull. His contentment of being with Ember, even in this cold, spartan place, welled up in him. It almost made him feel secure. Almost.

Yet he had to ask. "Ember, are we good? I'm so sorry . . ."

"Will, I think we should be together, don't you?" She smiled at him, and the world expanded. His heart seemed to swell, and his pulse raced.

"Yeah. Yeah, I do." He smiled back at her, lost in her eyes.

A cloud crossed his thoughts. He'd seen the way Xander looked at Ember, and he resented it. He wanted to high-five the guy and laud his savvy ways, and at the same time, he wanted to deck him. He said casually, as if making conversation, "What do you think of Xander?"

"I met him when I was in school. He seems pretty much the same now, just older and more brazen. We had a run-in then, and I got the blame."

Will squeezed her hand. "He hurt you?"

"No. Not physically. He was just hateful. I never thought I would meet him again, especially like this."

"What's your read on him?"

She hesitated and dropped his hand before she spoke. She looked away. Her voice deepened and became heavy, as if the words brought some special fervor. "I have an *acute* awareness of him. He's full of fire. Definitely a force to be reckoned with."

Will felt his stomach twinge. What lay behind her tone? Ember wasn't telling him everything.

Just as quickly her inflection changed. "He's gonna be great for us, though. What he's discovered is the evidence we need against the Magistrate and all the Elite. And, I can read him —easily. If there's something off, I'll let you know."

"Thanks. I don't totally trust him, especially if he was out of line with you. But you're right, we wouldn't be where we are without him." He sighed. They did need him, but more than ever he wished the guy wasn't so good-looking or as smart as he seemed to be. He would be a tough competitor, if it ever came to that.

THEY'D BEEN DRIVING LONG ENOUGH that Will's butt was now numb, but with no windows, he had lost his sense of time. When the transport began to slow, he grabbed Ember's hand again in solidarity. They had to be ready for what the dreaded Outside held. When the vehicle came to a hard stop, he released Ember's hand to push the interior button for the door to slide open. His hands trembled. He took a deep breath. The Outside represented both a horror and an unconditional freedom they had never known. He smoothed his palms along his upper legs, waiting for his typical heroic spirit to kick in. The door slid open with a gratifying hiss. *This is the door to the future for all of us.*

The sight greeting Will as he and Ember peered out the back was a somber one. Blackened ground and charcoaled wood pieces were scattered about a primitive clearing. This then must be the burn site. It was painful to see, just slightly less torturous than watching the flames devouring the victims. The evidence of Will's suspicions lay before them, Tranquility's broken dreams.

He turned to Ember and took her in his arms. It was a bitter conclusion to Talesa's story. He hoped she could be brave, and then remembered she didn't have to be. Her emotions were now her own. Will let her go after a tight body-melding hug.

She said, "I'm ready. Let's jump."

Will beamed his thousand-watt smile, and they hopped down in unison from the transport's three-foot elevation. Will said, "The end of the road, but the beginning of a better life."

Xander and Wee rounded the corner from the front of the vehicle. Will hadn't realized Xander still had one of the rifles, but there it was, slung across his shoulder.

"The burn site, as you may have gathered," Xander declared with a sweep of his arms. "But over there, not so obvious." He pointed to the straggly trees nearby. "That's where numbers are carved."

Will said, "For the victims?"

"I imagine," Xander replied. "If the rings were numbered as you said . . ."

"My mom's number. It'll be there." Ember's voice was a thin whisper.

Will put his arm around Ember, wishing he could be alone to comfort her, but an overly emotional Wee threw his arm about Will's shoulders.

"We're all here for you, Ember," Wee said.

Ember said, "Thanks, guys."

Will turned to Xander, who stood a couple of yards away with his arms crossed. "You coming, Xander?"

Xander said, "We're a team, aren't we?" Xander closed the gap by taking Ember's side, further erasing the space as he eased his arm across her shoulder.

Will bristled, his face flushing. His muscles spasmed, but now was not the time for combative words.

In strained solidarity, they walked toward the trees, the crunching of crispy, blackened coals under their feet the only sounds in the desolate wasteland.

Their feet tracking powdered soot, the group approached the slender thicket. The trees, anemic and shadowy in the twilight, seemed to whisper "shh" as a sudden cold wind ruffled their tattered branches.

Then, the numbers. Merely half-inch tall, they seemed larger than life. Stark. Forlorn. Lonely.

Ember reached out and reverently touched the first number she saw. She put her hand to her mouth and started to weep, catching her breath in between jags.

This number was once a person, Will thought. He choked back a surge of pain welling up in his throat. Inconceivable.

Xander cleared his throat and said, "We can all search for a while. We'll find it quickly enough with the four of us."

Will said, "Agreed. Number 1025, everyone."

He hesitated to leave Ember's side, but time was passing, and they still had prisoners to manage. He would do like the others and fan out.

Within minutes, Will found his adopted tree's numbers began with a stark number of 0101. Other numbers were carved on the tree in various places, none of them in a row. And none of them the number he was seeking.

"Where are the thousands?" Will called out.

"Here!" Xander's voice echoed.

Ember streaked to Xander's spot, pushing Xander out of the way. She searched the tree, finding and touching each number before moving on. The numbers were scattered, some high, some low, but there were very few on the tree. Ember stood on her tiptoes to see one of them a couple of feet above her head.

The rest of the group gathered up around Ember's tree, standing aside, their respect for her search reflected in their faces. Will found himself holding his breath, watching. At last she stopped, looking almost frozen. 1024. So close. This was it. No doubt this was the series of numbers they came to find. She searched up and down the tree's expanse, checking and rechecking each number, even casting her gaze up into the stubby limbs.

"Is that all? *All?*" Ember cried. "Where's 1025?" She looked frantically at the rest of the group. "Why isn't it here?" She yanked on her hair, sobs engulfing her again. She crumpled to the ground and pounded her hands against the tree.

"Hey, are we sure?" Wee said, his voice radiating a forced optimism. "No more numbers?" Throwing up a "wait" gesture with his giant hand, he loped from tree to tree one more time. The rest of the little party joined in, again spreading out, reexamining the trees. But the numbers were clear. Each tree had a series, and none of them had more than a few numbers on them.

Will's heart broke. *Wasn't this the least she could have? A number?* All he could do was clutch Ember to his chest and let the rush of her tears soak into his clothing. She grabbed his shirt with her fists, her head buried in his chest in defeat.

"Ember, there's got to be more to this. We'll figure it out. The Magistrate will answer for this," Will said with clenched teeth.

He smoothed his hands through her hair until her sobs quieted. She looked up at him through her drowned lashes, and he vowed to himself to be the man she trusted him to be.

In the meantime, he could simply offer her hope for the future. "I'm so sorry, Ember. One day, no matter the risk, I'm gonna make this right."

Xander smirked at Will, but then turned to Ember. "No quest is too great for me, either. I'm ready and—," he raised one eyebrow—"willing."

Will picked up on Xander's implication, and immediately changed the subject. "Ember . . . we have prisoners to release, and then we need to head back. The three of us will get the Plauditors untied and let them go. Until then, if you want to stay…"

"No." She took a deep breath and stood up straight.

Xander nodded at Will, and they strode back to the transport, where each of them first ungagged the Plauditors. Once their mouths were free, Austel screamed and yelled. "Finally! You lean-witted maggots! Were you going to leave us all day?"

"Yes, that *is* the plan, and not just for the day," Xander replied. Xander roughly cut the zip ties around their wrists and pushed the prisoners out of the van. "There ya go." One babbled and screamed, practically falling from the van. As their feet hit the dirt, they hugged themselves and shivered in the chill wind.

He saw their eyes pan the scene, the skin on their faces tight, their eyes as wide as bloated balloons. The charred space gave its testimony.

"Now maybe you'll believe," Will said to them.

"C'mon. We want to go back to the city," one fair-haired Plauditor implored. "We made a mistake!"

"Don't abandon us here! Can you be that heartless?" another moaned.

Austel began a whiny all-scale campaign. "Look, we can work something out. I know things. I can help you."

Xander said, "Seriously? *Now* you want to join our cause? Well, I don't blame you. Life is harsher than you can imagine out here."

In spite of everything, except for Austel, Will felt a twinge of sympathy. Nor did he want to leave anyone in this place who could be useful to them later. "No way of knowing if they're worth saving without Ember confirming," Will said.

Wee spoke. "Can you reassess them, Ember? They've suddenly become converts to our cause."

Ember grimaced, but turned her attention to each of the discredited Plauditors. Fascinated, Will watched her put her hands on every person's shoulders and make eye contact with each. It didn't take more than thirty seconds to judge the entire group.

"They're frightened, but I can't tell their thinking. Their auras are diffused out here beyond Tranquility. We simply can't trust them. We need to leave them behind."

She sounded regretful, but determined. Will was struck by how much she had changed, even in the short time since they had first met. She was beginning to trust herself.

The captors immediately began yelling again in protest, their emotions practically growing into full-size monsters. Austel, of course, was the most verbal. He lashed out. "Your coup won't be successful, and then you'll all wind up out here too. But you, Will, you're gonna burn eventually for this. You're a disgrace, a traitor."

The words hurt for a moment, but Will bounced back. "One day, when you realize you're wrong, maybe we'll come back for you. So, you better hope we're successful."

Austel merely grunted.

Xander said, "Go. Walk away. Suggest you head East." He pointed in a direction beyond the trees.

"I won't forget this, Will," Austel said. He suddenly raised his arm to throw a punch, but Will blocked it, twisted Austel's arm around his back, and shoved him forward.

"Get going," Xander hissed. He grabbed the rifle and brought it forward.

Austel turned his back and began walking, still calling out

insults as he went. The rest of them drifted off slowly, as if in a trance, shuffling their feet and looking back at them in case there was a sympathetic change of heart.

The little Phoenix party stood their ground, watching the captives until they slipped behind a cactus-covered hill obscuring them from view.

"We can't leave until we leave our own mark," Wee said. "I have an idea." He turned to Xander. "You got somethin' on you we can use to carve?"

"Of course." Xander pulled a spartan knife from his uniform pocket. "Here you go."

"Did you make this or somethin'? It's pretty sad," Wee joked, as he turned it over in his palm.

"It does the job."

"C'mon. Follow me," Wee said. He led them back to the trees.

Placing the blade into a broad space on the trunk of the nearest tree, Wee carved his name into the bark. It was crude, but it was distinct.

He handed the shank over to Will. He etched his name underneath. He spoke each letter. "W . . . I . . . L . . . L . . . I'm finished."

Xander stepped up next. "I'm representing all the REMs here—not just me. I'm proud of that and of who we are." Using the tiptop point of the blade, and holding it steady with his two hands, "REM" soon solidly appeared below Will's name.

Flashing her a smile, Xander asked Ember to open her palms. He reverently placed the knife across her hands. "Now, for you, Ember. Your mother's number may not be here, but your name will be here for a long time to come."

Her right hand closed around the handle, and Will watched her approach the tree. She stood there for a minute, staring at their names. She turned around to look at her friends, an expression of joy on her face, as if she had just inhaled a sunbeam, lighting her up from the inside.

She began to carve, but not below the others. Her name went right next to Xander's, where he had carved his tribute to the REMs.

As he watched the third letter of her name emerge, Will realized what was happening. Within a moment, so had the others.

Wee

Will

REMEmber

The four huddled together, each calling out their part of the message with triumphant voices and pumping their fists in the air.

With the final whoop, Will broke from the group and raced back to the transport van. He leapt up on the bumper and spread his arms wide. "The fate of all Tranks rests in our hands, and so does the city of Tranquility!"

The others ran to Will, lifted him off the bumper, and carried him around above their heads in a spirit of victory.

"To real happiness!" Ember cried.

"To rising from the ashes!" Wee said.

And, finally, Xander. "The revolution begins!"

Also by Tanya Ross

Facing Off, **Book Two of the Tranquility Series**

A rising revolution. Renegades on the run. Relationships transformed.

Ember, Xander, and Will return from their justice-seeking trip to The Outside to deliver a brewing revolution to Serpio Magnus's doorstep. But when Tranquility's Magistrate goes on the hunt for them, it sends them scattering into the wind in a desperate attempt to survive.

As Ember battles her way back to find the others, her nightmares urge her to discover the final, staggering truth about her mother, and she must embark on a dangerous quest. Her relationship with her adoring boyfriend compromised by betrayal, she turns to a unlikely companion to forge a new confidence in herself and in her unique superpowers.

Left with impossible odds, the risky actions each one takes will change everything.

Will their spark of rebellion grow into a blaze of self-destruction?

Gripping Dystopian adventure laced with hot

romance continues with *Facing Off,* the highly anticipated sequel in the Tranquility Series!

Don't want the story to end? Scan the QR code to
begin Book Two! Or, use the exact link to Amazon:
My Book

Before You Go...

Thanks for reading *Rising Up*! I hope you enjoyed it! As an indie author, reviews mean everything. Not only do they let other readers know whether a book is worth investing in, reviews also give the author insight into what a reader loved (or didn't) about a story. **If you have a minute, please take the time to leave a review.** It doesn't need to be long, just say how you felt about *Rising Up*, the writing, the story, the characters, or whatever. My everlasting gratitude if you do!! And again, thank you so much for your support and being a new fan!

Please leave a review for me on Goodreads or wherever you purchased this copy!

Discover more on my website and sign up for my newsletter at http://www.tanyarossauthor.com

Acknowledgments

When I began this book, I was excited about the fulfillment of a lifelong dream. However, this work of fiction was one of the most difficult projects I have ever attempted.

As an educator I tried to push my students to always think positive and to "rise above." That, in part, fueled my plot. But what I told my students daily was so much easier to preach than to perform. What I thought would be easy, was certainly not. It challenged me beyond what I thought possible. So, I have many to thank for their help and support on this very demanding journey.

To my husband, Kerry, I thank you for your unwavering belief in me and your continual flow of ideas. I could never have completed this project without you. And to the rest of my family, especially my daughter, Ashley, who have stayed interested and encouraging throughout the past three years as I wrote this novel, thank you.

To my Writer's Group: thanks for your support and feedback. Pete Peterson, in particular, I owe you my gratitude for your critiques, encouragement, and help with publishing.

To the Beta Readers at Woodland Park Middle School, for your evaluations and "five star" ratings. Thanks to Kim Saito and Heidi Patchett, excellent language arts teachers, for your willingness to help secure those very important readers in spite of your insanely busy schedules.

Great appreciation goes out to all the San Marcos Unified staff members who have supported me as I launched this novel: Jamie Yorba, Heidi Patchett, Kim Saito, Trish Lucia, Steve Ottaviani, and the ELA Curriculum council.

Also, love and thanks go to the thousands of students in my career, whose collective and sometimes singular personalities inspired me to develop believable characters.

And finally, to my Lord and Savior, Jesus Christ, through whom all things are possible.

Biography

Tanya Ross was born and raised in San Diego County. Although Southern California is paradise, she desires a world where everyone is kind, compassionate, and upbeat, which became one of the themes of this novel, *Rising Up*. For thirty-two years she was an educator of English, history, AVID, and student leadership. She loved teaching and kids, her students a daily inspiration. Her exit from the educational arena allowed her to indulge her hopes, dreams, and goals in what she taught for so many years—writing. When she's not creating new worlds, you can find her reading, spending time with her husband and two kids, or walking her golden retriever, Honey.

Find her on:
Facebook: https://facebook.com/fictionauthor54
Instagram: https://instagram.com/tjross_author
Goodreads: https://rebrand.ly/rorwqi3
Bookbub: https://rebrand.ly/g9s3387
Website: https://www.tanyarossauthor.com